THE NIGHT SHIFT

GEMMA ROGERS

Boldwood

First published in Great Britain in 2025 by Boldwood Books Ltd.

Cover Images: iStock

A CIP catalogue record for this book is available from the British Library.

Paperback ISBN 978-1-80549-511-6

Large Print ISBN 978-1-80549-512-3

Hardback ISBN 978-1-80549-509-3

Ebook ISBN 978-1-80549-513-0

Kindle ISBN 978-1-80549-514-7

Audio CD ISBN 978-1-80549-505-5

MP3 CD ISBN 978-1-80549-506-2

Digital audio download ISBN 978-1-80549-507-9

This book is printed on certified sustainable paper. Boldwood Books is dedicated to putting sustainability at the heart of our business. For more information please visit https://www.boldwoodbooks.com/about-us/sustainability/

Boldwood Books Ltd, 23 Bowerdean Street, London, SW6 3TN

www.boldwoodbooks.com

For all the Type One Warriors –
May your highs be greater than your lows.
In May 2024 just before I started writing this book, my
youngest daughter was diagnosed with type one diabetes.
It has been a tumultuous few months of learning and
navigating new routines, however I am constantly in awe
of her strength and resilience in the face of something that
has ultimately been life-changing. I couldn't be prouder.
<u>She</u> is my Nina.

1

6 P.M. – 10 P.M.

'You're late, Nina!' Stacey snapped, her voice muffled through the glass. She stood with her arms crossed, glaring at me, neck mottled, as I tried to unlock the door, inputting the wrong code into the keypad twice.

At six o'clock when my twelve-hour shift started at Storage Queen, the twenty-four-hour accessible storage warehouse, the entrance switched from opening by sensor on approach to being locked. After that time, the warehouse was accessed by entering a six-digit code into the keypad outside. My job was on reception, three nights a week, caretaking basically and making sure visitors signed in. The unsociable hours paid well and the solitude was perfect, giving me a quiet place I needed to study for my medical degree.

I squeezed through the tiny gap as the entrance slid open at a snail's pace into the modern reception of the warehouse. My nose was red, eyes puffy from crying, but thankfully my boss hadn't noticed, or if she had, she was too infuriated to comment. Her lined face resembled a battered cushion with half its stuffing missing, muscles no longer strong enough to lift her jowls into a proper scowl. Not that I could blame her for being disgruntled when she was waiting to go home.

'I know, I know,' I said, swinging my bag onto the tall yellow gloss counter with a thump, not wanting to meet her eyes. 'I'm sorry, my car wouldn't start.'

It was a lie, my beat-up 2007 Ford Focus was as reliable as ever, but I couldn't tell my unsympathetic manager about the row I'd had with my now ex-boyfriend, Dom. She wouldn't care that despite being heartbroken and crying off all my mascara, I'd still hauled my arse to work when I could have called in sick. I had thought about it, pulling the duvet over my head and weeping into it all night, but being a relatively new employee, still on probation, if I didn't work, I didn't get paid.

'If *you're* late, then I'm late leaving,' she moaned, gathering her bag and keys, eager to get home.

I rolled my eyes when she wasn't looking, it was ten bloody minutes, but I understood, twelve-hour shifts sucked, but she was the manager and earned way more than I did. Enough to drive a brand-new three series BMW. Her lacklustre camel-coloured coat, almost the same shade as her wayward hair, was already on and I waited for her to waddle around the counter and give me what little handover there was.

'There's a couple on the second floor, in unit two hundred and forty-seven, arrived about half an hour ago. They're unloading from a trolley up there. Other than that it's empty, I did the last check at five and we've had no calls either. Should be a quiet night.'

I nodded, hoping so, waiting for her to leave so I could have a meltdown in private. I had university work to finish and was counting on being undisturbed. That's if I could concentrate on anything at all after breaking up with Dom. I unpacked a sugar-free Red Bull and leftover macaroni cheese from my bag onto the desk to keep me going and looked up, surprised to find Stacey still standing there.

'I've stocked up the snack drawer.' Her voice softened as she glanced first at my food and then the small continuous glucose monitor attached to my upper arm, about the size of a ten-pence piece, its rim poking out beneath the sleeve of the purple Storage Queen T-shirt. Along with the optional fleece, the T-shirt was the only uniform we were contracted to wear, so I was able to throw my slouchy jeans on without anyone batting an eyelid. Something I was happy about as I lived in denim and comfy trainers.

'Thanks,' I replied, cheeks flushing.

Stacey could be a grumpy cow at times and I guessed by her age that, like my mum, she was probably going through the menopause. She was a stickler for the rules, but on the whole Stacey wasn't a bad boss when you delved beneath the layers. The snack drawer was always filled with crisps and Pot Noodles for the night workers, but a few weeks after I'd joined, packs of chewy sweets and fun-size chocolate bars had appeared in a transparent plastic box with my name on it. Purchased by Stacey specifically for the diabetic employee and woe betide anyone else who had a sugar craving in the middle of the night, as Karl, another night-shift worker had found out after nabbing a tiny Snickers bar. He didn't hear the end of it.

'Have a nice evening and sorry again for being late,' I said as cheerily as I could manage.

She smiled, her lips pressed into thin lines, and

moved past me, punching our staff code – 461822 – into the keypad just by the door.

'Call if you need me,' she mumbled, waving her hand in the air as she exited into the car park, not looking back.

I'd never called her, not even on my very first night shift, which had been a baptism of fire. A squirrel had got in through one of the air vents somehow and had set off lights that operated on sensor during the night shift, scurrying around each floor trying to find its way out again. I didn't know what it was at first, convinced the place was haunted or another member of staff was playing a trick on me, like a Storage Queen night-shift initiation I knew nothing about. That was until I saw the rodent whipping down one of the corridors at lightning speed, its tail flapping.

It took a certain amount of mettle to work nights, not only tricking your body clock into staying alert during the witching hour but also braving the solitude. Silence could be overwhelming when you weren't used to it, but I loved my own company and the majority of customers who wanted access to their storage units in the evening were out the door by ten o'clock despite us being open twenty-four hours a day. Most nights, I had around eight whole hours of peace and quiet to study, other than the regular checks.

The first time I had to do a walkaround, which involved checking no one was onsite that shouldn't be and all the units were closed and locked, I broke out into a cold sweat. The corridors were long with high ceilings, painted a pale grey with each unit having its own bright yellow metal door. The units ran the length of each corridor on both sides in a u-shape with a staircase at either end, as well as a lift at the west stairwell. When I'd had a tour during my interview three months ago, it had reminded me of the inside of a prison, from what I'd seen on television, but nothing could prepare me for what it was like after dark. To say it was eerie was an understatement.

The fluorescent lights were powered by motion sensors and I was forever terrified of being plunged into darkness halfway down a corridor. So much so, I always walked with the torch on my phone permanently switched on whenever I was alone. It got so quiet inside the massive building you could hear a pin drop, nothing but the sound of your own footsteps slapping along the concrete walkway and the thud of your heartbeat. With three floors to cover, the checks took around twenty minutes and that first night I was a nervous wreck, screaming to high heaven when the squirrel I'd seen on the camera darted out in front of me on the first floor.

In my interview, Stacey had assured me I'd be quite safe working alone during the night shift. The warehouse was tucked away at the back of an industrial estate in Crawley where I lived, the only lit building after seven o'clock at night. Its plot included a small car park of twenty spaces, covered by cameras, as was inside. Employees used one keycode for access after hours and there were only five of us working at Storage Queen – four employees and Stacey, the manager, who was on call twenty-four, seven, if there were any emergencies.

In addition, there was also a panic button installed under the desk in reception that alerted a security firm who would attend the site if pressed. Each entrance and exit using the keypad was logged on the system and storage renters were given their own unique keycode should they wish to access their unit between six o'clock at night and six o'clock in the morning. Everyone who came through the door had to sign in and put down the number plate of the vehicle they were using.

During the day shift, when I'd been shown around, the place was a hive of activity; customers moving house and packing things away into their units or emptying them, dragging trolleys with precariously balanced boxes out to their cars or vans. It amazed me how many people rented storage and for all kinds of purposes I hadn't considered before joining Storage Queen. Businesses rented units because they didn't have enough office space, or for archiving paperwork. The general public stored furniture from downsizing or between house moves and entrepreneurs filled their spaces with stock ready to sell. The place was a treasure trove, although we rarely got to see inside the units unless we were called upon to assist, which had only happened once since I'd started.

Hoping Stacey would be right and the night would be quiet, I put the energy drink and macaroni cheese in the fridge behind my desk and settled into the cushioned chair Stacey had petitioned the owners for. Waking up the mouse, I logged onto the company desktop computer and opened my email. Stacey's radio played in the background, Smooth FM on low to populate the silence and Coldplay's 'Shiver' soothed my fractious mind which was still replaying my last conversation with Dom.

We'd ended our seven-month relationship barely half an hour ago and I'd like to say it was amicable, but rather we'd got to an impasse. He was going travelling around Thailand in three weeks with a friend, Drexl, from years back – someone I was yet to be introduced to. It was a trip that had been planned for ages and he'd told me he could be away for six months. When things began to get serious between us, he'd invited me to join them, but I was just coming to the end of my second year of a five-year BSMS Bachelor of Medicine, Bachelor of Surgery degree at the University of Brighton and wasn't prepared to miss any of my course.

What followed was a lot of arguments about the future of our relationship. We were poles apart, Dom was hedonistic and had studied agriculture at Plumpton College, where he became friends with the guy he was going travelling with. He'd dropped out while I was still doing my A levels and had secured a job as a gardener for an oil exploration company at Gatwick, long before we'd met at a nightclub in Crawley. When he'd approached them for a six-month sabbatical, they'd agreed, but I didn't have that luxury. I'd worked hard to save the university fees after thankfully acing my A levels and had to save up before I could apply, doing whatever job the agency would throw at me. It was why I'd started the degree later than some. The first year alone had cost over nine grand and I was lucky to still be living cheaply with my mum. The job at Storage Warehouse would pay for the following years' tuition and I couldn't jeopardise that, no matter how enticing the trip sounded.

Dom loved to have a good time, but his values were centred around the environment and reducing the damage humans were doing to the planet. I was a woman of science, an academic determined to become a doctor specialising in diabetes, something that had been part of me since I was diagnosed eight years ago, aged thirteen. I didn't want to waste time travelling when I could be helping people with their life-changing illness, plus I'd finally found a well-paid job that didn't interfere with my studies. I guessed opposites attract because, despite our differences, I was smitten and I'd even offered to fly out and visit during the summer break, but for Dom that hadn't been enough. He'd wanted me to join him for the entire trip.

'Last one,' a voice called from the entrance before an empty trolley crashed into the reinforced glass door.

I winced and stood up, peering over the counter.

'Shit, I'm sorry,' a man said, readjusting his hold and offering me a weak smile before frowning at the door, asking the silent question of why it hadn't opened. He was of slim build and handsome, with a ruddy complexion, but his eyes were slightly too far apart. Speckles of grey at the temples of his closely shaved hair contradicted his youthful face.

'It's okay, happens all the time. You need to input your code after six o'clock to enter and exit the building. The doors lock automatically overnight.'

'Ah okay,' he replied, nodding his head. 'Where did the other lady go?'

'There was a shift changeover, she's gone home.'

He nodded again and I watched as he fished his phone out of his combat trousers, tapping at the screen to find his code. Something which would have been emailed to him once his rental agreement had been signed and a minimal deposit paid. A second later, he entered it on the keypad to the left of the door and it slid open. The wheel of the trolley squeaked as he pushed it through to his van outside and began loading it with boxes as the door drew to a close. I shivered. Although it was March and spring was supposed to be in the air, the temperature hadn't got the memo and I was grateful Storage Queen still had their heating on in reception.

Outside in the car park, the floodlights were glowing, illuminating the already dark ombre sky. One flickered ominously and I returned my attention to the computer to check the cameras, switching between them to survey each floor. The man's wife or girlfriend was nowhere to be seen, but unit two hundred and forty-seven had the door wedged open, so I guessed she was inside, organising the stacking. The first and third floors were quiet. The images on screen were monochrome as the cameras switched to infrared in the darkness, indicating no one was up there.

The beep of the keypad pulled my focus back to the door and the man entered with his trolley now full of boxes, secured together with blue rope.

'Are you here all alone at night?'

There was something about his tone, not just the question, that sent the hairs on the back of my neck standing upright. My mouth went dry.

'You could get up to anything in here,' he added with a chuckle, running his tongue across his lips.

He pushed his trolley over to the lift and pressed the button, waiting for the doors to open. When they did, he looked back at me over his shoulder.

'You let me know if you want some company, eh.' He winked before pushing his trolley inside, not taking his eyes off me until the doors drew to a close.

2

I shuddered in my chair, annoyed at my vulnerability. It unsettled me, being a lone female where random men could intimidate or harass me for fun if they chose to. I was sure that guy was harmless. He was here with his partner after all and probably just flirting or trying to have a bit of banter with the girl on reception, but I never forgot how susceptible I was working here by myself. It wasn't as if I hadn't felt safe since I'd started working at Storage Queen. Nothing had happened so far, I'd had no strange visitors, other than the squirrel who'd been just as terrified as I was, but I wasn't about to advertise the fact I was alone.

Karl had told me once, during his shift, he'd had a man try to gain access in the middle of the night, shouting through the glass and pretending to have forgotten his code, but the policy was we didn't open the doors for anyone except security or the emergency services. If someone had misplaced their code to get in, then they had to come back during the day. All previous codes provided to renters were deleted from the system as soon as their agreement was up too, so only existing customers could come and go. I was sure it would happen to me at some point, I'd get a weirdo knocking on the glass, but knowing we had the panic button and cameras made me feel safer.

Turning my attention back to the monitor, through the camera I watched the creepy man and his Lycra-clad partner lifting boxes from the trolley and carrying them inside their storage unit. He paused to give her backside a squeeze and she slapped his hand away, unimpressed. Perhaps they were splitting up, storing items from the house they'd have to sell, or maybe she was just fed up being manhandled. I enjoyed coming up with stories for the renters and what could be inside their units to pass the time. The one they rented was one of our smaller sizes, about the dimensions of a large bathroom, so I imagined it was full to the brim by now.

My viewing was interrupted by my phone vibrating with what I initially assumed was a message from Dom. His final words to me just over an hour ago of *'well I guess that's it then,'* as he traipsed back towards his car, still ringing in my ears.

My heart had shattered watching him drive away. It wasn't supposed to end like that. I'd hoped we'd make it to the emotional goodbye at the airport. Our foreheads touching as we held hands, eyes misty with tears. I'd wanted to wish him well, tell him to take care and be safe in Thailand. Content knowing neither of us were going to make any promises for what would happen when he returned, but he'd kept pushing me to book my ticket, refusing to understand why I wouldn't defer for a year. He couldn't comprehend how my desire to become a doctor could stand in the way of a once-in-a-lifetime opportunity.

But the vibrating of my phone wasn't a message from Dom, it was my continuous glucose monitoring app, signalling my blood sugar level was 3.9 and action was needed. Every five minutes, the monitor attached to my upper arm automatically checked my blood sugar levels via a tiny canula inserted into the skin, alerting me if I was below 4.0 or higher than 10. I hadn't had a chance to eat before work because I'd been arguing with Dom, plus stress always sent my blood sugars plummeting.

I reached for the drawer and pulled a packet of

gummies out of the labelled plastic box, chewing rhythmically but barely tasting anything. My stomach was tightly knotted and I wasn't in the mood for food, hating having to eat when I wasn't hungry, but that was the life of a diabetic.

When I glanced back to the camera, the couple were gone, their yellow door now closed and secured with a padlock. Seconds later, the lift chimed and they both emerged, empty trolley in tow.

'Thanks, shall we just leave this here?' the man asked, pointing to the neatly stacked collection of trollies in the corner. He sounded completely normal now the woman was with him and I guess he'd just been chancing his arm earlier.

'Yes please.'

He pushed theirs into the stack and I made a mental note to oil that wheel later because the squeak set my teeth on edge.

'Could you sign out please?' I asked, tapping the open book on the counter.

He came over and squiggled his signature, entering the time, giving me another wink before joining his partner by the door. He entered their code, letting the frigid air in again, holding hands all the way to their van, reminding me of everything I'd lost tonight.

I sighed, rubbing my puffy eyes, and threw the empty sweet wrapper into the bin. At least I was alone to wallow in self-pity, to try to come to terms with the fact my relationship was over. It wasn't something I wanted to accept, but Dom had made me choose between him and the dream of becoming a doctor I'd been pursuing since I was thirteen. Now twenty-one, my goal hadn't changed, I'd worked hard and made sacrifices to earn the grades needed to get into university, and as much as I loved Dom, it was no contest. But breaking up still hurt like hell. I swiped away angry tears, wishing I could call my best friend, Laura, again, like I had on the drive over here. Or even Mum, who would at least offer me some words of wisdom, but they were both working tonight, Laura waitressing and mum at the hospital.

The urge to scroll through my phone watching TikToks for hours, to go down that wormhole of mindlessness was calling, but instead I begrudgingly pulled my textbook and pad out of my bag, making a start on the work I'd been set at today's lecture on the human airway. If I wasn't going to Thailand to save my relationship, I needed to make damn sure I got my bachelor's degree so my broken heart wouldn't be for nothing. After what seemed like a long dark and dreary winter, I really could do with some sun, but there was no way I could justify jetting off before I had completed my second year.

I turned the radio off, unable to bear another Ed Sheeran love song, and was fully engrossed in labelling a diagram of the respiratory system when headlights swung around the glass front of the building, catching my eye. A VW Golf pulled into the space next to my Focus and a man in a black baseball cap got out and opened his boot. It was dark and I squinted to see better in the flickering street light, chewing the end of my pen.

Through the gloom, I could tell the man was short, around five feet seven inches, and thickset. He had a huge neck and those rounded ball-like shoulders from hours spent lifting weights in the gym. I watched as he retrieved a large suitcase, finally turning to face the entrance, allowing me a better view. Despite his stocky appearance, the luggage appeared cumbersome, but luckily for him, it had wheels and he dragged it towards the glass doors. Whatever was inside was really heavy, I could tell by the way he was leveraging his weight as he walked, leaning forwards onto the balls of his feet. Perhaps it was dumbbells or a whole load of steroids and keratin powder for bodybuilding. I giggled to myself at my assumption.

When he reached the doors, he entered the keycode without pausing to look it up and I pulled my features into a welcoming expression. Studying wasn't the only reason I chose the night shifts, I wasn't great with people. I'd be that person at a party in the corner, avoiding eye contact and hoping no one spoke to me. I guess you could say I was guarded and it didn't always make me the most approachable, although if I was going to be a doctor, it was a skill I'd have to learn. *Fake it until you make it.*

'Hi,' I said as brightly as I could manage, standing up to greet him, but the man just nodded in my general direction.

He was dressed like he could have come straight from work, in a plain black long-sleeved T-shirt, dark indigo jeans and faded tan work boots. Barely giving me a second glance, he headed directly towards the lift, pulling his cap down as he went. It clearly wasn't his first time at Storage Queen and he waited with his back towards me, looking down at his phone.

'Um, could you sign in please.'

He looked over and frowned before leaving his suitcase by the lift and coming over to the reception desk, scribbling in the book and dropping the pen on the counter.

'Have a great night,' I muttered under my breath as he returned to the lift, sinking back into my seat. I was going to offer him the use of a trolley, but he obviously didn't want to be bothered.

Checking the time, I found I'd been studying for about forty minutes, actively forcing all thoughts of Dom from my mind. It was only half past seven, the first hour and a half had gone quickly, yet it was easy to clock-watch on a night shift, where the minutes seemed to tick by slower than usual. When I looked up again, my new visitor had disappeared, but the rumble of the lift sounded as it made its way up the shaft. I flicked through the cameras, wanting to see what floor he'd come out on, and found him on the third, dragging his case, still with some difficulty, right to the end of the corridor before the bend.

I remembered asking Stacey during one of our joint shifts where she was training me on the job, whether she ever had the urge to see what people stored. For all we knew it could be contraband, guns, drugs or stolen goods. The thought excited me, the idea of the police raiding the building during one of my night shifts like in a television drama, SWAT teams with guns or hazmat suits swarming every floor, cordoning sections off behind spirals of tape.

'They have to sign as part of the rental agreement; nothing that's deemed illegal is allowed to be stored on the premises' was the stock answer she gave me and I knew then she had no interest, but I burned with desire to peek behind every single yellow door. Mum and I spent hours curled up on the sofa binge watching the show where people bid on old or discarded storage units for their contents, hoping to find treasure and turn a profit. Some of them made a fortune, others weren't so lucky.

The stocky man in the baseball cap had disappeared from the screen and I couldn't tell if any of the doors were open at the far end of the corridor, the camera wasn't sharp enough. I never felt totally relaxed unless I was the only one inside the giant warehouse, but tried to go back to my diagram regardless. At least the gummy sweets were raising my blood sugar and would tide me over until I reheated the macaroni cheese, although the thought of it right now curdled my stomach.

I knew I had to do my checks, but at the same time was reluctant to leave the sanctuary of reception. We were supposed to do a walkaround every two hours when no one was in the building, every hour if there was, and I didn't want Stacey to look at any of the recordings in the morning to find I hadn't done my job.

Peeling myself out of the chair, I went to the toilet, taking time to splash water on my face before returning to the desk, pocketing my phone and making my way towards the stairs. It felt good to stretch my legs and perhaps the climb up and down three floors, checking the stairwells as I went, would work up an appetite, although I doubted it.

To the right and closest to the counter was the door to the east stairwell. Inside, its bright lights assaulted my eyes, not helped by the fact the steel staircase had been painted the same illuminous yellow as the doors. That was the colour scheme for Storage Queen, purple and yellow, even down to the cheesy crown logo that adorned the building, glowing at night. The owners had been a little too keen with the yellow, it was everywhere and so vivid it burnt my retinas.

The only sound was the rubber soles of my trainers making the metal clang and echo with each step. When I reached the first floor, the porthole window in the door from the stairwell into the corridor was encased in darkness. Anyone could have been the other side of it, waiting in the pitch black to jump out, but I knew it was just my overactive imagination, which played up every single night shift. I hoped by the time I'd worked here for six months, I would have rid my mind of the tricks it played on me.

As I loitered, steeling myself to open the door, I

heard a thud from above, reminding me I wasn't alone. It sounded like the visitor upstairs might have dropped something and, weirdly, it gave me a little bit of comfort, knowing if something happened during my checks, another human was on site to help.

As always, almost as soon as I pulled the door open, the overhead lights sprang on, illuminating the empty corridor. There were no monsters hiding in the shadows and I breathed a silent sigh of relief, shaking my head at my foolishness. Time to get on with the job I'd been employed to do.

A walkaround wasn't rocket science, I moved along the corridor, checking left and right to ensure the unit doors were closed, opening ones without padlocks on that weren't currently being rented. We had to make sure no one was inside. Stacey told me she'd had to call the police on a poor homeless guy once who'd managed to sneak in during the day and found an empty unit to hunker down in. It was ingenious really, somewhere dry and relatively warm compared to out-side, especially in winter, but most of the units on this floor were rented, all with padlocks securing their se-crets inside. Thankfully I found no strangers lurking as I was sure I wouldn't have been as calm as Stacey, had I discovered someone hiding.

Each floor was identical, long passages of bland

grey with what seemed like a never-ending amount of acid yellow doors. It was easy to forget where you were, what corridor, on what floor or even which stair-well, if you got distracted.

Once content all the doors on the floor were secure and the ones that weren't padlocked were empty, I came back on myself, double-checking, then climbed up the stairs towards the second floor to start the process again, freezing mid-step when, from some-where, an earth-shattering shriek filled the dark and empty steel cavern and stopped me in my tracks.

3

It only lasted a few seconds, but the shrill scream turned my veins to ice. I stood rigid in the stairwell, body trembling as I peered through the porthole into the darkness of the second floor, breath fogging up the glass. A chill ran up my spine as the air shifted around me, all at once becoming heavy and oppressive. Could it have been an animal, and if so, how had it got in, or had I been mistaken? Was it another squeaky trolley wheel?

No, I'd heard it and it didn't sound like a trolley, it sounded human. I chewed the inside of my cheek. It couldn't have come from this floor as no lights were on in the corridor, which meant no one was moving around. Unless it came from inside a unit. I stared back down the centre of the stairs, the light reflecting off the yellow metal, trying to be as quiet as a mouse, waiting for the sound to come again before I moved, but standing alone in the crushing silence made me jittery. What if someone or something was hurt? Trying to replay the sound in my head, I doubted myself, could I be sure it was human?

I debated where to go next. The acoustics were off in the warehouse due to the amount of steel. Noise seemed to bounce around and you never quite knew exactly where it was coming from. What I did know was that up to a few minutes ago, there was only one other person in the warehouse and I didn't think the sound had come from him. The policy was, if in doubt, call security, but I didn't want to get in trouble for calling them if it was a false alarm.

I eased the door open to the second floor, cringing at the squeak of the hinge and balling my hands into fists as the lights sprang on again, illuminating an empty corridor. Goosebumps ran the length of my arm as I waited for someone to appear. I couldn't see around the corner so had to assume I was the only one up here. I'd been the one to set the lights off after all. Stepping back inside the stairwell, I paused to listen again, looking up and down to the neighbouring floors, but unable to hear anything besides my racing pulse going ten to the dozen.

I breathed in and out slowly. Part of me wanted to remain right where I was, call Stacey or Dom even, tell them I'd heard something and I was scared. He'd come wouldn't he, despite our break-up, he'd show up if I needed him to? The thought of confronting who-ever or whatever had made that sound filled me with dread, but what choice did I have?

Eventually, common sense won and with slow, measured footsteps, I made my way up to the third floor. Before I reached it, I could see the light from the corridor beaming through the porthole. Obviously the lights were going to be on, the renter in the baseball cap was using his storage unit. As gingerly as before, I eased the door ajar and peeked around to see a unit open at the far end of the corridor just before the bend. My neck prickled, sending waves of electricity down my spine, my nervous system giving out the body's natural fight-or-flight response. Despite knowing the biological reason, it didn't make the situation any less intimidating, but someone could need my help and that propelled me forwards.

I reminded myself that I worked here, I was in charge and whatever happened was my responsibility while I was on duty, but it didn't ease the dread that crawled up my back. That sound had spooked me.

I tried to make my approach along the corridor as quiet as possible, stopping at a tiny red speck on the grey concrete walkway. My red Adidas Gazelles, just centimetres away, were a perfect match in colour. The speck seemed to glimmer as the overhead lights bounced off it and I bent down for a closer look, swallowing the lump that grew in my throat.

Was it blood? Dabbing my finger into the speck, effectively wiping it away, I brought it up to my face, recoiling. Its metallic odour was barely noticeable, but I'd had enough sessions in laboratories, working with vials of the stuff, to know that what I was rubbing between my fingertips was blood.

'Everything okay?'

I jumped at the deep voice booming down the corridor, nearly losing my balance as I straightened up. I couldn't place the accent, Polish maybe or Czech. It sounded quite harsh and abrupt, but the man in the baseball cap standing at the far end of the corridor wore a perplexed smile. His arms were folded across his chest and he resembled a bouncer at one of the many nightclubs Laura had dragged me to over the years, preparing to ask me for ID before he'd allow us in. He was no height at all but stocky as hell and not someone you'd want to pick a fight with.

'Fine,' I replied, my voice coming out a little high-pitched, 'just doing my checks.'

I pulled my face into an apologetic expression and tried to make my body appear relaxed as I walked towards him, but my shoulders remained rigid with tension. He stayed motionless as I approached, legs reluctant to move and feeling self-conscious, eyeing me curiously while I tried to work out if he was a threat. His red-rimmed eyes seemed to bore into me and my resolve to remain calm withered away with the blood I'd rubbed between my fingers. Whose blood was it? Had it been here earlier meaning Stacey missed it on her last check, or had it happened since I'd arrived on duty?

The man pulled his black cap low as I closed the distance between us. Was he trying to conceal his face? Unsettled by our interaction, I suddenly remembered I should be checking the doors and immediately swivelled my head from side to side as I passed each unit.

'Checking they're locked?' he asked, his lip curling upwards. Was he mocking me or making conversation? It had been an effort for him to nod his head in greeting when he'd arrived.

'Yep,' I replied, my voice as light as silk, betraying my thudding pulse.

He stepped aside at the last minute, moving out of my path, and despite being determined I wouldn't, curiosity got the better of me and I glanced inside the open door of his unit as I passed.

To my surprise, it was empty except for the suitcase, which was closed and lying flat on the floor. I could sense his eyes on my back, burning into my T-shirt but I tried to keep my pace steady, fighting the urge to take off and run out of sight around the corner to the west stairwell.

'Have a great night,' he called as I reached the end to turn left, sounding insincere.

'Thank you,' I said, over my shoulder, a quick glance revealing he was still standing there watching me go. I shuddered, something about him gave me the creeps, but I forced myself to stop and turn around. 'Did you hear a noise a few minutes ago? It sounded like a scream?'

He shrugged, mouth turned downwards and shook his head. 'Nope.'

I nodded, unsure if I was convinced but eager to put some distance between us. The noise had put me on edge and I continued half-heartedly doing my checks around the rest of the third floor. Hopefully he'd be finished doing whatever he was doing soon and I'd have the warehouse to myself. I'd have to check the cameras to make sure no one had come in whilst I was doing my walkaround but if they hadn't then maybe I'd be able to relax a little.

Nothing was amiss on the rest of the third floor and I quickly walked the second floor, having missed it on my way up, before heading back down to reception, intending to check the toilets and then do a little digging. I'd heard a yell or a scream, I was sure of it, trying to recall the sound, but already I was doubting myself. Was it a sound of pain or terror? The only thing remotely similar was foxes I'd heard over the woodland at the back of our house in the middle of the night. Whether they were mating or fighting, I didn't know, but the noise was horrific. I wanted to double-check I hadn't somehow missed anyone entering Storage Queen.

When I reached my desk, the screensaver had kicked in. I logged on and scrolled back through the camera footage of the entrance from five o'clock, an hour before I'd arrived. Two lots of renters had left before the couple I'd seen arrived in their van, collecting the trolley with the squeaky wheel and loading boxes onto it. I moved the feed forward. A VW Golf in battleship grey drove into the car park and sat for a while before driving out. I couldn't tell if the driver was the man in the baseball cap currently on the third floor, but the car looked to be the same.

Had he forgotten something or was he waiting for a better time to visit? A time when there were no other customers on site. The idea made me shudder and I made a note of the registration number on my pad, underlining it twice, because what he'd written in the visitor book was barely legible. I carried on watching right until Stacey left, hurrying to her flash BMW, and then the couple left in their van before the Golf returned. It was definitely the same vehicle, it had the same registration plate. I paused the footage and shrank the camera feed down on the desktop and clicked into the database where each unit had a name attached to it.

Number three hundred and twenty-one was rented by a Sasha Cizmarova on a six-month rolling contract, no registration plate listed. I opened the scanned copy of the agreement and saw it had been signed off by Stacey and to date there were no overdue payments or notes on the account. I assumed Sasha was female, so who was the man up there now?

Checking the visitor book again, I couldn't tell what name he'd put down either. I pulled my phone from my pocket, unsure whether to give Stacey a ring just to see if I was overreacting, but I'd already made her late home, I didn't want to disturb her evening further, not on a Friday night. She might already be in her pyjamas, half a bottle of wine down by now. I didn't even know if she had kids, I'd never thought to ask. I hadn't noticed if she wore a wedding ring and had no idea about her world outside of Storage Queen; she hadn't volunteered anything about her personal life during our interactions.

While I had my phone in my hand, I checked my notifications on autopilot, disappointed to find no texts from Dom, no regret for the way we'd left things. It was a bitter pill to swallow and the thought of him not being in my life any more made my chest constrict. My blood sugar sat at 6.1, a safe range, no action required, so I turned my attention back to the computer screen, closing the recording and opening the camera feed for the third floor.

I had so many unanswered questions, who was the creepy man in the baseball cap? Assuming he wasn't Sasha, had she given him the access code? It was frowned upon, the codes were only supposed to be used by the renter. If anyone else was discovered using the code, their agreement would be terminated with immediate effect. Could he be storing the suitcase on her behalf, and if so, what was in there that made it so heavy?

The blood I'd found belonged to someone; it wasn't flaky, therefore relatively fresh, so had the stranger cut himself by accident? It was a possibility, but he hadn't appeared wounded, just a bit off. In fact, his whole demeanour was weird, watching me until I left the corridor. What didn't he want me to see? At the forefront of my mind, the cause of my unease wasn't only the blood, I knew I'd heard something resembling a scream. I hadn't imagined it, so who'd made it?

4

To my right, the door to the east stairwell squeaked, almost making me jump out of my seat. The man in the baseball cap appeared. This time, he had a friendly smile on his face as he approached the counter, a marked improvement from the sneer I thought I'd seen before. His unit was on the east side of the building, so I guessed he thought it was quicker to use the stairs than to walk around to the other side for the lift.

'Hi,' he said, resting his forearms on the counter. A faded eagle tattoo poked out from beneath his sleeve on his right hand and I saw his nails were bitten to the quick on stumpy fingers. Up close, his round face was smooth with no stubble visible, and his hair, although mostly hidden beneath his cap, was a mousy brown. His nose was large but flat, like it had been punched many times, and I imagined him in a bare-knuckle boxing match, his opponent towering over him. He may have been vertically challenged, but he was wide, arms like tree trunks, and I had no doubt he could look after himself.

'Hi, how can I help?' I replied on autopilot, the words catching in my throat, betraying my composure. As I waited for him to speak, my face grew hot, there was something intense in his molten eyes which un-settled me, not to mention the proximity between us. He was so close, it was disconcerting, and I found my-self rolling backwards in my chair a few inches.

'I need to go, but I can come back.'

I frowned – was it a question or not? The language barrier had me confused, but I answered as if it was.

'Yes, we're open twenty-four hours a day,' I replied, swallowing the saliva that pooled in my mouth.

'Good, good,' he said, leaning further forward and glancing down over the gloss counter to the desk, eyeing the contents before stepping back. What was he looking at? My pad and pen, my textbook? He'd gone from blatantly ignoring me to now being overfa-miliar. 'I see you in little while.'

He turned towards the door, tapping in the code

again from memory and left. I stared after him, letting out my breath in a gust. A sense of calm drifted over me as he climbed in his car and drove away, but it was short-lived. He'd said he'd be back. Would he come alone or with someone else?

My phone vibrated – a welcome distraction from the dark thoughts that whirled around my mind. It was Mum, probably on her break at work.

Don't forget to eat. X

I sighed and checked my blood sugar, it was now 5.8. I calculated the carbohydrates in the portion of macaroni cheese, inputting my current levels and the total carbs into an app on my phone. With the information I'd given, it displayed how many units of insulin I had to give myself and I rummaged in my bag for my insulin pen. After fitting a new needle, I twisted the dial at the end, loading the smallest amount of insulin I could, and plunged down, injecting a tiny drop of liquid into the bin to make sure there were no air bubbles.

The potent smell of manufactured insulin, the hormone that regulated blood glucose levels, made me wrinkle my nose. Even after all these years I couldn't stand the artificial odour. I twisted the pen again, clicking up the numbers on the dial to the amount of units the app stated I needed to inject and steeled myself.

I couldn't say it got easier exactly, each pinprick hurt a tiny bit, but I'd become used to it. I'd given myself thousands of injections since I'd been diagnosed. My preferred site was on my stomach, I'd always been on the lean side and it was the only place I could pinch an inch of flesh. The rule was, the fleshier the injection site, the less it hurt. Holding my T-shirt up with my teeth, I pressed the needle slowly into the skin of my stomach, waiting for it to pierce. Once in, I pressed the plunger down, sending the insulin into the fatty tissue to do its magic.

I put the pen away and retrieved the macaroni cheese from the fridge. It had been Mum's leftovers from lunch and she always made sure I went to work with at least one hot meal to get me through the night.

Caring was in her nature, although since I'd started working at Storage Queen, during the week we were often ships that passed in the night. She was a nurse and worked shifts at the local NHS Urgent Treatment Centre, seeing patients with minor injuries or illnesses that weren't serious enough for Accident and Emergency. She triaged the unwell when they came in and prioritised the urgency of their treatment.

It had been the two of us for as long as I could re-
member – like peas in a pod, she'd always said.

I had no siblings and hadn't had a father figure in
my life either, mine hadn't even stuck around for my
birth, deciding to hot-foot it as soon as Mum let slip
she was pregnant in the early stages of their relationship. I was sure she was lonely, but she told me she
had no time for all that, and in all these years there
had only been a handful of dates and one short-lived
romance when I was much younger. Maybe once I'd
moved out that would change.

I'd started saving for a deposit to rent a flat now I
was earning a decent amount and working around my
studies. It was something Dom and I had discussed,
but I hadn't been brave enough to broach the subject
with Mum yet. I knew she'd feel deserted and I didn't
want to hurt her. She had put me first always and
when we'd curl up on the sofa together and watch
television with a cup of tea at the end of a long day, I
knew she was at her happiest.

We were close – in fact, she was my best friend,
besides Laura, who I'd known since high school. She'd
stepped up and been a dad as well as a mum, happy to
include Laura in anything we did. The three of us had
gone to the pub when we'd both turned eighteen only
weeks apart for our first legal drink and she'd taught

me to drive in her tiny 1980s Mini around deserted car parks after the shops had closed. She'd been the one to vet my boyfriends, help me with my homework and visit the closest universities before deciding which one to apply to, delighted to find I could do a bachelor's degree in medicine at the University of Brighton just a short drive away so I didn't even have to be a resident on campus. Even then, she'd wanted to keep me near because I was her world. Laura, as much as she loved my mum, used to say she smothered me, but it never felt like that and I knew she was already dreading an empty nest.

As Mum's leftover macaroni cheese lunch whirred in the microwave, permeating reception with a funky smell, I realised I hadn't yet washed my hands. Something I should have done before I injected. On inspection, miniscule spots of blood were crusted in the tiny ridges of my fingerprints, reminding me I hadn't given much more thought as to where the blood had come from since I'd got back to reception. Not from a paper cut on baseball cap man's hands that was for sure. Perhaps I could find out?

Dinner momentarily forgotten, I checked the camera feed for the third floor, scrolling back to when the lights had come on. The man emerged from the lift dragging the cumbersome suitcase down the corridor, stopping at the end to unlock Sasha's unit. Once inside, there was nothing to see for around ten minutes and I fast-forwarded the footage, playing it again when he flashed back onto the screen.

What was he doing? He seemed to have a funny gait, walking towards the camera, one foot lagging behind, face directed at the floor. I squinted at the screen and rewound it, spotting a cloth beneath his tan boot. Was he cleaning the floor? My breath caught in my throat as I rewound and watched a third time. Had there been more blood and he'd missed the speck I'd seen? I pushed my chair back, needing to look again, and took the stairs two at a time to the third floor, pausing for a second to pant at the top.

I walked slowly down the corridor, eyes glued to the concrete for any hint of red but couldn't find a single drop. Loitering outside unit three hundred and twenty-one, I gave the padlock a tug for good measure, but it was locked. I pressed my ear to the cool metal door, listening for sounds of anyone inside. Someone could be hurt, although the most obvious explanation was that the man in the cap had accidentally cut himself somehow, perhaps on the sharp edge of the suitcase. But it didn't sit right with me, something in my gut told me that wasn't the case.

Reluctantly, I headed back down the metal stairs,

my foot slipping out from under me like I'd trod on a sheet of ice, and I clung on to the banister for dear life.

'Shit!' I hissed, regaining my balance, waiting for my equilibrium to return. Beneath my trainer lay a dark green credit card, the emblem of the bank displayed on it. I flipped it over and found the name Cizmarova printed in white letters. Maybe the guy was Sasha? Perhaps I'd been too quick to assume. The card seemed to thrum in my fingers as I held it on the way back to reception, an idea springing to my mind. There was only one way to find out if the guy really was Sasha.

I logged on to the database and called up unit three hundred and twenty-one, waiting impatiently for Sasha's details to appear on the screen. They included a mobile number and I dialled it before I could change my mind, listening to it ring sporadically, the reception patchy. Eventually, it went to voicemail, the standard automated spiel was jittery due to limited coverage in the warehouse and didn't tell me the sex of Sasha, so I didn't leave a message. I wasn't sure about handing the card to the man in the baseball cap either, especially as I didn't know whether he was Sasha or not.

I could ask him for some identification, but the thought of doing that made me uneasy. What if he got confrontational? I was here alone and I needed to consider the implications of that. My mind spiralled in all directions, imagining the worst-case scenario, as Dom told me I often did: what if the man wasn't Sasha and she was trapped inside the unit?

Scribbling down the number on a Post-it note, I jogged back upstairs. I'd have to eat soon, the insulin I'd administered was already lowering my blood sugar and I should have tucked in already, but I'd only be a couple of minutes. I just wanted to put my outlandish theory to bed so I could get back to my assignment with a clear conscience. When I reached unit three hundred and twenty-one, I used my phone to dial the number on the scrap of paper, waiting for it to connect. When the shrill ring began, I lowered the phone away from my ear.

My hand trembled and I ran my tongue over bone dry teeth, expecting to hear it ring from inside the unit, but no sound came. I was about to hang up, but before I could, the line cut out and I lost reception. Sasha's phone wasn't in there, not that I could hear, but it didn't mean she wasn't.

5

What would I have said if Sasha had picked up? Are you trapped inside? Shall I call the police? Did baseball cap man abduct you?

Maybe I'd got it completely wrong, he could actually be Sasha and had just dropped his bank card. My mind was conjuring up all sorts of conspiracy theories, anything to pass my lengthy night shift and avoid university work. Anything not to think about Dom. At any rate, I needed to eat, my blood sugar level was dropping and soon my phone would go off, alerting me I was low. I should have eaten as soon as I'd injected, a schoolgirl error.

I slipped the paper in my pocket and walked back

down the stairs, calves aching, freezing between the third and second floor when I heard a moan coming from somewhere below me. My chin trembled as I descended the stairs quickly, peering through the porthole onto the second floor, which was cloaked in darkness. Despite no lights being on, I was sure the sound had come from this floor. The realisation I wasn't alone made my hands clammy; someone was in the building and the noise this time had definitely been human.

Steeling myself, I pushed open the door, the lights springing to action but the corridor appeared empty. Striding down the corridor, I got almost all the way around to the west stairwell when I heard a giggle come from one of the units I'd just passed. It was number two hundred and forty-seven. The one the couple had been using earlier. My tightly wound shoulders sagged before irritation came over me in waves as I put my ear to the door.

'Stop, you know I don't like it,' a voice simpered, followed by a throaty laugh and then a groan of pleasure.

I chewed the inside of my cheek, annoyance bubbling in the depths of my stomach.

Raising my fist, I knocked three times, unable to believe I was about to evict a horny couple getting it on in their unit. Didn't they have anywhere better to go?

'Hello?' a male voice called through the door before it was pushed open. The man who had winked at me stood shirtless at the threshold, his hair dishevelled.

'You need to go please. I'll give you five minutes, then I'm calling security,' I said in the most authoritative tone I could muster. I wanted to give them a piece of my mind for scaring me half to death. When had they got in? I'd watched the camera footage, but then it dawned on me. I'd watched the recording until the man in the baseball cap had arrived in his Golf, I hadn't watched anything after that. They must have snuck in when I was in the toilet, leaving their van in the parking spots at the side of the building rather than at the front.

'Umm sure,' he replied, shrugging, 'you know how it is, when the mood strikes.' Awarding me with what I assumed was supposed to be a cheeky grin.

'Five minutes,' I said stiffly before leaving them to it and going back to reception.

I checked the visitor book and saw the couple from unit two hundred and forty-seven hadn't signed in again, so I sat waiting for them to emerge red-faced at being caught using Storage Queen as a cheap hotel. I reheated the tepid macaroni cheese for another twenty seconds and shovelled half of it in as fast as I could. It was rich and gooey, but I didn't enjoy it, the pasta was sustenance and I wished I had a tub of Ben & Jerrys to pick at instead. As fast as I ate, my phone still vibrated with a low warning five minutes later. I'd have to wait for the carbohydrates to hit my system and my blood sugar to catch up. Feeling a little light-headed, I relaxed back into Stacey's comfortable chair, closing my eyes for a second and waiting for the floaty feeling to pass. I'd be chasing my tail all night now.

Finally, the pair from unit two hundred and forty-seven emerged from the lift, the man looking a little more put together than I'd last seen him.

'Sorry for your trouble,' he said, passing through reception as the girl shrank behind him, unable to stop giggling.

I gave the pair of them a death stare until he in-putted his code and they left. I'd been on edge since the first scream, which I now deduced was the woman squealing, and perhaps because of that I'd overreacted about everything that had happened since.

I sent Mum a text to reassure her I'd eaten and thanked her for the pasta. It was almost nine o'clock and I had another nine hours to get through. The thought made my heart sink, but at least the first three had gone relatively quickly. Karl, the other night shift worker, brought his iPad in and binged Netflix all night, sometimes getting through a whole series in one shift. Occasionally, Stacey left us little tasks to do, entering new clients on the database, filing paperwork or cleaning out a recently emptied container, but most of it was covered during the day. We were just bodies sat in the seat, guarding the premises, although I certainly wouldn't be much of a deterrent. I'd deliberately not brought any entertainment so I'd concentrate on the assignment I had to complete, something I was now beginning to regret.

I sent Laura a voice note, filling her in on the weird night I was having. She was waitressing at an American restaurant where she made more in tips than she did in wages. Her bubbly personality and girl-next-door qualities made her the perfect waitress, not to mention her ample cleavage, which was always on display. It was a job I'd be terrible at; unfortunately, I was one of those people whose face betrayed exactly what they were thinking the majority of the time. Plus, the general public could be rude and entitled and I'd find it hard to bite my tongue if someone complained about slow service on a busy night.

Like me, Laura was working to support her way through a degree at the University of Brighton, but her chosen path was business management. She was super smart and had a head for enterprise from an early age. When we were fourteen, she'd opened her own underground tuck shop at school, making a hefty profit until the headteacher had caught her dealing snacks in the toilets and shut her down. She had a month of lunchtime detentions, but that didn't stop her. After the heat had died down, she'd reopened her business outside the school gates every morning, trading for half an hour before the bell rang. I couldn't fault her tenacity, but whenever we'd studied together, I couldn't make head nor tail of what she was learning, her textbooks might have well been written in a foreign language for all I understood.

Trying to avoid the respiratory system assignment for a few more minutes, I clicked through the camera feed. Every floor of the warehouse was in night mode, the screen monochrome, with no activity until I switched to the car park, my shoulders climbing instantly to my ears when I saw the VW Golf was back. Swathed in shadows, I couldn't tell if anyone was in the driver's seat, but there it was, parked next to my car again. I rewound to see when it had arrived. It was over twenty minutes ago, when I'd been upstairs. He must have taken the lift or used the other stairwell for our paths not to have crossed.

I watched the man, still in his cap, enter the building and walk towards the counter as though I'd been sat there, disappearing off screen. Stacey told me there weren't any cameras directed at where we sat on reception any more, just the general vicinity. She'd argued against it, declaring it an invasion of privacy, which made me wonder what she got up to when she was on duty. Her internet search must be a riot, although I doubted it was anything more scandalous than clothes shopping or an addiction to Foxy Bingo. I checked the book and he had signed in again, another indetermined squiggle of a signature, but at least it was there, which reassured me somewhat because surely if he was up to no good, he would have bypassed the book altogether.

Nonetheless, an involuntary shiver descended my spine as though someone had walked over my grave. Instantly, I was on edge again, knowing I wasn't alone. The man was in the building somewhere as, according to the car park footage I'd fast-forwarded up to now, he hadn't left. I drew my arms around myself, suddenly feeling a chill that had nothing to do with the drop in temperature as the evening went on.

It was bad enough knowing the couple had slipped in without me noticing but him too. I brought up the third-floor camera, rewound it back and found him entering his unit on the third floor, then exiting again a few minutes later and walking around to the west stairwell. All of the floors were still in darkness currently, but he could be on the stairs or in the toilet maybe. I was sure there was some reasonable explanation for not being able to see him on the cameras. Perhaps he was looking for his bank card in the stairwell where no cameras were located. It seemed silly to call Stacey and worry her when I didn't know all the facts yet.

Now I was on high alert, contemplating what to do next. My bladder answered for me, announcing the need to be emptied with some urgency. There were only one set of toilets, located on the west side of the reception next to the lift. A door led through to a small lobby area with a bench running the length of the back wall and a mirror above, with two further doors at the end: one for men and one for women. We had to share with the public, there were no separate ones for staff. It gave me the ick, especially as the cleaners came in at seven in the morning. By the time I got to work, they'd been in use all day long.

I loitered by the men's toilet, trying to listen for movement inside. Could he be in there, using the facilities, and that's why the lights were out upstairs? It was perfectly acceptable for him to do so as a customer.

Curiosity got the better of me and I pushed the door open a fraction, peering inside, the potent smell of urine hitting me in the face like a rubber mallet. 'Hello,' I called, trying not to gag, 'anyone in there?'

I waited a beat, but no response came, only the sound of a tap dripping.

I stood for a few seconds, but the man in the baseball cap didn't emerge from either of the two cubicles, so I went into the ladies', to the furthest stall and began layering the toilet seat with paper before I sat down. You couldn't be too careful. After, I washed my hands thoroughly, then I checked my reflection in the mirror over the sink. Dark circles ringed my eyes and I tutted. My skin was pasty and my shoulder-length hair looked like it could do with a good brush. I'd cried off what little make-up I wore on the way into work while I'd been on the phone to Laura and had no time to fix my face as I was already late. Tonight was the first of three consecutive night shifts and I already looked like shit. No wonder Dom hadn't put up much of a fight for me.

I scowled at my harsh judgement; that wasn't fair, he was trying not to prolong the torture, he'd said. If I wasn't going to Thailand, it was better to end it now.

Like ripping off a plaster in one foul swoop. Perhaps I should have agreed to go. What if he was the one and I'd messed everything up? I knew I was still young, but I'd never felt this way about anyone before. Having said that, Dom was the first serious boyfriend I'd had. Laura had assured me there'd be others in the future, saying I was too young to get tied down anyway.

Perhaps the timing was off. Mum had suggested that could be the case when I'd confided in her about Dom going to Thailand, she'd said sometimes you meet the right people at the wrong time in your life. Had that been the same for her? I'd hate to think what she'd have said if I'd announced I was deferring my degree to join Dom backpacking. I didn't think I'd be able to handle the disappointed look she'd give me, throwing it all away for a boy, even though she liked him.

I sloped back to reception, rounding the desk and noticing immediately the bank card had disappeared. I'd left it tucked partly beneath my keyboard. Not only that, but the Storage Queen branded pad where I'd written down the registration of the Golf had gone too. I looked inside my bag to ensure it hadn't been riffled through. Everything seemed to be in order, the important items: my insulin pen, purse and car keys loose at the bottom amongst the crumbs and debris. I frowned, looking around the desk, something else was missing. I searched through the single drawer of snacks, then on the sideboard by the microwave and fridge. Where was my phone?

Panic began to solidify in my muscles, making my movements juddery. *Calm down, Nina, it'll be here somewhere*, I told myself. But as I moved bits of paper on the desk and searched the area behind me again, even looking in the fridge and microwave this time, I came up empty-handed. I needed that phone, not just because my whole life was on there, but I had no way to tell what my blood sugar was without the app. Stupidly, I'd left my manual machine, the finger pricker, at home in a rush to get out of the door after Dom had dropped his bombshell.

Shit! I plunged my fingers into my hair, pulling at the scalp as I blew air out through my cheeks. If the man in the baseball cap had taken my phone along with the bank card and pad his number plate was written on, why had he done so?

6

Instinctively, I checked the cameras again, at a loss of what to do. His car was still in the car park but he wasn't in it and when I rewound the footage back, he hadn't left. He was in here somewhere, but where? Concentrating on the inside cameras I checked each floor. The light on the first floor was on, although I couldn't see anyone. It flicked off and twenty seconds later, when I switched the feed, the third-floor light came on. I saw the door to the stairwell open and close again as though it had just been pushed to set the lights off, but no one came through it. Was the guy messing with me? Should I confront him?

Remembering my training, I picked up the landline on my desk and dialled Stacey's number which had been printed onto a label and stuck on the handset. It rang for ages without being answered, making me more anxious with each second that passed. It was half past nine, would she be in bed already? Even if she was, wasn't she supposed to answer whenever it rang? Wasn't that the point of being 'on-call'? It went to voicemail and I left a message, asking her to call me. I counted to ten and eyed the panic button. Was it really an emergency, was my life in danger? Stacey had said we got charged for callouts, so I wanted it to be a last resort, worried I'd jeopardise my job if I pushed it for something not deemed serious.

I gritted my teeth and bounded towards the stairs without overthinking it.

'Hey,' I shouted as I climbed, hoping the man in the baseball cap might pop up, but there was no reply. By the time I reached the third floor, the light was still on, but walking the length of the corridor all the way around, I didn't see anyone. Unit three hundred and twenty-one was still padlocked and I didn't find the man back down the stairs of the west stairwell either. My heart was beating so fast, I thought it might explode out of my chest and I gripped the banister to collect myself at the bottom.

It's just a silly misunderstanding, Nina, everything is fine.

Out in reception, the lift chimed, announcing its arrival, and I backed away, waiting for the doors to slide open, holding my breath as dread enveloped me, like I was expecting a monster to burst out. When the doors eventually opened, the noise of dragging metal sounding all too loud in the quiet space, the lift was empty.

He was fucking with me, there was no other explanation. But why? Irritation scratched beneath my skin. I wasn't paid to chase weirdos around the building.

'Sod this, I'm calling Stacey again,' I muttered to myself, hoping this time she'd answer and suggest ringing the police or pressing the panic button, but she could just as well tell me it was an overreaction, that working the night shift got people het up this way sometimes.

I didn't really want to call her either; she was the manager, but I should be able to handle this myself. What if she thought I wasn't responsible or mature enough? I didn't want her to think she'd made a mistake hiring me. I needed this job, it fitted around my studies and the money was decent. I debated for a minute, scratching the back of my neck where the hairs stood on end.

I could deal with this jerk by myself. Did he really have nothing better to do than torment a lone worker on a Friday night? Was that how he got his kicks?

His motivation scared me though. I was a female, alone in a huge warehouse with a stranger – a large and imposing stranger at that. Yes, there were cameras, but were they a deterrent? If he caught me in the stairwell or dragged me into a unit, there were no cameras there. Hell, he could attack me as I sat at my desk and that would be out of shot too. All my initial reservations about working the night shift resurfaced. He could do whatever he wanted and no one would have any idea, not for hours anyway. If I had my phone, I'd message Laura again, something light-hearted: *There's a guy here and he's really freaking me out. If you never hear from me again make sure my mum sues Storage Queen. LOL.*

Even if I had my phone, I knew she wouldn't respond, she'd be busy serving customers their ribs and fries, she likely hadn't even listened to my last message, but it would give me comfort to send her one anyway. I needed someone to shake me by the shoulders and tell me I was overreacting and that's just what Laura would do. She'd tell me to get a grip and we'd laugh about it tomorrow. When we spoke on the drive to work earlier, she'd suggested we meet up for a coffee and cake, and I was looking forward to crying on her shoulder about what had happened with Dom. I'd give anything to be able to talk to her right now as I was losing my mind.

The lift rumbled into action, jerking me from my thoughts, and my heart nearly leapt out of my chest. He'd summoned it from another floor. I stood, waiting for the number display to rise from ground to level one, unsure whether it would go further. It stopped at one and I raced up the stairs, bursting through the door on the first floor, but the lift was empty and, despite the lights being on, so was the part of the corridor I could see, before the bend.

'No more playing with the lift,' I scowled, stepping inside and pressing the bright red emergency stop button which emitted a loud beep. Then the lift powered down, leaving the doors stuck open.

Try moving it now, dickhead.

'Hello!' I called down the corridor, my voice echoing as the lights flickered ominously. *Please stay on.*

Walking the length of the first floor, the utter silence creeped me out. Not only was there a random guy, who had potentially stolen my phone, wandering

around Storage Queen, but he deliberately wasn't answering me. My gut fizzed with anxiety. Was I being
stalked like in some horror film where the antagonist
toys with his victim, revelling in her fear before
swooping in for the kill?

I shook my head, trying to dislodge my overactive
imagination, it was firing on all cylinders tonight,
zooming down rabbit holes I didn't want to go. No,
there had to be a rational explanation, maybe he was
in the toilet or I'd just missed him using the lift when I
was going up the stairs. But why he should be somewhere else other than the third floor, I didn't know.

I moved upwards to the second floor just in case he
was there, although he had no business being anywhere except where his unit was – or rather Sasha's
unit. Dom would tell me to 'chill out', blaming my
constant need to catastrophise a situation without
thinking logically, before following up with his usual
'you worry too much'. And I wished he was here to
talk me down from the ledge.

No sooner than I'd got back to the stairwell,
finding nothing out of place on the second floor, I
heard a crash from below and scurried back down the
stairs with my jaw clenched so tight I thought my
teeth might crumble to dust. Carrying on past the first
floor as I continued to hear sounds coming from fur-

ther down, I burst through the door to reception, ready to give the guy a piece of my mind.

I found him on his hands and knees by the entrance, gathering the contents of a box it looked like he'd just dropped and putting them back inside. Had he been in the car park all this time? No, not possible, someone had called the lift and set the lights off, but from the chill in the air, I could tell the doors had just been opened. He must have had time to go to his car while I'd been walking the first- and second-floor corridors looking for him... unless there was someone else here?

'Oh, hello,' he said, gesturing to the floor, 'I had an accident.' He looked innocent enough, seemingly with no idea of how uneasy he'd made me.

I stepped forwards slowly and bent to pick a book up. It was a dog-eared copy of a Lonely Planet traveller's guide to Asia, filled with annotations and pages turned over. The flaps of the box were closed and I didn't get a chance to sneak a look at what else he had.

'I thought you'd left?' I said, handing the book to him.

'I couldn't find key to the padlock, but it was in the car and now the lift isn't working,' he grimaced and for a second I felt a slither of guilt. He sounded convincing. Had we just been missing each other around the warehouse? 'Could you help me carry this up? Save me two trips.' He lent back on his knees, hands resting on his huge thighs awaiting an answer.

I couldn't reactivate the lift from the ground floor and as much as I didn't want to, perhaps if I helped him, then he'd be out of here quicker. The sooner he was gone, the sooner I could relax.

My throat was dry and scratchy and I let out a feeble cough before speaking. 'Um, sure,' I said, plastering on a weak smile.

He returned with one of his own and I noticed his two front teeth overlapped slightly. Getting to his feet, he handed me a black rubbish bag tied at the top. Although large, it wasn't overly heavy, so I assumed it was clothing or bedding inside.

'I couldn't find you on the cameras,' I said, wanting him to know we were being filmed as I led him towards the stairwell.

'Oh, you must have missed me,' he said dismissively.

I chewed my lip, gesturing for him to go ahead up the stairs. I didn't want him behind me; if he got weird, at least I'd be able to ditch the bag and run. I wasn't going to be one of those people who got themselves killed from being polite, not going with their gut when it told them something was wrong. Ted Bundy had asked his victims for help carrying something to his car before overpowering them... or was I thinking of *Silence of the Lambs*? I shuddered, trying to dispel the image of Buffalo Bill from my mind, it really wasn't helpful.

As we climbed, I looked for signs of my phone in the rear pockets of his jeans, but they appeared flat and empty. Had I just mislaid it after all?

'You haven't picked up my phone have you?' I asked, trying to make my question sound casual and not accusatory.

'No, you lost it?'

I couldn't tell if he was lying from his voice and his face wasn't visible to see if it gave the game away, but someone had removed the pad on my desk with his car registration on it as well as the bank card. It couldn't possibly have been anyone else.

'Really,' I said, incredulous and unable to stop myself, 'you don't have it?' I couldn't hide the sarcasm in my voice.

He stopped halfway up the stairs and turned around to face me, shaking his head. 'No, I don't.'

'Okay,' I replied stiffly and we carried on climbing. Maybe I'd left it in the toilet, although I was sure I hadn't taken it in there with me. He had to have taken it, but what was I going to do, wrestle him to the ground and search his pockets?

'Is it not safe for a girl to be working alone all night?' he asked, pausing to look over his shoulder. My back stiffened before irritation won over.

'It's quite safe for a *woman*,' emphasising the word, 'there are cameras everywhere and Paul is due on shift shortly,' I lied, hoping I sounded convincing.

'I see,' he said, a smile playing on his lips. Was this guy deliberately trying to unnerve me? More than anything, I just wanted him gone. I was tempted to lock the doors, switch off the lights and hunker down for the rest of my shift once he had. Stacey would understand. When she called back, I'd tell her I got spooked. Realistically how many more customers would there be? None, if my past shifts were anything to go by.

When we got up to the third floor and along the corridor to unit three hundred and twenty-one, I placed the bag down and stood back as the man fumbled in his pocket for the key to the padlock. He had acne scars on the back of his neck, around his hairline, and was taking his sweet time to get the door open.

'I need to get downstairs,' I said, hating the quiver in my voice as I backed away, feeling suddenly vulnerable, adding, 'I'm supposed to man the desk.' At least in reception, I was close to an exit, plus I needed to find my phone.

'Sure, thanks for the help,' he smiled, as fake as any I'd seen. Wide enough to give me a flash of lower jagged teeth, as a river of cold unease seeped into my chest.

7

The desire to get back to reception pulled at me like a fierce current. It felt like the safest space in the building, just a sliding door between me and the outside world. A few steps and I could be in my car, driving away, but leaving the place unmanned was absolutely forbidden, especially if there was a customer inside. I might as well kiss my job goodbye. I should have asked baseball cap man outright if he was Sasha, but I'd lost my nerve. I was too intimidated by his size and the strange vibes that emanated from him. Every bone in my body told me he wasn't the renter of the unit, and if I had misplaced my phone but he'd taken the pad with his registration on and the bank card, why not mention it? Why not ask me why I'd written it down or say, 'hey, I dropped my card, thanks for finding it'. Something didn't add up and my instinct was telling me that he wasn't all he seemed to be. Hopefully he'd be finished in his unit soon and would leave because his presence hung over my head like a dark cloud. There would be no work done on my assignment while he was there, I'd never be able to concentrate.

While I waited for him to come downstairs, I hunted high and low for my phone. Checking the toilets, then repeating my search under the desk, through the drawer and even in the bin in case I'd had a moment of madness and chucked it in there. However, it was nowhere to be found. I'd last used it to send Laura a voice note while I'd been sat at my desk. Then I went to the toilet to splash water on my face. It went missing the same time as the bank card and pad, so it had to be him, although I had no idea what to do about it. Especially as he'd denied it. Should I call the police and report it as a crime?

My blood sugar levels were now a guess, although the macaroni cheese would tide me over for a while at least. I should have eaten all of it, I'd given myself insulin for the entire portion but hadn't been able to stomach it. That was stupid, but at least I had Stacey's sweets and a glucose gel in my handbag if I ran low.

I woke up my computer from the screensaver and logged in again to check the cameras, surprised to find the lights off on every floor. With the cameras on night mode, I could see the stretch of corridor his unit was on, the door closed, unless he was inside. The VW Golf was still in the car park beneath the flickering street light so he hadn't left whilst I was in the toilets looking for my phone.

My skin bristled. I didn't like this one bit. I couldn't relax knowing he was roaming around somewhere. I waited for a few minutes, sure he'd turn up somewhere, and dialled Stacey for a third time, but she didn't answer. Where was she?

I pinched my lips together. Didn't the man in the cap have anywhere better to be, it was practically the weekend, shouldn't he be down his local pub chugging beers with his buddies. A faint noise made my ears prick up, a tune I recognised as my ringtone, a vintage phone sound. Someone was calling me.

Leaping up from my chair, I followed the sound to the east stairwell, getting almost to the first floor before it abruptly stopped. Where had it been coming from? Had I been mistaken about losing my phone when I went to the toilet and dropped it on the stairs instead? I hunched over, examining each step. Perhaps it had fallen out of my pocket. About to carry on climbing, hoping whoever it was would ring again, beneath me, somewhere on the ground floor, I heard the faint sound of metal clang against metal.

I froze, tilting my head. Seconds later, I was plunged into darkness. My breath hitched and I lowered myself onto the step where I stood, gripping the banister. Statuesque in the dark, I sought comfort from touching the cool metal. It was pitch black and even with my senses heightened, all I could hear was my own breath coming out in rasps.

Panic filled my lungs, replacing the air. I couldn't see a thing, not even my own hands held out in front of me.

It's okay, Nina, it's just a power cut.

I'd never been afraid of the dark, not even when I was a kid. Over the years, we'd had a few power cuts at home, Mum dotting every surface with candles and the both of us huddling together, playing gin rummy. We'd heat up some milk on the gas stove and eat crisps or crackers, spreading out a picnic on the rug with whatever was in the cupboard. It had even been kind of exciting, but I wasn't at home and Mum wasn't here. I was in a giant warehouse with a stranger who was either playing a spectacular prank or he meant me harm.

Anxiety had me spinning out of control. I had to

get out of here. Sod the job, Stacey could fire me, but I wasn't staying a moment longer. For all I knew, baseball cap man could be a lunatic, a serial killer hunting for his next victim and I wasn't going to take that chance.

A buzzing sound came from overhead and the lights flickered, coming back and giving the stairwell a soft glow, not the harsh light I was used to. The bold green emergency exit sign burst to life too and I guessed the generator had kicked in.

I eased myself up, feeling the stairwell shrink around me, and struggled not to hyperventilate, taking tiny pigeon steps down the stairs. At least it wasn't dark any more, but it was still eerie. When I finally reached the ground floor, I shuffled forwards, skin prickling, wincing at the squeak the door to reception made when I pulled it open a crack. I wasn't sure why I was trying to be quiet, just going on instinct. Through the sliver, the reception area looked the same, yet the lights blinked ominously, threatening to plunge me into darkness again.

For some reason, the silence seemed amplified and fear draped itself around me like a blanket. I didn't want to go in there. Was he in reception, waiting, ready to attack?

It was just a power cut, Nina.

Trepidation of what could be ahead glued my tongue to the roof of my mouth and I blinked back tears. I'd never felt so vulnerable and so frightened, feeling strangely exposed, straining my ears for any sound of movement that wasn't my own, but the man wasn't here.

Every nerve ending fired, goosebumps layered my skin and a sheet of cold sweat attached itself to my back. Reaching the counter and moving around to the desk, I crouched down, bony knees grating on the polished floor. Crawling awkwardly, I bumped my head into the cushioned chair and grabbed for my handbag, fumbling inside for my car keys. When my hand closed around them, I felt giddy. I had an escape, but I knew I had to enter the keycode to get out. With each digit pressed, it would omit a beep that in the silence would sound like a siren.

If it wasn't a power cut but something more deliberate, then there was only one person who could have engineered it and I couldn't think of any valid reason why. The knot in my chest remained tight because if it was accidental wouldn't he have come downstairs and made himself known, demand to know what the hell was going on? That's what I would have done in his situation.

'Nina,' a voice called from the other side of reception, sounding like it was coming from the far corner where the stack of trolleys were. The man's sing-song cadence sent a chill right down to my bones and I scooted beneath the desk, trying to make myself as small as possible. Something in his tone made me stay quiet. It didn't sound like he was calling for help, more like he was goading me.

How did he know my name? Then I remembered, the stupid name badge Stacey insisted we wear. 'It'll make you more approachable,' she'd said, but that didn't help me now.

I pressed my lips together, trying not to make a sound. Did he really expect me to answer?

His footsteps followed, coming closer until I could hear him breathing. The floor squeaked beneath his boots, just the other side of the counter, inches away, and every cell in my body was electrified.

'Nina.' He lingered on each syllable.

I swallowed, clamping my hand over my mouth and squeezing my eyes shut.

'Why did you write my number plate down?'

I needed to pee and a cramp kept threatening in my calf, but I didn't dare move. I held my breath, not wanting to make the slightest sound in case he heard. He was so close. Did he know I was here? Was this some fucked-up game of hide-and-seek? Why was he pissed about me writing down his registration? His car was recorded on the camera anyway.

The landline on my desk began to ring, sending vibrations through the metal above my head, and I almost peed myself. Stacey was calling me back, but I squashed down the urge to jump up and answer, scream for help. I didn't want to give away my position just in case there was a chance he didn't know where I was hiding. Eventually, it rang out and I heard him snigger, jumping as the cord was yanked from where it was plugged in at the panel by my feet. My mouth went dry as realisation hit, him removing the cord and rendering the phone useless had to mean he was a threat.

I tucked my head into my knees, waiting to be dis-covered, but seconds stretched into minutes with no movement. What was he doing? I had to stop my teeth from chattering until finally his footsteps moved away and I felt I could breathe again. I tried to gauge where he was, but after a while I couldn't hear anything, yet I visualised him standing just feet from the desk like a statue waiting to pounce.

8

Eventually, I heard a door open then close, believing it to be the far stairwell. The hinges squeaked, yet I remained rigid in case it was a trap, a ploy to get me to reveal myself. Sweat beaded at my brow, despite feeling cold, and I swiped it with the back of my hand. I hoped my blood sugar wasn't dropping because of the stress I was under. Without my phone, I had no way of knowing until I felt the effects in my body. Usually the first sign for me was sweating.

I hid for ten minutes, counting to sixty over and over again in my head, finding the repetitiveness soothing. When I was sure he'd gone, I crawled out, kneeling up to grab for the landline on the desk, but as soon as I realised he'd taken the cord, it was useless.

I pressed the panic button, expecting some kind of alarm, but nothing happened. Had it worked? Perhaps it was silent, I'd never used it before and tried to remember what Stacey had said about it, pressing it again for good measure. Either way, it didn't matter; I was getting out of here. With my car keys pressed into my palm, I stood, looking at both stairwells in turn, waiting for the man to burst through at any second.

My pulse smashed at my throat despite feeling calmer moments before. By moving out from beneath the desk I'd made myself vulnerable, but I couldn't hide forever and I only had to get to the door. I began moving slowly across reception, keeping my steps as light as possible. The staff code was 461822 and I repeated the pattern in my head, knowing once the first beep sounded, when I pressed digit four, I wouldn't have long. Not if, for reasons I didn't want to consider, the guy was trying to prevent me from leaving.

Steeling myself, I entered the first digit, hearing the loud beep, and then, all the lights went out.

Fuck! I screamed inside my head and hammered at the keypad, but it didn't make another sound. Why had I hidden for so long? I should have moved sooner because now there was no electricity, so the doors wouldn't open. Had the generator failed?

Resting my forehead on the frigid glass, leaving a

sweaty smudge, I inhaled deeply. Maybe a fuse had gone, or a breaker or something, and it could be repaired. I looked through the glass into the car park. We were at the end of the industrial estate and I couldn't see any other buildings from my viewpoint to see if their lights were on. Had he engineered this? Trying to cut me off from the outside world and trapping me inside?

Think, damn it. There had to be another way out.

I had no working phone, no email, no way to contact anyone and had to hope security had received the request for help when I'd pressed the panic button. My mind was jumbled, overwrought with anxiety, but I needed to think clearly, otherwise I was never going to get out of here. I gritted my teeth, I *had* to be good under pressure, I was going to be a doctor for Christ's sake.

I stayed frozen in the dark by the door, putting two fingers on my wrist and silently counting my pulse until it finally started to slow. If I was going to get out, I needed another exit and I was sure the one at the base of the stairs, which we were supposed to use if there was a fire, would still open despite the lack of power to the building. It was a fire exit door with a push bar release that led out down the side of the warehouse, where there were a couple of extra parking spaces

Stacey often used. It was where I imagined the horny couple in the van had parked before they snuck in earlier.

The problem was, the fire exit was in the west stairwell, by the lift. That was where I thought I'd heard the door close. It was only twenty or so feet, but it might as well have been miles. Fear had seized my muscles and I felt stiff, reluctant to move from where I'd pressed myself against the glass. I needed a way to defend myself from a man who probably weighed double what I did. What if he jumped me as I was trying to leave the building? I had my keys but surely, I could find something better.

With blood pumping hard in my ears, I edged towards the direction of my desk, hands outstretched in front of me, dropping to the floor and crawling when I felt the counter. Pulling my bag towards me, I rooted around blindly for anything I could use, feeling for the objects inside. Lip balm, a small perfume sample, tissues, paracetamol, a bookmark, glucose gel sachets and there, right at the bottom, my fingers grazed something sharp. Initial excitement gave way to disappointment when I realised it was an old pair of tweezers.

Still, having something was better than nothing, and I lifted up my jeans and tucked them in the elastic of my sock. Making sure my car keys were wedged safely in my pocket, I remained still, listening until I was positive I was still alone. The silence was overwhelmingly oppressive, closing in on me like the darkness. It was time to get out of here.

I shuffled across the expanse of space between the counter and the lift on the other side of reception. The floor was always kept clear due to customers coming and going with their trolleys, but I moved slowly, my brain imagining obstacles I could bump into with each step. I kept my arms spread out, hearing only ragged breaths from my own lips with each stride. The man with the baseball cap had to be looking for me, but how on earth was he moving around so easily in the dark without making any noise? I moved my clammy hands constantly, terrified I was going to crash into him at any moment, imagining my palms connecting with his solid chest, jolting me backwards. It would take him seconds to snap my neck with the power in his arms.

Why was he doing this? I'd hardly been the witness to a crime, yet he knew I'd written down his number plate. Was that all it was? Maybe doing so had sealed my fate. I had to be on to something, but how had it escalated so quickly? One minute I'd been helping him, carrying a bag to Sasha's storage unit, the next the power had gone out. My day had been bad enough before I'd arrived at work, now I was being hunted by some lunatic on steroids.

If only Stacey had answered the phone when I'd called. There was a chance I was going to die here, in Storage Queen of all places, and it wouldn't even be captured on the cameras now. If the police replayed the footage up until the power went out, would they have enough to identify the man in the baseball cap? Assuming my gut had been right and he wasn't Sasha Cizmarova, renter of storage unit three hundred and twenty-one, would the police be able to locate him?

Realistically, no one would be coming to use their storage now, it was too late, the next person to arrive if Stacey or security didn't show up would be Paul to relieve me, and his shift started at six o'clock tomorrow morning. No one was going to crash through the glass and rescue me like they did in the movies; I hadn't been able to tell anyone I was in trouble.

I forced the negative thoughts away, all they were doing were intensifying my panic and weren't going to help me to get out of here.

Maybe baseball cap man had left already, but all I could see in the glass door now was my reflection, half formed like I wasn't whole. I couldn't tell if the Golf was still in the car park, and despite knowing deep down he hadn't, I prayed he'd driven away and wasn't searching for me in this enormous warehouse. In the dark, it felt like a maze and I was the rat trying to get out.

Eventually, I reached the other side of reception where the lift and stairwell were. There'd been no sign of the man or any sound to signal where he was and my heart grew more hopeful with each step towards the fire exit. I was going to make it out of here, jump in my car and put my foot to the floor. The creak that sounded when I opened the door was exactly like the noise I'd heard before. It must have been where he'd gone after calling my name.

Inside the stairwell, I looked up towards the third floor, it was like looking into the sky on a cloudy night when the stars were hidden. Even the yellow painted steps which I'd assumed would glow in the dark weren't visible and I tripped as I tried to move around them, dragging my hands along the pimply wall until I reached the first corner and the next. It was so disorientating; spaces seemed bigger and smaller at the same time.

My stomach somersaulted when I found metal and glass and I heaved my hands down on the bar and shoved the door with all my might. The bar gave but the door wouldn't budge more than an inch. I tried again, jostling my weight against it, but it was jammed and there was no way I could open it. Crouching, I ran my fingers along the floor at the bottom of the door. Was there a catch or something else I had to release for it to open? Stacey had given me no instructions on my tour, just pointed the fire exit out. It was pitch black and I couldn't see a damn thing. Enraged, I kicked at the glass with my trainer, which didn't even shudder. Pain ricocheted through my toes, making my eyes water, but I didn't care.

The sound echoed around the stairwell along with my sobs. Slumping to the floor, I hammered it with my fists, tasting salty tears on my lips. All of the glass was reinforced and shatterproof; as soon as I started trying to break it, he would know where I was, if my crying hadn't alerted him already. I doubted I'd make it through before he reached me.

Sweat gathered between my breasts and adrenaline coursed in my bloodstream shocking my brain into action. I had to use what advantages I had; I was smaller, quicker, I knew the building. In a few hours, the sun would come up and Paul would arrive and get help. I just had to make it until then.

9

'You can't get out of here, Nina, I secured the fire exit when I went out to the car. It's the only other way out, right,' came a voice from above.

How did he know that?

'And I took care of the generator too. I don't think those doors work without power, do they?' His mocking tone set my teeth on edge.

My breath hitched and I scrambled to my feet, clapping my hands over my ears when he began to sing.

'Run rabbit, run rabbit, run, run, run,' he crooned as deliberately loud footsteps thudded downwards, echoing around the stairwell, the light from a torch sweeping above.

Forcing myself through the door back into reception, I ran blindly towards the east stairwell on the opposite side, tripping over my own feet and crashing hard onto the floor. All the air was knocked out of me, but I had no time to gather myself. Clambering up, I rushed forwards, hands outstretched until I smacked into the wall. Feeling my way to the door to the east stairwell, I pulled it open at the same time as I heard the creak of the door I'd bolted through moments before.

He was right behind me, in reception now, whistling the tune to 'Run, Rabbit Run', trying to freak me out, and it was working. Part of me wanted to scream at him, tell him to get away from me. What did he want? I wasn't going to hang around to find out. He was hunting me in the dark and, worse than that, it seemed like he was enjoying it. Why me, what did I do? Was it a case of wrong place, wrong time, or had I been targeted? I guessed the answer didn't matter, I just had to keep moving.

Fear kept my muscles pumping as I took the stairs on all fours as quick as I could. What floor should I stop at? Two, three? I had no idea where to hide. Should I go up to the roof? I wasn't even sure if it was unlocked, I'd only been up there one time, the memories of it flooding back.

Dom had come to visit me during one of my first night shifts and, fascinated by the enormity of the warehouse, he'd asked me to show him around. I did, but once we'd completed the third floor, he'd wanted to see what was on the roof, although we hadn't made it that far. There was a door for staff only on the third-floor east stairwell, leading up another level to a room where the heating and ventilation systems were situated. It was open plan and, although large, was half the size of the floor below. Dimly lit with lots of dark corners, we'd spent ten minutes fooling around behind a water tank, lost in each other, before I insisted we come back down. I didn't want to be caught messing around on the job and get fired when I'd only just been employed.

If I went up to that room now I'd be able to hide, but I'd be trapped. On any of the other floors it was the same, but at least there were two exits, the east side and the west side of every corridor. We could run around like Tom and Jerry all night if we had to, as long as I had sugar to keep my levels up. I'd do what I needed to if it meant staying alive.

I carried on climbing, sweat dripping at my temples, intending to go out onto the second floor and keep moving. The only way to stay safe was to make sure I was ahead of him, because if he got his hands on me, it was game over. Unless, the thought entering my head like a light bulb going off, I activated the fire alarm. Those red boxes were on every floor and all I had to do was smash the glass. Yes, that was it!

I counted the steps, as I climbed, excited to have a plan, but just before I reached the second-floor stairwell, I missed a step going up too quickly, and lurched forwards, hand skidding down the banister. Before I could right myself, my knee crashed into the metal edging of the step below, seconds before my forehead hit the top one. White-hot pain flashed across my eyes and I felt them roll back into my head, plunging me into unconsciousness.

* * *

I blinked at the bright light. I seemed to bounce, the sensation of travelling, but my legs weren't moving. Muddled, I couldn't put it together. My forehead throbbed with its own unique pulse and when my eyes finally focused, I saw arms dangling limply. Were they mine? Wavy brown hair hung over my face and a pair of tan boots and jeans moved below me. Was I upside down? Pain clouded my brain, leaving me unable to think clearly, it was indescribable and I struggled to connect the dots.

After a few seconds, I realised what was happening. With the intense pressure on my abdomen and black cotton brushing my cheeks and nose, eventually I was able to untangle my thoughts and piece it together. I was being carried, bumping along over someone's shoulder. The dark stairwell I'd been in seemed extremely far away; it was bright now, but not from natural light. The unforgiving fluorescents hurt my eyes, so I closed them again, shutting out the dazzling glow. The man in the baseball cap had turned the power back on. I vaguely remembered tripping and banging my head, it had to be how he'd found me, unconscious, slumped on the stairs and unable to put up a fight. The hair at the nape of my neck stood to attention as I tried not to think about what he wanted with me and how I was at his mercy.

I remained limp, pretending to still be out for the count, hoping my rocketing heart rate wouldn't give me away. It was easy, I didn't think I could move even if I'd wanted to. Although the desire to reach up and touch my head, where the pain would not stop, was hard to ignore, but I couldn't risk it. Maybe he thought I was dead already. I had little hope he was trying to help, being a good Samaritan and carrying me to a waiting ambulance. So where was he taking me and how long had I been unconscious for?

Eventually, he came to a halt, balancing me precariously over his shoulder as he fumbled with something I couldn't see. I recognised the sound, the jangle of his padlock, the scraping of a key against metal. He was unlocking Sasha's unit. Knowing where I was, I fought the urge to scream, kick and thrash, but the pain in my head was so intense I wasn't sure my body would comply. He was going to put me inside. Roughly, he deposited me onto the cold concrete floor, my T-shirt riding up and exposing my midriff. Thankfully my hair had fallen over my face which was turned away from him, but I kept my eyes shut, waiting for him to do something, for the moment I'd have to fight, knowing already I'd be the loser.

A gut-wrenching ball of anxiety formed as I lay still, pretending to be unconscious. What did he want from me? I pushed away the dark thoughts that popped into my head. But no cold fingers touched my skin, no hands wrapped around my neck or pawed at my clothes. Instead I heard the door close and the latch go across, then the padlock clicked into place, encasing me in his tomb. Why was he keeping me here and how on earth was I going to get out?

I waited until I could no longer hear his footsteps and attempted to sit up, groaning with the effort. It took three attempts, the nausea almost making me vomit. I raised my fingers to my forehead, the pressure overwhelming. It had a long horizontal bump across it, bruised and swollen from the metal edging strip I'd collided with. I was probably concussed, which made sense as my mind was so foggy and muddled. The rest of my body appeared unharmed, but my knee felt a little bruised. I flexed my toes and moved my arms to check. It was just my head, the constant pounding making me feel sick.

At least the light was still on. Although that also meant he had to be coming back soon. I looked around the unit, medium-sized, about the floor space of a large garden shed, but other than the suitcase he'd brought in earlier and the extra bits I'd helped him carry, there was nothing else inside. The suitcase hadn't moved from the spot I'd initially seen it in when I'd walked past. That felt like hours ago, when I could have got in my car and driven away from this nightmare, but hindsight was a wonderful thing.

As my fate dawned on me, palpitations rose up in my chest, small ripples that grew bigger, like waves building at high tide. I held my hands up to the light squinting; they both had a slight tremor. Was it my head or had my blood sugar dropped? How long had I been laying in the stairwell for? The tremor could be stress manifesting physically, but there was the possibility I was having a hypoglycaemic attack. It wasn't something I wanted to face because trapped here in this unit there was nothing I could do. Why hadn't I pocketed the glucose gel from my handbag instead of the stupid tweezers that were currently digging into my ankle. I knew better than to go anywhere without one. Yet I hadn't thought I was going to be locked in anywhere.

I crawled over to the suitcase, dizzy from the movement. It was old, a faded black canvas material, not like the newer ones with the hard outer shell, and there were no ties or padlock securing it. I fumbled with the zip, dragging it around the suitcase, nearly retching from the repugnant smell. I hadn't seen the blood, hidden by the dark canvas, but now some was on my hand. I lifted my T-shirt over my nose and pushed open the lid, letting out a shriek when the contents were revealed.

10

'No, no, no, no, no...' I whimpered, scrabbling in reverse until my back was pressed against the cold wall. Fear lodged in my throat at the sight before me and I heaved involuntarily. She was contorted, folded into the suitcase in a foetal position, her head unnaturally bent forwards, showcasing the bumps of her spine through her flimsy blue T-shirt. Thin as a rake with sparrow-like arms and tiny wrists, her clothes were baggy but couldn't mask her fragile frame. Blonde hair, matted with blood, hung in clumped strands over her face, while milky pupils seemed to bulge from lids painted in heavy black eyeliner. She stared at nothing, her mouth agape like she was mid scream. It was a ghastly vision and one I was not pre-pared for.

In places, her skin had discoloured, turning from a pallid grey to a violent purple where the blood had begun to coagulate and sink with gravity. I forced my-self to look away from the horror just feet away from me, unable to stop myself gagging. Hugging my knees to my chest, I buried my face, trying to slow down the uncontrolled panting. The poor woman was so young, maybe in her late teens, and here she was, obscenely stuffed into a suitcase. Her life ripped from her and discarded like a piece of rubbish. It was heartbreaking.

The light flickered, amplifying my panic. I wouldn't be able to cope if they went out. There was no air and it was claustrophobic in here anyway, without sharing the space with a dead body. I didn't want to vomit, but my head was swimming and the throbbing wouldn't subside. I squeezed my eyes tightly shut, trying to block out the image of the once pretty woman with her unseeing eyes, now twisted in death, but she was burnt into my vision. Something I'd never be able to forget.

The walls began to close in and I sucked air in like a marooned fish. I had to focus on something else, take my mind off the here and now to avoid a full-blown panic attack, but it was difficult when even with my eyes shut, the odour of death in the room was undeniable.

Amidst my hysteria, I struggled to think clearly, thoughts jumbled. We'd covered stages of decomposition last term and I hadn't looked too closely, but if I had to guess, the woman had been dead for a few hours, less than twelve. The smell spilling out of the suitcase was a potent mix of blood and faeces, but even though it was unpleasant, it wasn't unusual. Many people defecated when they died due to their muscles relaxing: if their bowels were full, then out it came.

Could that be Sasha in there? Tombed inside her own storage unit to be found months later when the bills were no longer being paid. Would anyone notice the eventual decaying smell on the third floor, the putrid aroma coming from unit three hundred and twenty-one?

If I didn't do something, this would be my catacomb too. Would a search be organised of every unit when my disappearance was reported, when I didn't come home and Mum couldn't get hold of me? Would they assume I was still in the building or that I'd run away? Surely the camera footage would give them a clue and my car would still be outside. Either way I'd be dead long before they reached me, but it wouldn't be from dehydration or hunger.

I already felt weak because I'd given myself too much insulin for the small amount of pasta I'd eaten, it had been slowly lowering my blood sugar levels ever since I injected. Without sugar to bring them back up, a hypoglycaemic attack would take hold and in a matter of hours I'd lose consciousness. It was a juggling act. I'd die trapped in here without insulin if my blood sugar was too high, and I'd die without sugar if it was too low. The end result would be cardiac arrest, otherwise brain or organ failure.

I gritted my teeth, I was not going to die here. I was twenty-one, with my whole life ahead of me. I was going to be a doctor and help people live normal lives with the illness I had, not to die from it. Pulling myself up and avoiding Sasha, I swayed along the wall towards the door, running my fingers around the edges for weaknesses and checking the hinges for any give, but it was rock solid. I knew deep down there was no way out, not with the latch put across and the padlock closed, but I still poked my car keys and tweezers through every gap, just in case. Perhaps by some miracle I'd be able to find a way through the door.

My limbs felt weak and I was light-headed, sure now it was low blood sugar playing havoc with my bodily functions. If I didn't eat something soon, whether I could get out or not wouldn't matter. I prayed that panic button had sent a signal to security and they were downstairs right now letting themselves into the building.

I rummaged in my pockets, checking I didn't have a glucose gel stuffed somewhere I'd forgotten about, but they were empty. Turning my attention to the box the man had brought in earlier, I upturned it onto the floor, going through the contents. Lots of clean silver bowls, plastic baggies, digital scales, masks like we wore back during Covid and weirdly a few sealed tubs of baby's formula. Checking I hadn't missed anything, I crawled clumsily over to the bin bag, tearing it open at the top.

As I'd thought from carrying it up here earlier, it was partly filled with clothes. Mainly men's, but then as I pulled the contents out onto the floor, I discovered a large green T-shirt near the bottom, stained with blood on the sleeves and chest. Then I found two pink towels, also covered in bloodstains. Were these from the woman's crime scene, brought here, to be burned later? Could baseball cap man have hid the evidence here before he intended to get rid of it all?

Still searching for anything to raise my blood sugar, I rummaged through the clothes, attacking the pockets of three pairs of trousers and a jacket, desperation forcing my uncoordinated hands on, but I found nothing to eat or drink.

Deflated, I slumped back down on the concrete floor, laying on my side. I'd rest, just for a minute, my eyelids so heavy they fluttered. Slipping asleep would be like easing myself into a warm bath, all of the pain would go away. My forehead was so sore, the swelling seemed to pulsate, stretching the skin tight. I rested my head on my clammy arm and felt the sweat drip from my hairline, seeping into the concrete. It wasn't hot inside the unit, they were temperature controlled; the sweating was a symptom of the hypoglycaemic attack. I knew if I was to look in the mirror I'd be as white as a ghost, fading into nothing.

It wouldn't be long, I'd put my body through too much tonight and now it was giving out on me, it would slowly shut down as my organs failed one by one. Hopefully I'd be unconscious and unaware of any pain, but I wept for the life I could have had. It was all so unfair, leaving my loved ones behind when I wasn't ready to go. I'd die with Dom never knowing how much I loved him, how the decision to stay and not go travelling had torn me in two. I thought of my mum, who would be devastated at losing her only daughter.

I knew she'd struggle to go on, the grief would be torture.

What would happen when I died? Would baseball cap man leave me here to rot with Sasha or move us both somewhere else under the cover of darkness? Would we be buried in a shallow grave in woodland somewhere in Sussex never to be found? I was a woman of science, I didn't believe in the afterlife, but it was all so final and I had more left to give.

Tears of frustration cascaded down my nose. I'd been so stupid, a rookie mistake my diabetic consultant would have berated me for. Carrying hypo treatments wherever I went was the number one rule, yet I'd sealed my fate and had to accept it.

The only thing I could possibly pray for now was that my captor would return and take pity on me, but I knew deep down that wasn't going to happen. Why would he? I had nothing to bargain with. Even if he did return, I didn't have the strength to fight him. If he came back he didn't have to kill me, he wouldn't have to lift a finger. I'd done the job for him.

11

The pain in my head began to ebb away as my eyelashes flickered, fighting against sleep. Glancing around, the bare concrete walls of my prison cell closed in on me with every breath. It felt like my body was made of stone, and like a starving dog, I barely had the strength to lift my head. Wordlessly, I begged for my life, for someone to rescue me, crying tears of pity that slowly gave way to indignation.

This wasn't supposed to happen, I was going to be somebody, achieve something. How dare he take that away from me. I half crawled, half dragged myself to the suitcase, the smell no longer a concern now I was facing death. Revulsion slithered over my skin at what

I was about to do. As awful as I felt about the poor woman before me, I didn't want to touch her, but I had little choice.

Sasha, if that's who the body belonged to, was stiff to move, but not so rigid I couldn't manipulate her limbs to unfurl her position. Full rigor mortis hadn't set in yet, which corroborated my initial assumption that she hadn't been dead for long. Her slender arms were tanned, weird for so early in the year, and stuck out beneath the T-shirt she wore. Her skin was clear and smooth and, despite being slight, she looked relatively healthy. I gently lifted her lip to assess her teeth and gums, a straightforward way to check for drug addiction, but they looked normal. I shuddered when I removed my finger and her lip remained stuck in position, turning her silent scream into a snarl. I wiped my hands on my jeans, wishing I could wash them.

As I pulled myself up to a proper sitting position, I recoiled at the gaping hole in the back of her head I hadn't seen before, but, to be fair, I'd deliberately not looked too closely. There was clotting around the wound now, but it left no doubt in my mind that massive blood loss and blunt force trauma was what had killed her. Her nails, painted a deep red, were glossy and unblemished, with only one chipped. I hoped she'd fought for her life. Beneath them could be DNA evidence of her assailant, skin cells potentially, and I avoided touching them, not wanting to contaminate my cells with theirs.

Whoever she was, she deserved justice and I wanted to be alive to see it. I looked her over, slowly, methodically, trying to get my foggy brain to work. It gave me something to focus on; despite being so weak, I had to stay awake. On her wrist, she wore a plain analogue watch with a black leather strap and I gently unclasped it, putting it on my own, struggling to get my fingers to work. I intended to give it back as soon as we got out of here, but it would be useful to know what the time was. I couldn't believe it was almost ten already. Laura would likely still be serving drinks and desserts before clearing down her tables and getting the restaurant set up for the following day. She probably hadn't even had time to listen to my voice note yet.

My vision was already beginning to blur and it was an effort to coordinate my hands as I tried to focus on the task again. If I didn't find anything in the suitcase, I'd open the baby formula and give that a go, knowing the dry powder would most likely make me sick.

'I'm so sorry,' I said to the woman as I eased my hand inside her jeans pocket, pulling out a receipt and some silver coins. Ravaging her corpse was unconscionable, but I was desperate and out of options. Manoeuvring her inside the suitcase took the last of my strength and I almost cried when, out of her other pocket, I pulled out half a packet of Polos, the foil twisted into a perfect spiralled point. Relief hit me like a tsunami when I checked the packet to make sure they weren't sugar free.

As though I hadn't eaten in days, I put five in my mouth at once, crunching and swallowing, taking no time to relish the cool saliva that moistened my parched lips.

'You absolute angel,' I breathed, my shoulders loosening.

Each sweet would likely have around three or four grams of carbohydrate and what I'd eaten would get me out of the danger zone. I sank back onto the floor, pausing my search until the dizziness passed. I stared at her, our faces barely feet away. She looked back at me with her unblinking eyes. She'd just saved my life, yet I'd never be able to thank her. I reached out to stroke her cold, limp arm, tears rolling down my nose again.

'Thank you,' I whispered, vowing to make sure someone was held responsible for the death of this poor woman.

It took around twenty minutes to feel some semblance of normal again and I stared at the watch face as the hands slowly ticked around. Twenty minutes until I was no longer a sweating, shaky mess of confusion. Despite the throbbing of my forehead, my mind gradually sharpened, although I knew I couldn't push myself too much. A low episode like that could take hours to recover from. One particularly bad hypo I'd had at home had left me snoozing on the sofa for the rest of the day. But I wasn't going to lay here and wait for baseball cap man to come back and kill me – if he came back at all. If I couldn't get out, I at least wanted to be ready for him.

I put the Polos in my pocket; there were around six mints left to save for later. Who knew how long I'd be stuck in this unit for. Reluctantly, I sat up and moved back to the body, checking the remaining pockets of her jeans, finding only a tiny round pot of Vaseline. It was too much to hope for a bottle of water tucked away somewhere. I was dying for a drink because all I could taste was minty bile in the back of my throat.

A flash of gold caught my eye and I reached inside the collar of her T-shirt and retrieved a necklace. The name Sasha in gold on a thin chain confirmed my suspicion.

'Hi, Sasha,' I whispered, placing it delicately on top of the fabric. 'What did he do to you?'

I couldn't find any bruises, no marks on her neck or arms. She'd likely been struck from behind, no warning or time to run, and my heart hurt for the tragic loss of someone so young. I wished I had a blanket to cover her, something to provide the dignity she deserved, but I wasn't about to cover her in the bloodied towel I turned my attention to the lid of the suitcase. In the large elastic pocket which I'd thought was empty, I found a hammer wedged at the bottom, dropping it like a hot potato to the concrete when I saw the head was matted with blood and long blonde strands of hair.

Jesus! He'd put her in the suitcase along with the weapon he'd used to murder her, disposing of the evidence here for her to rot, unless it was a temporary measure. I retched at the tangled hair wrapped around the hammer and clamped a hand over my mouth. I couldn't lose any of the mints I'd eaten.

As gently as I could, I closed the lid of the suitcase, pulling the zipper around, and stuffed the bloodied items back into the bin bag. When he came back maybe, I could deny having seen what was inside, try to talk myself out of this awful situation.

Breathing deeply through my nose, I picked up the brown wooden handle with its rusted metal head and looked towards the door – could it help me escape?

Hammering on it would do nothing but cause a racket and I couldn't prise the door open either, but at least now I had a way to defend myself for when he came back, and if he didn't, I just had to pray that someone found me.

12

SASHA – BEFORE

Fresh out of the shower, I whizzed around the room in my towel, water still dripping from my skin, making tiny dots on the carpet. Moving like a whirlwind with the radio blasting, I stuffed items I couldn't bear to leave behind into my holdall. I had to get out of the maisonette before Luca got back. I didn't want the confrontation. He'd only try to stop me, making promises he couldn't keep before the threats inevitably came. He always got angry if he didn't get his own way. Usually, I'd be able to talk him around to a compromise, but I wouldn't this time, not about me leaving.

I'd been putting money away for the past four months, stashing it behind the bath panel amongst the cobwebs – somewhere Luca would never think to look. He'd seen me bringing home face creams and make-up, clothes and handbags, knowing I had expensive tastes and cursing social media for causing it, believing what I'd purchased were the high-end brands I'd normally buy, when in reality they were designer knock-offs. My tactics had worked though and stopped him asking questions about where all my money was going. He assumed I flitted money away on superfluous things and that suited me fine. If he knew I was saving, he'd want to know why.

After the last trip, my fourth in total since Luca and I had been roped into the hare-brained scheme, I'd finally accumulated enough money to comfortably start over. Despite the pittance I got for all the risk involved compared to what the others earned, eight thousand British pounds was not to be sniffed at and mentally I'd spent it already, putting my plans in motion a couple of months back and getting organised for today. Luca and I had always wanted to see the world, a continent at a time, but not like this.

My ticket to Manchester was booked for eight o'clock from Euston and nothing was going to stop me from being on that train. Luca would understand eventually; it wasn't as if we hadn't talked about moving away from Crawley, although it hurt to leave him behind. I'd miss him terribly and I knew for a while it would be hard, going it alone, especially becoming a mother. Whenever I thought about it, a giant hole opened in my chest, but this wasn't the life I'd anticipated when we'd planned to relocate to England from Poland and it wasn't the right place to raise a child. England was supposed to be a fresh start for me, to get away from my overbearing father and open a world of opportunities, but we were too young and too naïve. We never stood a chance.

I gazed at our photo on the sideboard. A selfie of the two of us giggling at something during a picnic in Hyde Park, although I couldn't remember what. We'd had a day sightseeing – the usual haunts, London Bridge, Buckingham Palace and my favourite place, Soho – a few weeks after we'd arrived, pinching ourselves at our good fortune. I was debating whether to pack it when my stomach rolled violently, mouth filling with saliva. Nausea hit me like a truck, and I ran to the toilet, just making it before vomit cascaded out of my mouth, firing at the bowl in a forceful stream. I hoped I'd make the train journey without any sickness, but everything seemed to set me off at the moment, the slightest smell or taste. Hiding it was becoming more difficult by the day, another sign it was time to leave. I didn't want the father to find out; it had been a stupid drunken mistake and not one I was going to repeat.

After a cool glass of water to soothe my throat, I brushed my teeth and returned to packing, leaving the photo where it stood. I wanted to pack light and had plenty of photos on my phone anyway, Luca's face would be one I'd never forget, no matter how long we were apart. Standing in front of the mirror, I pulled on an old pair of jeans and a T-shirt, not especially flattering now, but with most of my newer clothes packed, they would do to travel in. I wasn't looking to draw any attention to myself; if anything, I wanted to be unmemorable and blend into the thousands of commuters hurrying about at that time of day, because as soon as Luca knew my holdall was gone, he'd come looking.

I'd booked an Airbnb for three nights in walking distance from the train station for when I got to Manchester. In a city of over half a million residents, I hoped it would be easy to disappear and reinvent myself as someone new. The prospect excited me, a new name, a new look perhaps. How many people get the chance to do that, not someone still finding herself at nineteen. It was a chance for a do-over, no more orders or instructions to follow, I'd be as free as a bird.

My intention was to change my visa to allow me to

study initially and enrol at college on a nail course. Once qualified, I could apply for another visa that would let me work, intending to start my own business offering gel manicures and acrylics. They were all the rage here, even teenagers were wearing fake eyelashes and nails, it was a fast-developing industry and I wanted a piece of the pie. Eventually, I would open a salon or rent a space in one and create my own brand.

I loved Instagram and followed so many nail techs, ensuring mine were always on point. I spent hours planning all the sick videos I'd film using the current trending transitions. It was an area I was fascinated by, using social media to build and advertise business, and I knew I'd be great at it. I could create a good life for myself and my unborn child. I wanted to do something positive with the money, considering how I'd earned it, although it would never fully cleanse my conscience.

When I finished packing, I applied a little make-up – eyeliner and enough concealer to cover up the green tinge my face seemed to permanently have at the moment – whilst nibbling at a ginger biscuit. I'd lost weight, my appetite had disappeared, but I wasn't sure if it was down to stress or the fact everything seemed to turn my stomach right now. Spritzing perfume behind my ears and on my pulse points, I put my watch on. It wasn't my usual style, too plain and not blingy enough for me, but I wore it for sentimental reasons. It had been a gift from my mother when I was sixteen. The rear of the face was inscribed with the words *mój anioł* – my angel – and I never went anywhere without it so that she was always with me, despite the clasp now being loose.

Distracted by my phone ringing from somewhere, I turned the radio down and found it on the edge of the bed, flipping it over to see Luca was calling. He was probably letting me know he was on his way home. He called every day when he got off the train, asking if I wanted anything picked up from the shop he passed on his walk back from the station. I bit my lip, thrusting socked feet into my trainers. It meant I had to get going if I was going to make it out of here without bumping into him.

I retrieved the money I'd stashed in a brown jiffy bag from the bathroom and shoved it to the bottom of the holdall, rearranging my clothes around it. In went the make-up I'd just applied, then hairbrush and toothbrush, before one final check around for anything I might have left behind. When we'd arrived in the UK, we'd looked at various locations intending on the London suburbs but ending up further out where it was cheaper. It cost so much less to rent in Crawley, yet we were only thirty minutes away by train to London, with the bonus of being near to the coast too, which I loved. Although if we'd never come to Crawley, I wouldn't be running away now.

Aware the clock was ticking, I swept my eyes over every surface, checked every cupboard, cementing the memories of happier times here into my mind to call upon later. Scribbling Luca a simple note telling him I loved him, I carried the holdall to the door, stopping abruptly when the doorbell rang. My back prickled, thinking Luca was home, although why he hadn't used his key I had no idea. Frozen in the hallway, a few seconds later the bell sounded again.

We didn't have a peephole, but if it wasn't Luca impatiently waiting for me to open the door, it could be a courier needing a signature. Luca was expecting his monthly delivery of protein powder. I debated whether to wait, but if it was a courier, it would be quicker to answer, grab the parcel and then follow them out. With one hand carrying the holdall, I stepped forward and pulled the door open, recoiling at who my visitor was.

'Hi, Sasha… going somewhere?'

13

10 P.M. – 2 A.M.

I crouched by the door of the unit with the weapon raised, poised in case baseball cap man returned. Hamstrings aching, I'd been frozen in position for I had no idea how long, when the lights suddenly went out. Reluctant to move, time slipped through my fingers, either the countdown to my demise or my rescue, I wasn't sure which. I knew I'd only have one shot to strike when he opened the door, but as soon as I was pitched into darkness, I gasped and dropped the hammer, the sound of metal clanging against concrete echoing around the unit for a second time.

It was pitch black, the air musty and I shivered in my T-shirt, wishing I'd worn the Storage Queen fleece.

The acrid smell emanating from Sasha had filled up the tiny space and lodged inside my nostrils; it slowly turned my stomach. In the darkness, it seemed stronger than ever and I dropped to my knees, dragging my hands blindly along the floor for the hammer until I found the wooden handle.

I bit my lip, trying to stay calm, but my heart was pounding. Why had the lights gone off again? What the hell was he up to? I'd taken being able to see for granted and now I was back to being blind, racking up my anxiety by the second. I was even more vulnerable than before and the last place I wanted to be in the dark was in here. My mind kept playing tricks on me, hearing sounds around the unit I knew weren't real. Images of Sasha unzipping the suitcase and shuffling along the floor on her belly towards me, dead eyes imploring, a hand raised begging for help, entered my head.

'Get your shit together, Nina,' I hissed, palms sweaty around the wooden handle of the hammer. I gripped it tighter, trying to ascertain whether I could hear footsteps approaching or whether that was another figment of my imagination. In the sliver beneath the door a light flashed past. Was he back?

I crouched again, ready to strike as soon as the

door was pulled outwards and he stepped inside, arms raised aiming for the head. Hands shaking with a mix of terror and adrenaline, my triceps burned with lactic acid. Finally, I heard the padlock being unlocked and the hinges protest as the door opened, followed by a beam of light shining into the unit harsh on my eyes.

'What the f—' He didn't get a chance to finish his sentence as I swung the hammer high, bringing it down but missing his head entirely. The jolt landed on his shoulder and he cried out in pain, dropping to one knee. The torch he'd been holding slipped from his grip, rolling onto the floor, and I snatched it up as his hand flailed for me. Jumping back, I swung again in the half-light, this time catching his cheek and sending him reeling into the wall head first. The hammer flew out of my hand with velocity and bounced onto the floor, skidding beneath the bin bag as he crumpled into a heap at my feet.

Leaping over him, I ran from the storage unit, the torch's beam bouncing from left to right on the floor until I reached the east stairwell. Descending the stairs as fast as my legs would carry me, I burst into reception like a tornado, heading straight for the door. I tried the keypad, but it wouldn't work. Of course it wouldn't, there was no power. The landline was useless too without its cord and I rummaged blindly through my handbag, grabbing the glucose gel and stuffing it into my pocket. I was so thirsty, my throat burned, but there was no time to stop.

I berated myself for not searching him for my phone. He must have had it on him. Why didn't I think before I ran, but I'd been so terrified. I still was. I was out of the storage unit but no better off than I had been before, still trapped in the dark with a madman, unable to escape. At least now I had a torch.

I checked the fire exit door in the stairwell, but it was still jammed, something on the other side was preventing it from opening and I couldn't smash the glass either. It barely cracked when I kicked it. Panic setting in, I returned to reception, aware he could be down here any minute. Why hadn't I locked him in? Even without a phone I could have held out until Paul arrived in the morning. *Stupid, Nina!* I struck one of the windows by the keypad with the torch, a crack bloomed but didn't give. Was this stuff bulletproof?

'Shit.' I had no choice but to go back to the third floor and try to find a phone. At least then I'd be able to call the police and hide somewhere until they arrived. They'd have a battering ram, that would do the trick surely.

My gut twisted with anxiety at the thought of

having to retrace my steps, terrified at the thought of coming face to face with the burly man I'd just knocked unconscious. There was around six or seven hours until sunrise, and although the warehouse was large, there wasn't an endless supply of hiding places. Not ones I knew about anyway, so that wasn't an option. I needed to get out of here in one piece, but right now it was as much of a prison as the tiny storage unit I'd been locked in. Where was security? I'd pressed that stupid panic alarm, why hadn't someone come? They didn't have anything in the employee manual for this scenario.

The torch flickered, making me start and I banged it against my palm, praying the batteries would last. Unable to put it off any longer and with my heart knocking against my ribcage, I moved back to the east stairwell and began the climb to the third floor. With legs like lead, I moved slow, breathing shallow, listening for any sound and trying to be as quiet as possible. I'd hit him hard, but it was the wall that had done the job and knocked him out. I cursed myself again for not checking his pockets at the time, but I'd just fled, fearing he would jump up and grab me. They did in the horror movies I loved so much, but humans were delicate, much more than they realised. Just a mass of cells, fragile and easily broken.

When I reached the third floor, I swung my torch-light along its length. The door to unit three hundred and twenty-one stood open just as I'd left it. Was the man still inside, crumpled on the floor like a wounded stag hit on a poorly lit country lane? The thought of searching him for my phone made me break out into a cold sweat and the torch slid around my clammy palm. I squeezed it tighter. The last thing I wanted to do was touch him, I didn't want to be within ten feet of him, but what choice did I have. A phone would get me out of here. Once I found one I'd lock him in, at least then I'd be safe.

If he was awake, then the stream of light might have alerted him to my presence. There was a chance he was waiting for me, ready to strike as soon as I rounded the door. I didn't want to end up like Sasha, convinced he'd been the one to kill her, although I had no idea why. Had she stolen from him? Were they a couple? I had so many questions, but whatever she'd done, she didn't deserve her fate and it was down to me to make sure she didn't die in vain.

I tiptoed towards the door, my breath catching in my throat as every hair on my body stood to attention. I couldn't hear anything past my own pulse, which seemed so loud I was sure he would hear it. I steeled myself, I was just going to go in, get the phone and lock the door. I'd gone through Sasha's pockets, I could do the same to him, although my head was screaming at me not to.

I rounded the door, torch held low and peered into the unit, trying to make sense of what I saw. The man I'd attacked had gone.

14

'Nina,' the deep voice echoed down the corridor, sending shockwaves through my body.

I peered around the unit door and pointed the flashlight towards the call of my name. He stood at the end by the door to the stairs I'd come through minutes before, a palm raised up to shield his eyes from my beam. In his hand he held a phone, but I couldn't tell whether it was mine, the torch was on but pointed at the floor. He looked different without his baseball cap and with his curly hair matted to his head, it emphasised the roundness, like a bowling ball stuck on top of broad shoulders. I noticed his cheek was red and swollen from where I'd hit him with the hammer.

Pointing to it, he said, 'You shouldn't have done that. I *was* going to let you live.'

'No you weren't,' I blurted, finding my voice. What did he expect me to do, not defend myself? He locked me in a fucking storage unit with a corpse.

'I came back to get the password for the system; there's footage I need to delete.'

Now it made sense, he'd turned the power back on while I was locked in the unit so he could access the computer system, specifically the cameras. Turning it back off again when he came back to get me. That's where he'd been all this time. He wanted to erase himself from tonight, so it would be like he was never here. That's why he'd taken my pad with his registration on, but without me he couldn't log in to the computer. Would he have left me to rot if he could? I didn't doubt it.

'If you give me the password, I'll consider letting you walk out of here. I'll delete the footage and then leave. You'll never see me again.'

I nearly laughed at his attempt to be sincere. There wasn't a chance he was going to let me go, not when I could identify him. His DNA would be inside that unit, on the torch handle, the hammer likely too and no doubt all over Sasha's lifeless body. Although it wouldn't help the police if he wasn't already on their database. It was possible he could disappear and never be found.

He cocked his head to one side, waiting for me to answer, eyes squinted and palm still raised, blocking out the light. I kept it pointed at his face, enjoying how uncomfortable it made him. 'You shouldn't have been so curious, Nina. Why did you write my number plate down?'

That's what had done it, he'd seen it written on my pad and knew I was suspicious. Otherwise, he would have put Sasha inside her storage unit and left and I wouldn't have been any the wiser as to what was inside. It was finding the blood and the bank card that had sent me on the hunt for answers. My mum always said my gut feelings were usually spot on and this time she wasn't wrong.

'You killed somebody!' I blurted instead of answering his question.

'I didn't mean to.' His voice changed, the hard edge disintegrated and he looked genuinely remorseful. Sasha must have been his girlfriend but she'd deserved better than the thug at the end of the corridor. How many partners had killed their other halves in the name of love? Women beaten to a pulp daily who were too afraid to leave, knowing they'd be hunted down, never to be free.

We stood, glaring at each other in the shadows, caught at an impasse and where could we go from here? He was injured, yet he'd easily overpower me if he got close enough. I couldn't let that happen. My blood sugars were holding and I was back to firing on all cylinders, but for how long?

'Give me the password, Nina, and this all goes away.' He sounded irritated now as though I was a fly in his ointment. I'd delayed his plans for a quick get-away and the night had got messy, but I couldn't give him the password. That camera footage would prove my story later, it would identify him and be critical in bringing justice. I had to make sure Sasha's killer left here in handcuffs. It was down to me.

Although my circumstances hadn't changed. I was still trapped here in Storage Queen, unable to get out and he had my phone. I flinched as he took a step towards me, the beam of light wobbling in my shaking hand and he turned away, displaying the side of his face which was covered in blood. He seemed remarkably steady on his feet for someone who had been unconscious a short while ago.

'Tell me the password,' he barked, taking another step as I mirrored him, going backwards. Like an athlete waiting for the starting pistol, I couldn't take my eyes off him, counting on my reactions being faster than his. I was younger but not by a lot. I guessed he was in his early to mid-twenties, but he was carrying a lot of bulk. To my advantage, I was light, so technically I should be quicker.

His shoulder twitched and he lurched forwards, but I was already away, sprinting around the corner towards the west stairwell. Footsteps slapping concrete boomed down the corridor behind me, but I had a good head start.

Once through the door, I ran down to the second floor and around the corridor to the east stairwell, where I smashed the glass of the wall-mounted red box to sound the fire alarm. Except nothing happened. Did no power to the building mean no alarm? I guessed that was what the back-up generator was for, but the man in the cap said he'd taken care of that. I didn't have time to give it more thought and ran back up the stairs, determined to shake him off. Carrying on upwards past the third floor towards the roof, I prayed the door at the top would be unlocked. How badly was his head injury affecting him? He'd hit the wall with some force and I was surprised he could walk, let alone run.

Waiting in the darkness for his approach, I pulled the tweezers out of my sock and leaned over the railing. As soon as I heard a squeak of hinges from below,

I dropped them down the stairwell into the black abyss, hearing the clatter of metal against metal a few floors down. I switched off the torch, plunging the stairwell into darkness, hoping for misdirection.

Listening to his footsteps and spying a low beam of light descend the stairs, my spirits lifted when the door to the roof opened, albeit stiffly. It was marked as Staff Only with a no entry sign below to keep the general public out, although I wasn't sure how much of a deterrent that would be for him. I squeezed through the narrow gap in the door and paused, ears pricking. My plan had worked, for now at least. Perhaps there would be another way down from the roof? A ladder or a different stairwell I didn't know about. I prayed there was, otherwise I was heading into a dead end.

I turned the torch back on for extra light, but the room already had a low red hue from blinking LED lights on numerous consoles that made no sense to me. They had to be battery operated and flashing in protestation because of the lack of power. One looked like it was a back-up generator and I took in the buttons and switches, could I do something to turn it back on? That way, I could get out of reception, maybe by creating a diversion of noise somewhere else in the building.

Buoyed by my new plan, I moved around the small

space, examining the buttons, but there were no labels and I had no idea what any of them did. I wasn't an engineer and could just about change a fuse at home. The control panel was so far out of my comfort zone that I was reluctant to press any of the buttons in case I set off an alarm, giving away my location.

Resting my head against the green water tank to gather my thoughts, I remembered the last time I was here, Dom's hands sliding up my T-shirt, the feel of his soft lips on mine and the throb in my groin that manifested whenever he kissed me. I'd barely noticed the uncomfortable cylinder pressing at my back, only stopping him when he moved to unbutton my jeans. The thought of never seeing him again twisted the knot in my stomach and it spurred me on. I couldn't let how we'd left things be the last memory he had of me. I wanted the chance to tell him how sorry I was, that I wished things could be different.

I hoped I hadn't backed myself into a corner by coming up here, like a mouse in a trap with nowhere to go. Pushing off from the tank, muscles aching from all the cardio I'd never normally do, I moved around the room, running the torch from floor to ceiling, covering every inch, searching for another way out. With my plan to get the power back on abandoned, I needed another exit. In the far-left corner, I found steps soldered into the wall, six rungs leading to a rusted hatch above that looked as though it hadn't been opened in a while. It reminded me of a submarine movie I'd seen with Mum.

'Here goes nothing,' I said to myself as I put the torch between my teeth and climbed.

15

The hatch was stiff but opened once I'd turned the circular handle and cool night air rushed in from above, sending a chill down the back of my neck. Arms laced with goosebumps, I popped my head through the hole to find a large expanse of flat grey felt, similar to the roof of Mum's shed at home. Heaving myself through, the wind immediately whipped my hair around my face and I shuddered beneath the stars illuminating the night sky. It was so high it took my breath away and I could see the blinking lights of Crawley town for what seemed like miles around, confirming what I already knew. It wasn't a power cut, more of a sabotage. I cast my eye over the rooftops of all the houses with people at home, asleep in their beds, or others like me working the night shift because the world never really slept.

A plane flew overhead, sinking lower, on its way to land at Gatwick airport, and I gulped in lungfuls of fresh air, boosted from being outside for the first time in hours. It had started to rain and I was cold, shivering in the flimsy fabric of my Storage Queen T-shirt with no protection from the wind, but I was alive and grateful to be. Despite my initial excitement, even with the noise, up here I felt truly alone. I was vulnerable with no shelter and nowhere to hide, but there wasn't time to dwell on that fact. I had to find a way down to the ground before he came looking for me.

The rooftop had no lip or raised wall, nothing to prevent you dipping beneath the single waist-high iron railing and sailing off the edge if you chose to, plummeting four storeys to the asphalt below. I turned away, the thought churning my stomach, determined to find something useful up here, but the space was barren. I checked every inch with the torch, but there were no external stairs, no ladder attached to the side of the building and no escape other than the way I'd come up.

'Shit,' I hissed, dropping the torch as tears of frustration filled my eyes. I'd wasted my chance coming up here. Now I was a sitting duck. Swiping them away before they grazed my cheeks, I heard a low rumble through the wind that tugged at my clothes. Jogging in the direction of the sound at the front of the building, I leaned precariously over the edge to look down at the car park, but my beat-up Ford Focus and the grey Golf were the only vehicles there. The rumble got louder, and a few seconds later, headlights swung through the barrier, making my heart leap into my throat.

'Hey, hey, up here,' I shouted, waving my arms and nearly tripping over my feet. I steadied myself on the railing, turning my face away from the biting gale. 'Up here,' I repeated, projecting my voice, which tailed off along with the plume of warm air from my lips as I recognised the car. It was an old orange VW Beetle, Dom's pride and joy. The car had over a hundred thousand miles on the clock and more rust than paint, but he loved that thing. My spirits soared to the heavens, he'd come to see me. I was getting rescued. 'Dom!' I yelled, but my shout was carried away on the wind.

He came to a halt right in front of the entrance, the beam from his headlights shining into the unusually dark reception, a place usually lit up like a Christmas tree, but even the neon sign was swathed in darkness.

I imagined his surprise, rocking up to find the premises looking like it was closed with me nowhere to be seen. Surely he would see the cracked pane of glass and realise something was wrong, especially as my Ford was sitting in the car park.

'Get out of the car, Dom!' I waved my hands around like I was landing a plane, trying in vain to signal, but he couldn't see or hear me up here.

He was likely warm and toasty inside the vehicle with its engine running, reluctant to get out because of the rain. I imagined him calling my phone again, trying to work out why I hadn't picked up and wasn't at my post behind the counter in reception.

'Dom!' I screamed into the night, leaning too far over the railing before jerking backwards, infuriated tears streaming down my face. He had to hear me. He had to be the one to call the police and save me from this nightmare. He was so close but might have well been light years away.

An agonising minute passed with me shouting until I was hoarse, but Dom didn't get out of the car and I was torn between risking running downstairs to show myself and potentially being caught or staying on the roof. I looked around for something to throw, but the rooftop was empty. No rocks or rubbish laying around, just the occasional lump of bird poo crusted onto the felt and then I saw the torch I'd dropped.

I dashed for it, returning to the edge just as Dom reversed out of the space and left the car park. I sank to my knees and watched him head into the night, sobbing uncontrollably. The fight in me had gone. It was hopeless, I wasn't going to be rescued. Pressing my palms into the grit on the felt, creating indents into my flesh, the adrenaline drained out of me and I melted onto the rooftop in a puddle. Laying with my face against coarse sandpaper, I let the tears leak out. Why hadn't he waited? Why hadn't he got out of the car and looked around for me? Surely he must have guessed something was wrong.

Eventually, I rolled over, my body like a dead weight, staring up at the stars, questioning if I'd still be alive in a few hours to see the sun come up. Despite the rain, I wanted nothing more than to lay here and watch the sky change from midnight blue to rust. The wind, now soaring above me, took the clouds with it and the night was quiet once more. My muscles were spent, and although the flat roof wasn't the most comfortable place I'd ever bedded down, my eyelids fluttered, longing for sleep. If I was lucky, I'd wake at home in my doughy bed, wrapped in the marshmallow duvet and tonight would have been a bad dream.

'There you are.'

I hadn't even heard footsteps approach, but now he was feet away, standing with his arms crossed. I sat up, watching his brows pull tightly together. The dried blood resembled tar glued to his face and neck in the moonlight and I shrank back, shoulders rising to my ears.

'I wondered where you'd got to.' He sounded like a teacher reprimanding a student. 'Why do you make me chase you?'

I got to my feet and began walking backwards, increasing the distance between us as he smirked.

'Where are you going to go, Nina?' he called, arms outstretched as he looked around the roof, concluding like I had that there was no other way down. He had me cornered and he knew it. I'd been an idiot to come up here.

'Who are you?' I asked, stalling for time until I figured out a way down from the roof that didn't involve going through him. He was standing between me and the hatch, the only way off the roof without dying in the process. 'It seems unfair you know my name when I don't know yours.'

'You can call me Luca, it's my nickname. Now let's

go downstairs, we can wipe the cameras and I can leave.'

'So I can end up in a suitcase too?'

Luca's jaw clenched and he flexed his fingers, eye twitching in irritation. There was definitely no way he was going to let me live now he'd told me his name. I'd been stupid to ask. 'I've been patient, now either you come willingly or I drag you down there,' he snapped, pointing towards the hatch.

What was I going to do, run around the roof all night, trying to stay out of Luca's reach? Hope he felt dizzy from the blow to his head and attempt to get past him and down the hatch. He looked pretty solid and I'd never make it down the ladder before he caught me with those hands that were like fat slabs of meat. Perhaps my only choice for now was to go along with it and try to make my escape once we were back inside.

He shifted from foot to foot, his impatience obvious, and I didn't want him to lose his shit while I debated what to do.

'You promise you'll let me go once you have the password?' I asked.

'I will.' He looked convincing enough, but I knew he was lying. Every bone in my body knew. There was no way he'd let me live, having seen all that I'd seen.

Why would he leave a witness, he'd be stupid to do that and maybe I had to start thinking like him if I wanted to get out of here. Maybe Dom would come back and this time I'd be in reception, able to signal I needed help. It was the best I could come up with.

'Okay,' I agreed, walking towards the hatch, shoulders slumped because, after all, what choice did I have.

16

'Wait,' Luca commanded when I'd descended the ladder into the control room. I stepped back to let him come down, watching as he lowered his heavy frame through the hole and his feet found each rung. There was a bulge now in the pocket of his jeans that had to be my phone, or his, and I thought about tearing it from him and making a dash for the stairs, but knowing my luck he'd fall and squash me. Blood wound his dark hair together and I was surprised he was still standing after that blow, let alone walking. Although I knew from a lecture that even minor cuts on the head could bleed heavily because the scalp has so many blood vessels close to the surface of the skin.

I'd debated too long and soon he reached the bottom, standing too close. I shuddered as though someone had walked over my grave when he brushed his large hands together to dispel the dust, particles tickling my nose. I'd never been in such close proximity to a murderer before, not that I knew of anyway. It made my blood run cold that he looked normal, an average man, yet he was capable of such atrocities. Had he toyed with Sasha beforehand like he was toying with me and had she any idea what was coming before he hit her, ending her life with one strike?

'Cold?' he sneered. 'Some of the places I've been, you'd know about it if it was cold.' My discomfort seemed to amuse him.

'Like where?' I asked, trying to keep him talking, to make a connection so he'd see me as another human being, but he regained focus, the smirk slipping off his lips.

'Enough talk. Give me the torch.' Luca held out his hand and I passed it to him without argument.

Pointing towards the door to the stairs, he raised his chin. 'Go.'

I did as he said, him following a couple of steps behind as he shone the beam to guide our way in the dark. I wracked my brain to come up with a plan, a way to run, but I knew I wouldn't get two feet away without him catching me. I had no weapon except for the car keys in my pocket; they might work, enough to cause damage but not enough to disable. Unfortunately, the tweezers were gone now and my head was starting to feel fuzzy, although I couldn't be sure if it was lack of sleep, low blood sugar or an adrenaline crash. Stress did funny things to blood sugar levels and tonight was unprecedented. Without my phone to read the sensor attached to my arm, I was running blind, but at least I had sugar if I needed it.

'Any chance I can have my phone?' I asked, not daring to look over my shoulder as we descended the stairs down to the ground floor. I gripped the banister, my legs not feeling quite like my own.

'I don't think so,' Luca chuckled, no longer bothering to pretend he didn't have it, now things were going his way.

'I'm diabetic, I need it to read my blood sugar levels,' I tried to explain.

'Ha! Course you are!' He let out a booming laugh, which sent my hackles soaring.

'What do you think this is?' I snapped, turning around and lifting the sleeve of my T-shirt to show the small glucose monitor. Luca stared at the round disc stuck to my arm as I glared at him, his eyes narrowed.

'Keep moving,' he said, nudging me forward and showing no emotion whatsoever. Didn't he understand the implications of diabetes or did he just not care? Maybe I'd given away too much. He didn't have to kill me if my own body was going to do it for him.

I took comfort knowing I had the glucose gel and the rest of the Polos in my pocket. I let my hand brush over the lump in the denim for some reassurance.

When we reached reception, I veered towards the counter, but his hand clamped my shoulder.

'This way,' he said, steering me towards the west stairwell over the other side and gesturing for me to open the door. 'Stay,' he instructed as though he was talking to a dog and I complied, remaining by the fire exit, the torchlight disappearing as he moved around the back of the staircase.

Run, now.

But I didn't run, I just stood with legs like jelly, staring at the cracked glass in the fire exit door, the lever flopping uselessly at my touch. With Dom gone and at least another six hours until sunrise, I didn't hold out much hope of seeing it. Beads of sweat formed at my hairline and the base of my spine and I reached for the glucose gel, jumping when there was a loud click and the lights sprang back on. I jerked my hand away and closed my eyes, seeing spots of yellow in my vision.

'Let's go,' Luca said, shoving me back towards reception.

What was back there? A fuse box? I'd never seen one in the warehouse but never had any reason to go looking, especially not behind the stairwell. I stumbled, tripping over my uncoordinated feet, glad when I got to my desk and could slump down into the chair.

'Wait, please, I need to eat something.' My head lolled forwards like my neck was made of rubber.

'We don't have time for a snack break.' He put the torch down, nudged the mouse and tapped at the monitor, the blue screen whirling to life, 'now focus.'

I wheeled the chair up to my desk, blinking rapidly, trying to clear my vision. It was definitely a hypo, my hands trembled so much, I kept mistyping my log-in and perspiration ran down the side of my face.

'You're sweating!' Luca said, wrinkling his nose, his disgust evident.

'I'm having a hypoglycaemic attack. If I don't eat something I'll pass out,' I pleaded, 'then you'll never get the footage deleted.'

He stared at me, our eyes locking, but I refused to blink. I was exaggerating, it was a hypo, sure, but I didn't think I was at a critical level yet, not like when

I'd been locked in the unit. I waited a couple of beats until he spoke.

'Okay, so eat.' Luca chewed on his lip, watching me like a hawk and grunting when I retrieved the gel from my pocket. It would be faster-acting than the Polos and I hated not having my phone and having to rely on my body's warning signals, but I knew I was sinking fast. Thank goodness I hadn't lost the ability to feel them yet; some people who'd been diabetic for a long time stopped having any physical warning signs their blood was high or low. It was so dangerous. 'What is that?' he asked as I tore the top off and squeezed the orange-flavoured gel into my mouth, running my fingers up the length of the sachet to get every drop out.

'Glucose gel,' I said, my mouth still full.

'You have medicine... insulin?'

I nodded. 'In my bag.'

'Show me.'

I reached down and rummaged in my bag, reluctantly handing Luca the blue pen of NovoRapid insulin, still with its needle attached. I hadn't removed it after I last injected. Something my mum always berated me about: 'You leave needles everywhere, you should know better, Nina! Use a needle and then put it in the sharps bin straight away.'

'Hmmm,' he frowned, a deep trivet forming on his brow, examining the pen as though he'd never seen one before and perhaps he hadn't. He looked at the dial at the top, taking in the numbers, then turning it around, clicking up the insulin dose and taking the lid off to see the needle.

'Small needle, huh.' I nodded, grateful to have a minute's reprieve. My brain wasn't working properly and I had no idea how I was going to get out of this situation. Surely as soon as the camera footage was deleted I'd be expendable. He could kill me sitting here in my chair, but right now I wouldn't be able to run anyway, my limbs were slow to respond as was every other function. All I could do was stall for as long as possible.

'Right, you've eaten, now do it,' he said, pointing back at the screen, but before my fingers reached the keyboard to try to log on again, the sound of a car engine made both our necks snap round to peer out of the glass.

I took in a sharp intake of breath, watching as headlights shone into the car park, breaking through the shadows and approaching the building. Was Dom back? I craned my neck to try to see the vehicle.

'Fuck!' Luca cursed, squatting down and wedging himself underneath the desk. I was about to jump up and wave for help when his giant hand wrapped around my calf, pinching the skin.

'Ow,' I bit my tongue as he anchored me in the chair, skin prickling with excitement. Was it Dom? I couldn't let him in, he'd be no match for Luca, but perhaps I could signal that I needed help.

As the car pulled into the bay opposite mine, I immediately recognised the distinctive white and yellow of a police patrol car. A balloon inflated in my chest, I'd been saved.

'Who is it?' Luca asked impatiently.

'The police.' My voice quivered with a mixture of anticipation and fear. Someone must have called them or perhaps the security team had alerted them. Either way, it had to be over now, they'd see the smashed glass and once I'd let them in, they would arrest Luca for Sasha's murder. My night of being terrorised was done.

17

Luca squeezed my calf, reminding me he was in control, and I winced, looking down to where he'd folded himself beneath the desk at my feet, hidden from view.

'Did you call them?' His eyes drilled into mine, serious as a heart attack, turning my veins to ice.

'No,' I whimpered as he squeezed harder, bruising my flesh.

'Don't get any ideas; we're not done here.'

The police officer who got out of the car was in full uniform, tall and gangly with glasses and a patchy goatee. He was alone and looked like he'd be of little physical threat to Luca, causing my initial excitement to falter. As he strode towards the entrance, he waved to catch my eye and announce his presence, surveying the area. With the power back on, reception was lit up like a Christmas tree and he nodded a greeting as he approached the door. I smiled tightly, distracted by Luca pushing my jeans over my ankle, touching my bare skin. What was he doing?

'Make him go away,' he commanded and I looked down, eyes bulging as I watched him twist the dial at the end of my insulin pen all the way around, as far as it would go, and discard the lid on the tiled floor. Each click represented half a unit and he loaded it fully, ready to inject. The pen carried thirty units which would send my blood sugar plummeting rapidly and there weren't enough sweets in Stacey's box to counteract a delivery that high. If the needle went in and he plunged the dial, I might as well sign my own death warrant.

Everything in my body told me to stand up or kick out, but I froze. Luca poised, the needle millimetres away from my skin as the police officer knocked on the glass, signalling for me to open the door, frowning now as to why I hadn't got up already. At the counter was a release button which overrode the keypad, but we hardly used it. I always forgot it was there because it was only for emergencies; we were all told to use the keypad to get in and out because the codes identified and logged who was entering the building. Storage Queen collected that data if there was any damage or theft from their property. Unfortunately, as with the keypad, the release button didn't work if the power was out.

'I've got to lean to press a button to release the door,' I whispered, chin pointing downwards, trying not to move my lips, knowing I was being watched. Luca's grip tightened as I leaned to the right to reach the button, my hand clammy.

Once pressed, the door slid open, letting in a gush of frigid March air and I nearly yelped when I felt the needle graze my skin, Luca's fingers digging into my calf muscle as an unspoken warning: Don't do anything stupid, your life depends on it.

'Can I help?' I asked, plastering on my best customer service face and hoping my sweaty brow and wobbly voice wasn't too much of a giveaway that something wasn't right.

'Good evening, or, rather, good morning. We had a call from a concerned member of the public asking us to do a welfare check.'

I frowned, initial confusion giving way to clarity. A member of the public, not security? It had to have been Dom who called. Internally I beamed, he had seen the glass and wanted to make sure I was okay.

'Ummm, we're fine. We had a power outage, but as you can see it's back up now and we're still open,' I said, trying to control the wobble in my voice.

'We?'

I cringed internally at my slip and Luca's grip tightened like a python crushing its next meal. 'Sorry, I meant Storage Queen; it's just me here.'

'You got a nasty bump to the head there,' he grimaced. 'What happened?'

I raised my hands to graze the lump on my forehead, which awakened as soon as I touched it, throbbing. 'I tripped up the stairs... when the power went out, smacked my head on one of the metal stairs.' I let out a weak chuckle.

'I think you might have to get that looked at.' Deep trivets settled between his eyebrows as he looked me over. I dreaded to think how I appeared, pale and sweaty with a huge bump across my forehead, hardly the picture of health.

'I will, as soon as someone can come and relieve me.'

'You're open twenty-four hours a day right?' he continued and I nodded while he checked his notebook, licking his fingers to lift the pages. 'And you are... Nina Soloman?'

'I am.' I swallowed the fear in my throat, feeling

the needle scratch against my leg again, Luca's grip
sending my muscles spasming. Panic engulfed me, yet
I tried to remain calm, externally at least, as my
bladder strained for release.

'And you're on the night shift here at Storage
Queen?'

'Uh-huh.' I nodded.

'The caller we had was concerned they couldn't get
hold of you, the lights were off when they came by and
they noticed...' he gestured with his pen to the cracked
pane of glass where I'd tried to smash my way out of
the building. Luca squeezed and I bit my lip, he was
cutting off the circulation to my foot and I could no
longer feel my toes.

'Umm, one of our customers had an accident with
a wayward trolley, I've informed the manager and
she'll call the glaziers when they open,' I said,
thinking on my feet and surprising myself.

The officer narrowed his eyes and I hoped he was
just being thorough rather than seeing through my
lies.

'Okay, mind if I have a quick look around?'

'Be my guest,' I said, forcing a smile.

He walked around the reception area, footsteps
loud on the polished tiled floor, and I heard Luca
whisper from my feet.

'You better get rid of him.'

My heart rate spiked at his threat and I focused on taking slow breaths as perspiration dampened my underarms despite the chill since the doors had opened.

The police officer did a lap of the reception area, taking in the collection of trolleys, the lift and peeking his head through both stairwells, seemingly finding nothing of concern.

'It was my ex-boyfriend who called you,' I blurted when he approached the counter again. 'We broke up tonight, that's why he came here.'

'Is he a threat to you?'

'No.' A laugh escaped me, Dom couldn't be threatening if he tried. 'He's not like that,' I assured the officer.

'Perhaps then,' he paused, a slight smile betraying his serious expression, 'you should let him know you're fine.'

'I will, my phone ran out of battery and then the power went down so I had to sort that out, it's been a stressful night,' I admitted, my voice a little shrill. It was the understatement of the year, I'd not had a worse one in my twenty-one years of being alive, but I'd never been locked in a warehouse and chased by a psycho in the dark before.

'Okay, I'll close this off, but do call us if you need

to. Have a great night, Nina, and get that head checked out.'

He walked towards the exit and I remained silent despite my head screaming at me to stop him. Ignoring the urge, I pushed the button to open the doors, smile strained. My second chance to escape tonight was about to drive away, leaving me in the clutches of a monster, but I'd saved myself from a massive insulin overdose and certain death – for now anyway.

I watched as the police officer started his engine and pulled away, my shoulders sagging and tears of defeat pricking my eyes.

'Good girl,' Luca breathed as he tried to unfold his massive frame from under the desk. His condescending tone made my jaw clench but I wasn't going to miss the tiny window of opportunity to get away.

With the needle still in his hand but now safely away from my leg, I lifted the receiver of the landline phone from my desk and brought it down hard on his skull as he emerged like a bear coming out of his cave after hibernation.

The thud sent chills down my spine and he let out a grunt, dropping the insulin pen which rolled onto the floor. I scooted to the left in my chair, kicking out as he grabbed a handful of my jeans. Disorientated, he lurched forwards on his knees as I fought to get him to release me, eventually writhing out of his grip. Using the desk to pull himself up, he struggled to his feet, still hunched over, blinking rapidly, trying to focus, leaning against the desk for support. He stood between me and the door release button I'd been hoping to press.

I darted towards the door; brain slow as though I was trying to wade through treacle. My limbs were liquid, the effects of the hypo hindering me. I rested my forehead against the cool glass, gripping onto the keypad to keep me upright.

'Bitch,' Luca snarled, bringing me back to the present. He was fully upright now, stumbling forwards, hands outstretched towards me.

'Shit!' I hissed, tapping in the code, but the keypad gave out a low beep in defiance, the doors refusing to open.

I rapidly entered it again, trying to feel my way around the keys, the pattern I thought I knew so well – 461882 – that was it, wasn't it? The keypad beeped again, flashing red.

I tried to focus, but everything seemed as though it was in slow motion. Luca was only feet away, staggering like the undead, reaching for me, the vein in his forehead pulsating. He looked incandescent, eyes red and bulging, his lips peeled back into a snarl. I had to make a choice, did I go for the door release button back at the desk or run?

As he lurched forwards, I stepped backwards, his fingers brushing my T-shirt but not getting a hold. I was not going to get out; even if I got to the door release button, Luca was blocking the exit. He swung his hand out to grab me, but I sidestepped and turned towards the west stairwell, making a dash for the door, Luca yelling my name behind me.

18

I had no choice but to run. If I'd entered the code incorrectly again, I'd have lost my chance to get away. Luca would have nabbed me at the door and lashed out for sure. Low blood sugar meant slow reactions, brain fog and the inability to think clearly, but self-preservation took over. If Luca was mad before, he was furious now and I had no doubt he'd kill me with his bare hands, whether the footage was deleted or not.

I tried the fire exit door again, just in case, but it was still jammed shut, so I had no choice but to climb. Gripping the banister with sweaty fingers, I hauled myself upwards, heavy-footed like I had lead weight in my trainers, but where could I go? I couldn't return to the roof and there were no toilets except on the ground floor, nowhere I could barricade myself in. I was out of options and out of energy.

From below, I heard Luca shouting up the stairwell, screaming obscenities, switching from English to another language I didn't recognise – Polish maybe? No longer promising he'd let me go once he had the password. If he caught me, that would be it, game over.

I kept going up, past the first floor, onto the second, unable to hear Luca's footsteps on the metal stairs. Where was he? Not wanting to wait and find out, I pushed through the door into the corridor of storage units. Leaning on the wall, pausing to catch my breath, I was plunged into darkness for a third time.

It was eerily silent, the only sound my heavy gasps as I tried to visualise the surroundings I could no longer see. There was no time to wait for my eyes to adjust. Luca had cut the power again to prevent me from getting out and now he had the torch. *Think, Nina.* I had to get back down there and find a way to turn the power back on. I knew where the fuse box was now.

Wiping my sweaty brow with my forearm, I

pushed forwards. I had to keep moving, otherwise I was toast. My fingers found the wall to my left, skimming every bump and ridge in the plaster until I felt the door to the first unit and the padlock securing it. I kept going, my hand at the same height, bumping over each door and every metal padlock until I got to the end of the corridor and had to turn the corner.

The repetitive motion and the sound of my footsteps steadied my nerves, but where was Luca? Was he searching another floor? His absence, although a blessing, worried me, what was he planning? Had he turned the power off hoping I'd emerge like a moth searching for some light?

When I reached the second corner, I continued towards the east stairwell, trying to be as quiet as possible, looking towards the end of the corridor for any flicker of an oncoming torch.

Should I go up or down? Not knowing where Luca's whereabouts was giving me palpitations. I chose to climb again, onto the third floor, systematically running my hand along the units once more, the opposite side of where Sasha's one was located. The smell increased as I got closer, pinpointing where I was despite not being able to see. Death permeated the corridor and I held my breath as I passed the unit, unable to stop myself visualising Sasha's slowly decaying corpse inside. I turned the corner feeling steadier on my feet. The gel was kicking in and my mind was becoming less jumbled with each minute that ticked by.

'Ouch!' I caught my finger in one of the padlocks, bending it backwards. With both hands, I felt what had snagged me. The padlock wasn't closed and swung idly on the latch, scraping against the metal. The owner had failed to secure their unit and I'd missed it during my first check of the evening, probably because I'd been eager to get away from Luca. It was the first bit of good luck I'd had all evening.

I removed the padlock and folded the latch back, flat against the door before pulling it, a rush of relief nearly overwhelming me when I got it open. I quickly stepped inside, feeling around and tripping over boxes. It was packed tight with little floor space to move and quietly I drew the door to a close, checking it stayed in place. I hoped Luca wouldn't notice an unsecured unit, fearing if he learned I was hiding inside, he'd take the padlock off me and lock me in. Leaving me to rot like Sasha.

Although that wouldn't be such a bad thing. I only had to make it until Paul arrived for his shift, sure I'd be able to create enough noise to draw attention to where I was. I still had the Polos and with little exertion I could hopefully keep my levels in check until then. There was no reason I'd need insulin given all the time I hadn't eaten.

I sank down onto the floor between two soft bin bags, glad for some time to regroup and plan how I was going to turn the power on and get out. I had to be smarter than Luca if I was going to survive, but without power I had limited options. He'd sealed me in the building like he'd sealed Sasha in that suitcase.

I hugged my knees, trying not to rustle the bags, overwhelmed with emotion and blinking back tears. What was I going to do? Dom would know, he would be calm and level-headed, which was exactly what I needed to be if I was going to be a doctor. Mum was the same, as a nurse she'd seen it all and could always be counted on in an emergency. I had to be like her, think logically without emotion. I'd made it this far.

Around ten minutes later, I heard footsteps approaching, my shoulders creeping up to my ears the closer they got. It had obviously been too much to hope I'd injured Luca with the receiver significantly enough for him to give up his tirade, cut his losses and run. He wanted that footage that tied him to his crime and he was prepared to kill for it, that much was certain.

I held my breath as his footsteps went past, clocking the torch skimming beneath the door as he did. Further down the corridor, I clamped my hand over my mouth when I heard my ringtone again. I knew he'd had my phone all along.

'Hello... is that Laura?' he answered, his voice taking on a weird London inflection, trying to disguise his accent. Her name must have flashed up on the screen.

I strained to listen.

'Sorry I can barely hear you.' The silence seemed to stretch for an eternity.

'Nina? Yeah, she's a bit tied up, managed to get herself locked in one of the units,' he chuckled moronically.

Laura would never believe his bullshit, surely.

'Sorry, the reception is bad. I've called a locksmith, yes, he's on his way,' he continued, voice smooth as silk.

I heard him laugh again, so fake she couldn't be buying it.

'What was that?'

He waited a beat and I could hear him moving away, seeking a better signal.

'Yeah, she could probably do with a bit of moral support. I'm sure she'd appreciate that.'

My stomach rolled, nostrils flaring as his voice carried down the corridor. I wanted to scream, to shout he was lying, get her to call the police, but Laura would be going home to bed, she wouldn't come. Then his next words left me numb.

'Great, see you soon.'

19

I couldn't breathe. Laura was coming here. She must have listened to my voice note about the weird customer and called me back once she'd finished her shift. Surely she wasn't so naïve to let Luca convince her I'd locked myself in a unit, but he'd seized the opportunity and it sounded as though she was on her way. I couldn't hear him any more and assumed he'd gone downstairs to turn the power back on so he could let her in.

Laura couldn't come inside. I couldn't allow him to use my best friend as leverage in his sick game, especially when I had no idea of the lengths he'd go to. Or perhaps I did. He'd killed Sasha, he was angry enough to kill me, but if Laura came in here there was the possibility neither one of us would ever leave. I couldn't let her be a victim of this night.

I stood, indecision clouding my judgement. I wasn't sure what to do, reluctant to expose myself or my hiding place, but I couldn't use it for shelter any longer. I had to get downstairs and prevent Laura from coming inside.

As I opened the unit door, the power came back on, blinding me, and I shielded my eyes from the glare, waiting for them to adjust. A headache bloomed at my temples, neck rigid with tension as I debated my next move. I'd have to give myself up, delete the footage and try to get away when Laura arrived. She wouldn't be long, ten minutes max at this time of night from the restaurant to Storage Queen.

I left the unit, making sure the door was closed and it looked locked, putting the padlock back and committing its location to memory should I have to find it again in the dark. Number three hundred and twenty-four was displayed on the door and I silently thanked the owners for their mishap in forgetting to lock it. Trudging down the corridor, I made no attempt to be quiet or disguise my whereabouts, my main concern was getting to Luca before Laura got here, but when I reached the ground floor, she'd already arrived.

Luca was at the keypad entering the code as she waited outside, a bemused grin on her face. Jeez, that was quick. She must have called from the car, perhaps she had already been on her way here.

I peered through the porthole window, having missed my chance to intervene, and watched her sashay in carrying a takeaway coffee cup and a brown paper bag. She wore her pink fluffy teddy bear coat with a matching thin scarf, restaurant uniform beneath, blonde hair swept back in a French plait. I didn't want to risk her coming to any harm at the hands of Luca by bursting through the door.

'I brought some food home, but I think you guys need it more than me!' she said gleefully, plonking both down on the counter, grease darkening the bottom of the bag. 'It will keep you going, if nothing else. Freshly baked mozzarella sticks.' She often bought goodies back with her, leftover food or slices of cake for us to eat the following day.

'Thanks, that's kind of you!' Luca said, still with his London twang.

He sat back down behind the desk in my chair, looking like he belonged there. He'd found my Storage Queen purple fleece from my drawer and wrestled it on despite it being at least two sizes too small, muscles bulging through the arms. His face was freshly washed, the blood gone and he smiled at her with his crooked teeth, playing the part of a welcoming employee.

'Where is she then?' Laura asked, hands on her hips, throwing her head back and laughing. 'I can't believe she's locked herself in! It's typical Nina, but she's had an awful day, bless her.'

I gnashed my teeth together, was it typical me? Was I that much of an idiot? I didn't think so, or perhaps Laura was just trying to make conversation.

'She's up on the first floor, I just came down to let you in.' Luca's face was frozen in a grin that didn't meet his eyes, from here he looked unhinged.

'So how did she call you?' Laura's head tilted to the right slightly. 'If you have her phone.'

Attagirl Laura. My chest swelled with admiration for my whip-smart friend. I was the gullible one, not her, she questioned everything to the point of exasperation, her brain always having to know the answers, easily one step ahead of me.

Luca frowned but thought on his feet. 'I came in and couldn't find her, she left her phone on the desk and when she didn't appear, I walked around calling. I heard her shouting from inside one of the units.'

'Oh,' Laura replied, as she turned away, seeming to

look towards the cracked glass by the entrance. 'I thought she was alone on these night shifts?'

She wasn't about to make it easy for him and a shadow seemed to pass across Luca's face, his eyes narrowing slightly.

'We were due to do an audit.'

At that, her whole stance changed, her back stiffened and I could tell alarm bells were ringing in her mind. I'd never mentioned anything about an audit. An audit of what? Stacey had never done one to my knowledge.

'Come on, I'll take you to her,' Luca said, standing up. 'Mmm, these smell great.' He picked up the brown paper bag, inhaling hungrily and licking his lips.

'She's never mentioned you before, never said she worked with a Lee,' Laura carried on her gentle interrogation, said with a smile as though she could be flirting. She had a way with people, it was why she earned so much in tips.

'I'm new,' was Luca's response, his tone belying a hint of irritation.

He walked around the side of the counter and I saw Laura chewing her lip. I pressed my hands flat on the door, breathing deeply, caught up with indecision. Would he hurt her if I showed myself? Could I risk it? Then I saw another fire alarm, so inconspicuously mounted on the wall I hadn't noticed it was there before.

'Is that blood?' she asked, raising her hand and pointing to the back of Luca's neck.

He stopped, his shoulders sagging, not even bothering to turn fully around. The fleece strained against the broadness of his back, stretched taut across his shoulders. It looked ridiculous and I'm sure Laura had noticed. She noticed everything.

I smashed the glass and this time the shrill siren sounded, deafening in the corridor. Through the glass, I saw Laura taking a step backwards, her hands over her ears. At the moment I burst through the door, Luca swung around, moving across the floor at lightning speed for someone so large, his fist connecting with Laura's face. I screamed out as she hit the floor like a deck of cards, blood gushing from her nose. She immediately rolled onto her stomach, crawling towards the door away from her attacker.

'You can't get out without the code,' he shouted, sounding almost bored as he watched her go.

'Stop! Don't hurt her.' I held my palms out, trying to pacify, but my words came too late.

He wrenched her upright by her arm at a weird angle and although I couldn't hear it, I imagined the sickening crack of it breaking as her lips stretched open in a scream drowned out by the siren.

I rushed towards Luca, jumping on his back like a monkey, my forearms around his throat, clinging on as he bucked and thrashed trying to remove me. I dug my ankles into his abdomen as Laura scooted back on her behind towards the door, her face a mess of blood and tears, clutching at her elbow. She sobbed as she cradled it like a newborn. Luca spun around in circles, making me dizzy, trying to shake me off. Eventually, he heaved forwards, throwing me over his back and onto the floor before tripping over his own feet and coming down hard on top of me. Both of us winded, he rolled off and onto his stomach, trying to get to his knees. I scooted backwards and kicked out at his jaw, my foot connecting, knocking him over. He clutched at it, swearing loudly.

Jumping up, I stepped over him, going for the door release button, but he grabbed my ankle, shaking it like he was a dog with a toy in its teeth, the both of us nearly on top of Laura.

'Laura, get out of the way,' I shouted, straining towards the desk, trying to twist out of his grip.

She shuffled away from the door, but I couldn't move, Luca was too strong, grabbing the back pocket of my jeans and dragging me back down to the floor.

On her feet now, Laura swung her leg back and launched it at Luca, kicking him in the kidneys. He loosened his grip for a second, air rushing out of inflated cheeks, and I managed to free myself.

'Run!' I shouted, pulling Laura along with me by the coat sleeve of her good arm. Out of the corner of my eye, Luca was getting to his feet, hot on our heels. We climbed the stairs up to the first floor, the siren deafening, managing to get out onto the corridor before Laura shrieked in pain, tears cascading down her cheeks. She clung on to me and we slowed midway down the corridor.

'It's okay, it's okay,' I shouted over the din, trying to soothe her sobs as she held her bad arm to her body. 'Where's your phone?'

'In my pocket,' she pointed. 'I can't get it.'

I patted her down, finding the phone, frustrated to see there wasn't any reception.

'Damn it!' I gnashed my teeth together; we needed a break. I held it up high to the ceiling, waiting for the bars to appear, frustrated to see her battery was minimal.

'What happened to your head?'

'I fell on the stairs,' I replied, the truth sounding like a lie.

'Is he coming?' Laura mouthed, digging her nails

into my arm, her eyes were like giant watery orbs moving from me to the end of the corridor where we'd just come from. Blood had smeared around her nostrils, but her nose didn't look like it was broken. Still, she'd taken one hell of a punch.

I pulled her along the corridor, trying to get around the corner, out of sight, glancing back over my shoulder, knowing we had to find somewhere to hide.

'Nina, is he coming?' Laura shouted, looking to me to take control of the situation, but I felt as terrorised and helpless as she did.

'He will be.'

20

'What are we going to do?' Laura's chin wobbled. There was no way she could help me fight Luca, not with that arm. Even two on one, as downstairs had proved, we were no match for him. Gently, I pulled her scarf away from her neck, fashioning it into a makeshift sling and slipping it over her head, my ears ringing from the relentless siren, but at least it meant someone would be coming.

'Keep your arm in that, don't move it,' I shouted, making sure it was supported, 'and take off your watch and rings, in case of swelling. I'm going to hide you, I have a place. Then I'm going to get help,' I continued, sounding more confident than I felt. If it was that easy, I would have made it out already.

I leaned in close, so my mouth was at her ear.

'Luca won't want to leave reception for long because he can't guard the door. I'll have to draw him away. In the meantime, you hide and keep trying to get the police on the phone.' I pressed the handset into her palm and kept walking, dragging Laura with me, aware we were sitting ducks in full view of Luca if he looked through from the stairwell. What was taking him so long?

'I thought he said his name was Lee?'

I shook my head, there was too much to explain now and I didn't want to scare Laura more than she already was by telling her there was a dead body on the third floor and the murderer was the man who'd just broken her arm.

'Nina, I don't feel so good,' she said in a rush, stopping to vomit on the floor all over her black trainers before sinking to her knees, 'I don't think I can walk any more.' Her skin had paled, a sheen across her forehead glinted in the overhead lights. It was the shock, plus the break sounded nasty and no doubt she was in a lot of pain.

I kept looking towards the door, expecting Luca to burst through it any minute. My body shook with adrenaline. There was no way I was going to get her up to the third floor and into that unlocked unit, not in her current state. I chewed on my lip, casting my eyes around the empty corridor. At least without access to my computer, Luca wouldn't be able to see us on the cameras.

Think, Nina. But I couldn't think, not while that alarm was going off, until suddenly it stopped. Luca had managed to turn it off somehow, which, as the power was still on, meant he had to be in the control room on the roof and on his way down. We wouldn't make it down to reception and out in time together, Laura could barely walk.

My gaze rested on the air vent a few units down on the left-hand side, still a little skewed from where the squirrel had got in. We'd passed it already, but it hadn't occurred to me at the time. Laura followed my eye and shook her head.

'No, Nina, no fucking way.'

'You'll fit, look it's huge,' I said, already moving over to it and dropping to my knees, excited to be proactive. Two of the four screws were loose and I pulled my keys from my back pocket and proceeded to use my 'bad bitch' keyring Laura had bought me as a screwdriver to loosen the rest. It was the perfect thickness and I hoped it was a sign that we were going to get out of here safely.

'I can't, it's too small, I won't be able to move.' Laura

continued to protest, tears rolling down her cheeks as I lifted the grate off and looked down the dark shaft, considering using it as an escape route. The squirrel had got in from somewhere, there had to be another loose grate that opened to the outside of the building.

Although if Laura got in first, she wouldn't be able to crawl far with one arm and I wouldn't be able to secure the grate back on from inside. If I went alone, I couldn't leave her here exposed, while I went for help. Perhaps it was an option I'd come back to, but right now I just needed Laura to get in there.

'It's perfect, I'll put the grate back on, but it'll just be hanging, you'll be able to kick it down I promise,' injecting a breezy tone to my voice despite the urgency.

'No, I can't. What if I get stuck.' Laura began to sob again. I'd never seen her look so vulnerable. She was always the stronger of us, the most capable and I hated seeing her this way.

I walked back over to where she was still kneeling and crouched down, avoiding the puddle of sick, and cupped her face in my hands. 'It won't be for long. He's going to come looking and, with your arm, you won't be able to defend yourself. Please, Laura, he's dangerous, let me keep you safe.' I tried to make my voice as gentle as possible, but we were fast running out of time.

'What if something happens to you?'

'It won't, and I'm not going to trap you in there, I'm just going to hang the grate back on with two screws. It'll be like a flap and you'll be able to shuffle back out if you need to.'

We both jumped as a loud crash came from below, followed by muffled shouting. Luca was angry and frustrated. He couldn't get into the computer without my help, giving him no access to the cameras and his plan to use Laura as leverage had failed.

'Please,' I begged, stroking a strand of golden hair that had come loose from her plait back behind her ears.

'Nina!' Luca yelled, his voice closer now. He sounded incensed and Laura nodded quickly, terror etched on her face.

I helped her up with her good arm and walked her towards the vent. It was tight with her fluffy coat on, but she squeezed inside and shuffled down the vent on her good side, grunting with pain, every movement of her arm excruciating.

'You'll be okay, stay quiet, and keep trying the police, try the Wi-Fi too,' I said to the soles of her black trainers, sticky with vomit. Although I couldn't re-member what the password was.

I heard her whimper as I hung the grate back onto the ridge, tightening two screws so it wouldn't fall as Luca's yelling got louder still. He was coming.

I made to the corner of the corridor before Luca blew through the door from the stairs like a tornado, the too-tight fleece now discarded.

'I see you, bitch,' he shouted, picking up his pace as I raced ahead around the corner and the next. I pumped my legs, sprinting to the west stairwell and up the stairs, knowing he'd expect me to go down to-wards the exit, but I knew I wouldn't get out before he caught up with me.

'Where's your little friend?' he called from below as I pushed upwards, past the second floor and up to the third. There was only one place I could hide where there was a chance he might not find me. 'I've called 999, told them it was a false alarm. Your plan didn't work.' He sounded triumphant, breath catching with exertion, before I opened the door to the third-floor corridor, where I could no longer hear him.

I made it to the empty unit, gasping for breath, holding onto the handle, expecting it to be pulled at any second. He wasn't far behind me; if he looked hard enough, he'd see it wasn't locked, especially as the lights were on. I closed my eyes and prayed Laura and I would get out of here safely. We'd left behind a puddle of sick in the first-floor corridor, but as long as she didn't make a sound, I didn't think he'd consider she'd be hiding in the vent.

A minute later, footsteps went past outside and I held my breath, but they didn't linger and soon all was silent again.

It wasn't long before the power went out, Luca playing the one trump card he had, and I imagined Laura panicking. Hiding in a confined space, unable to see anything. At least she had her phone so had access to some light and with any luck she'd managed to call the police.

Luca wasn't about to give up trying to find us. Without the power on, he could search properly, knowing I couldn't get out even if I got past him. I sank to the floor, the chill of the concrete floor seeping into my back making its way into my bones. I had to get the power back on so I could get out.

It wasn't long before I heard movement outside in the corridor, followed by Luca's voice again. This time he wasn't shouting, sounding like he was going rip me to shreds, or taunting, there was just an angry rush of words as he walked past the unit.

'You need to come. I can't find these bitches and

we're running out of time. She might have called the police.'

I heard him entering Sasha's unit around the corner, the squeaking of hinges. I concentrated on the noises, trying to visualise what he was doing and jumping when the door slammed less than a minute later. He'd shut the unit, but I couldn't make out any other footsteps, no other distinguishable voice. Was he still alone, on the phone maybe?

'What? I can't hear you!... How long? Okay, text me when you get here, I'm going to try the roof, she hid out there last time.'

My stomach plummeted along with his footsteps retreating back down the corridor. He'd called for back-up. With Laura out of action, it would be two against one. Was he luring me into a trap, saying he was going to the roof knowing I could be listening? I needed a plan, but how could I escape when there were only three ways out of the building; the fire exit door which was jammed, the main entrance which was useless without power and the roof where there was no way down except to jump. The height was not survivable and wasn't an option. I had no phone, no method to contact anyone and no weapon. I had to hope Laura had got through to the police and any minute they'd arrive, sirens blaring. Every other possible scenario I came up with ended up with Luca's hand around my throat, squeezing the life out of me.

How long would it be before he searched each unit in the warehouse, knowing we were here somewhere. It was only a matter of time until he noticed one was unlocked. If I stayed here, he'd find me eventually; sooner if there was two of them looking.

An idea bubbled into my mind, but it was crazy. When Luca's friend arrived, he'd have to turn the power on to let him in the main door. I shook my head, it was laughable, a ludicrous plan that couldn't possibly work, but what was I going to do, wait here like a lamb to the slaughter? I had to think about Laura, she needed medical attention. There was no other choice, I had to go for help.

21

The only way up to the roof was from the east stairwell, so when I slipped out of the unit, I turned right, following the corridor around to the west stairwell, running my hand over the padlocks to guide me as I went. My bladder was close to bursting and there were toilets at the ground floor on that side of the building, they would be a good place to hide. Knowing Luca had gone up when I was going down didn't make me panic any less at the slightest sound and even though my eyes had become accustomed to the dark, moving around wasn't any easier either. I had to keep my steps slow and steady, hands placed on a surface at all times, visualising where I was and imagining the bright lights overhead.

As I crept down the stairs, my stomach was knotted at what I intended to do, which was to run as soon as Luca's friend entered the building, while the electricity was on and the door was still open. I had a few seconds at best, ten at most, to sprint from my hiding place in the toilets and reach the door before it slid shut. And that was without being caught in the process. In my mind, I saw the scenario play out, Luca and his friend would go straight over to the counter, perhaps to try to break in to my computer somehow without the password, giving me the opportunity to come from the other side of reception and out of the door. Where I'd have to run for my life.

I had my car keys, but that would take too long. I'd waste precious seconds getting in my car and starting the engine, especially if there were two of them chasing me. Luca would have smashed my windscreen and dragged me out of the Focus and across the bonnet before I could put it in gear. A better plan was to hide somewhere in the industrial estate – there had to be plenty of places – and then circle back and retrieve my car. Either that or find another person or location with a phone. Surely I could outrun him on foot? I just needed to get help, to call the police and an ambulance. Laura would be safe if she didn't move from her hiding place and I prayed she'd hold her nerve in the dark.

The plan was deeply flawed, but it was the best I could come up with, considering setting off the fire alarm hadn't worked. At the bottom of the stairwell, I shuffled around the back of the stairs against the wall, using what little time I had to see if I could get the power back on, but it was pitch black and I couldn't see a thing. If I had a torch, I might have been able to give it a go, but without one I'd have to revert to the original plan.

I paused to listen, hearing no sign of Luca, hoping he was still on the roof or searching the control room. I feared he was invincible now; I mean, how many times did he have to get hit in the head before he went down and stayed there? I got he was twice the size of me and I'm sure whatever force I'd thrown at him wasn't a lot in comparison, but still.

In reception, I moved my hand across the wall. I found the lift, gliding my fingers across its smooth metal, remembering it was stuck on the first floor, its doors open. It could potentially be a good hiding place if I could drag the doors closed, but without power, there was a chance I could get trapped inside which wouldn't help anybody. Through the next door was the small lobby with the men's and women's toilets inside. From memory, the women's were closest and I fumbled for the door. It was frustrating moving around in the dark, knowing I'd be covered in bruises from all the bumps and scrapes, let alone what I'd incurred scrapping with Luca. The lump on my forehead, which had thankfully stopped throbbing, was still swollen and sore to touch.

I sighed with relief as I finally found the toilet cubicle and lowered myself down onto the plastic seat to empty my bladder, not bothering to cover it with paper this time. It was hardly a priority now and instead I stuffed toilet paper down the pan to stop the noise from my urgent flow of urine. I couldn't flush in case it alerted Luca, so made my way over to the door, yelping when I brushed against something hard. Jumping backwards, I slipped and hit the tiles hard, pain radiating up my spine.

Had Luca heard my cry? Blood pumped in my ears as I remained absolutely still, waiting for him to burst through the door like a villain in a horror movie. I wasn't sure how much more stress I could put my heart through. Eventually it would just give up the ghost, but at twenty-one I was too young for that, my heart was strong. Mum always said I had the heart of a lion, the bravery too.

I thought of her now, busy at work. Weekends

were always manic at the urgent treatment centre. Accidents happened by the bucketload, especially when alcohol was involved. At least she was safe. Other people my age would be out living it up and I should have been finishing my assignment, but at least I had an excuse. Dom would be tucked up in bed unless he'd decided to have an all-night Xbox session. Laura should have been at home too, fast asleep with her aching feet elevated after serving tables all night.

Guilt washed over me. If I'd never have sent her that voice note, she would have gone straight home. *You brought her here. You're responsible.* Now she was hurt, hidden in an air vent and terrified for her life. If neither of us made it through tonight, at least there was some evidence on her phone to explain what happened.

You can survive this, the voice in my head piped up. *You will both survive this.*

My internal monologue spurred me into action and I got to my feet, rubbing my sore behind, realising it was the wall-mounted hand dryer I'd bumped into. I exited the toilet into the small lobby. Hiding here, I'd be in prime position for when the power came back on, but I had no idea how long Luca's friend was going to take to arrive. He could have said ten minutes or half an hour on the phone, I hadn't heard, but the power hadn't been switched back on since, so he wasn't here yet. My body rigid, I waited, listening and ready to run as soon as those doors opened, hoping Luca wouldn't decide he needed to use the facilities before his friend arrived, because then I would be screwed. With any luck, he'd think we were hiding on one of the upper floors.

Every nerve beneath my skin tingled with apprehension; like on a rollercoaster, the waiting in line is always far worse than the ride. I thought of Dom and what his reaction would be when the police officer reported everything was fine at Storage Queen. He'd think I'd been ignoring his messages, still upset from how we'd left things. How many times had he tried to call? Part of me wanted him to come back, but I was glad he wouldn't feel the need to. I didn't want him caught up in this mess too, it was bad enough Laura was here. I wasn't about to have his blood on my hands as well.

Torchlight swept past the door and my face drained of colour as I swallowed the lump in my throat. It was game time. I heard the creak of hinges and, seconds later, the overhead lights came on, dazzling me once again. Clamping my hands over my mouth, I let out a silent scream at what had been in the dark with me. In the far corner of the small lobby, propped up against the wall, sat the body of a man in a rumpled grey uniform, fleece and trousers, a red crest on his chest. His skin was pale, eyes closed as though he was sleeping. He looked to be at nearly retirement age, his chin covered in grey whiskers and face deeply lined. I couldn't see any blood, but his neck was bent at an unnatural angle.

I stared at him in horror, lips pressed together so I wouldn't let out a sound. The security man had come, he'd answered the panic button and I'd got him killed. Throat thick, I walked over, checking his pulse, but feeling nothing beneath my fingers. Reluctantly, I turned my back, wiping away my tears. Another death, but this was on my conscience. I'd called him here to help me and now he was dead. I seethed at the injustice.

There was nothing I could do for him now, but I could still save Laura and I couldn't miss my chance. Back at the door, I dared to pull it open a crack, looking through the gap to watch Luca, back in his baseball cap, disappear around the counter by my desk. He picked up the monitor he must have shoved onto the floor in a fit of rage and repositioned it on the desk before reaching for the door release button.

Muscles tensed and ready for action, I saw the entrance slide open and caught a glimpse of the visitor. A slender man, white but with long tobacco brown dreadlocks wearing a baggy purple acid face T-shirt, stepped across the threshold. He was so not who I was expecting, it delayed me for a second until I remembered what I was supposed to be doing.

Bolting through the door, I pumped my arms, legs moving faster than I ever had around the track in my years at school, glancing over at them.

'Police would have been here by now if she'd called them,' I caught the friend saying as I ran.

It was as I'd envisaged, Luca was pulling back my chair about to sit down with his friend stood behind him. Both of them looked up, eyes bulging as I whipped across reception like a streak of lightning. A few steps away from the door, it began to close as Luca pointed at me.

'Nina!' he shouted, but I arched my body forwards, sliding through the gap before it shut like there was some invisible finish line, but no ribbon awaited me, no one to announce me as the winner.

Outside, the chilly night air smacked me in the chest as I ran around the side of the building, my trainers hitting the concrete, through the barrier and onto the trading estate. A stitch threatened at my side, but I kept moving, pumping my arms and legs as fast as I could. I'd run to the nearest house if I couldn't find somewhere I could call the police.

The Storage Queen warehouse was set at the back of the estate, the only building manned twenty-four hours a day, so there was no comforting glow from any of the offices and business dwellings I raced past. No security guards on duty to take me in and the closest residential street was around ten minutes away up a steep hill.

It was eerie, the subtle glow of the street lights, the empty buildings as I ran past looking for any signs of life. It wasn't as if we were in the sticks, but overnight the estate slept, Storage Queen the only one awake during the witching hours. The stitch had taken hold, twisting my side, and I panted, trying to suck in as much air as I could, refusing to slow down. I had to make it. Laura was counting on me.

Just when I thought I was clear, that no one was in pursuit, a rumble came from behind me. I looked briefly over my shoulder at the headlights cutting through the night, approaching at speed. It was a Mitsubishi EVO, no way I'd outrun that. I widened my stride, trying to move quicker, zigzagging across the road, but the souped-up engine zoomed closer, its exhaust spluttering. It sounded like it was biting at my heels. I swerved onto the kerb trying to avoid getting run over, but the car accelerated around me, screeching to a halt at an angle, straight into my path.

The Nightingale

22

I slammed into the side of the car at full pelt and bounced back, tumbling onto the tarmac, gasping for breath. All of the air pumped out of me, I was dazed, barely comprehending a hand snaking beneath my armpit, lifting me into the back seat. Laying on the unforgiving leather, I curled my knees up, trying to inflate my lungs but unable to draw any oxygen in. I'd been winded badly, sure I'd bruised some internal organs.

'So you're naughty Nina, eh?' The dreadlocked man's green eyes glinted in the rear-view mirror as he turned his car around and drove me back to Storage Queen. All the time, I struggled for breath. The journey took less than a minute, I hadn't even made it out of the estate. Why hadn't I hidden, found a bush or something? But I'd been so caught up in getting away, it hadn't crossed my mind until it was too late.

When we came to a stop, I was unable to resist him hauling me out of the back seat and dragging me back towards the entrance, legs like jelly, where Luca waited inside, his face crimson with rage. Dropping his hold on me, I crumpled at Luca's feet, laying on my side by the desk, shivering in pain. I was sure I'd cracked a few ribs when I'd hit the car, it hurt to breathe and I fought the urge to vomit.

'Give me the fucking password,' Luca said, through gritted teeth. He'd dropped down on one knee, leaning over me as I rolled onto my back, wheezing. 'The password!' he snapped, straddling me now, his huge hands around my throat. He wasn't playing any more.

'How is she going tell you the password when she can't speak?' His dreadlocked friend was well-spoken, at odds with his grungy appearance, and I clawed at Luca's hands which tightened with each second that passed.

Luca's friend tutted and walked out of my eyeline just as my vision began to blur. My hands flailed, having given up trying to get Luca to release me, instead searching for something I could hit him with, anything I could use to get him to release me. Then I spied my insulin pen which lay under my chair next to one of the wheels. I remembered Luca had dropped it when I'd whacked him with the phone. I stretched for it, my lungs on fire, knowing I probably had less than a minute before Luca choked the life out of me.

'Give. Me. The. Password,' Luca said, releasing his grip a little to lift my head and bang it down on the floor with each word. Pain reverberated around my skull until I saw stars.

I was vaguely aware of my fingers curling around the length of the pen, my thumb finding the dial and the plunger at the end. The cap was gone, needle exposed, but Luca was so infuriated he didn't notice I'd picked it up. He'd loaded thirty units before and I was sure he wouldn't have wound the dial back to zero; in fact, I counted on it.

My wrist was weak, the lack of oxygen in my bloodstream making me limp, and I struggled to focus on anything but Luca's hands squeezing out my last remaining breath as I tried to thrash my legs beneath his weight. Even then I felt myself start to fade.

'Jesus!' The reprimand sounded like it was a hundred miles away and I was deep underwater with all sound muffled, but the second Luca's grip loosened, I inhaled oxygen, refilling my lungs. He turned to look over his shoulder at his friend and I brought my hand up to the pale expanse of exposed throat, thrusting the needle into the skin and pushing the plunger down, delivering thirty units of insulin.

'Fuck!' Luca yelped scrabbling off me, his palm covering the injection site but not before I saw a tiny drop of blood from the pinprick. Rolling onto my side, I began to cough, wincing from the shooting pains up my back and chest with each expulsion as I tried to clear my airways.

'What did you do?' Luca shouted down to me as the insulin pen rolled out of my palm, making a tinny noise on the tiled floor. His eyes swelled to enormous orbs, his jaw slack as he watched it go.

'What's the matter?' his dreadlocked friend asked, sounding more bored than concerned, too busy munching on one of Laura's mozzarella sticks.

'She's just stabbed me with insulin,' Luca shrieked, the blood draining from his face. 'She's diabetic.'

'All right, calm down.' He shrugged as though it was no big deal.

'Felix, call an ambulance. I will die.'

'You're not going to die and no names!' he snapped back.

'How long will it take?' Luca kicked me in the kidneys and I curled up into a ball, instinctively putting my hands over my head, protecting myself from the next strike, but it didn't come.

Without waiting for an answer, he stomped away and began pacing by the door, concentrating hard on his phone. I'd have laughed if it didn't hurt so much: was he googling how long he had to live? Not long if I had my way.

'Seriously, I need to go, now.' Whatever he'd seen on his phone had frightened him, his entire body was jittery, as if he had too much energy to expel. That wouldn't last long, soon he'd start to sweat and shake, his pallor would change and he'd feel weak. Disorientation would kick in, then he'd struggle to coordinate his body, rendering him helpless and unable to stagger more than a few steps. Eventually, if there was no intervention, he'd pass out and his organs would stop working. I felt no guilt, it was self-defence and there would be one less violent man in the world.

'Mate, just have a *Mars* bar or something, you'll be right as rain.' Felix rolled his eyes, still not cottoning on to the gravity of the situation, and I wasn't about to intervene.

'How much did you give me?' Luca shouted, striding over to put the boot in again, this time in my leg. I winced as pain radiated up my thigh.

'Thirty units.'

'Fuck!' He tapped at his phone again and I pictured the google search. How many units could kill you? Inside I was celebrating.

'How bad is it?' Felix asked, his hands on his hips, staring pointedly down at me.

'He'll die if he doesn't get to hospital,' I wheezed, making myself as small as I possibly could, ready for another attack, but Felix chuckled, shaking his head at me as though I was a wayward schoolgirl.

'I'll have to take you to the edge of the estate, we can't bring an ambulance here...' Felix said to Luca, scratching his chin, 'but we need to do something with her and there's another one, you said, in the building somewhere.'

'Fucking kill her,' Luca spat, wiping spittle from his mouth, and I cringed.

Felix came around the counter and stared at me laying on my side, curled into a ball, all the while chewing his lip, a deep trivet in between sparse eyebrows. I shrank smaller still, my body a mass of pain.

'Where's your friend?' he asked, crouching down, his tone as light as a feather.

I pressed my lips together, they'd have to kill me before I gave up Laura. Her absence meant she was still safe in the vent.

'Did you say she was injured?' Felix stood again, the question directed at Luca.

'I think I broke the bitch's arm.'

'Okay, we'll be quick then and I guess this will have to do,' he said, pulling the cord out of the back of Stacey's radio and unplugging it from the socket. Lifting me from the ground, clearly stronger than he looked, he plopped me in my chair and tied my hands together, looping it around and fastening it to the stem of the backrest.

'You killed that man, the security guard,' I blurted at Luca through a haze of tears.

'I told you, it was an accident,' he growled, looking first at me and then Felix, who stiffened behind me.

'What did you do?' Felix barked at Luca, but I wasn't finished.

'And you killed Sasha,' I said, watching Luca's head jerk in my direction so fast I thought it might come off.

'What do you mean?'

'You killed her and put her in that suitcase, you're a monster!' I screamed.

'Shut up,' Felix said, yanking my hair back so hard, I yelped.

There was a moment's pause, the air in the room seemed to shift as Luca's eyes drilled into Felix.

'You told me it was some junkie who attacked you,

you said not to look as it was messy,' Luca said, staggering backwards a couple of steps, not shifting his gaze from Felix, and I realised he had no idea who'd been in the suitcase he'd put in unit three hundred and twenty-one. Did he know Sasha?

'She's talking shit. Come on, I'll take you to the edge of the estate.' Felix took a step towards him, but the red mist had crossed Luca's features, twisting them into an ugly snarl.

'I'm going to fucking kill you if you've touched her,' Luca shouted, letting out a guttural howl that came from the depths of his lungs, looking like he was ready to stampede.

Felix held his hands out to pacify him, his voice shaky. 'I'll take you up there right now, mate, it's bullshit, but you don't have time to waste, do you. Look, I'll call an ambulance now.' He pulled his phone from his pocket and began dialling, coming back to the desk to press the door release button.

The entrance slid open and a gust of wind blew in. Felix stepped out into the car park, phone pressed to his ear to make the anonymous call. I looked at Luca who seemed to have shrunk, his fingers intertwined at the back of his head, eyes red rimmed and on the verge of tears. Not knowing who to believe.

'I'm not lying,' I said out of earshot of Felix.

'You opened the suitcase?'

I nodded. 'She's got a necklace, it's her name.'

He seemed to fold in half, dropping to his knees onto the floor as the information sank in. Whoever she was, he cared about her a great deal and I'd got it wrong. Robotically, he got back up, marching towards me, nostrils flaring. I shrank back in my seat, pulling against the cord, but he stopped at the desk to hit the door release and ran, gunning for Felix in the car park.

I could just about see the scuffle outside, two figures fighting in the car park, but I needed to make the most of the time. Straining against the cord, I managed to wriggle my left wrist free in under a minute, but the right one wouldn't budge. Even with one hand at my disposal, I couldn't call for help as the phone had been unplugged. I considered wheeling myself towards the door, but not with the two of them out there, especially as I was stuck in this stupid chair. One of them would come back soon, but I didn't have any fight left in me, my body was battered and bruised, everything hurt and all I wanted to do was curl up and die. I'd give whoever it was the log-in and pray they'd leave without any more blood on their hands.

Whatever happened, I couldn't let the footage go completely, someone had to know what happened here. Someone had to be caught and made to pay for Sasha and for what was going to happen to me and Laura. An idea sprang to mind and, with my free hand, I wiggled the mouse, bringing the monitor to life, and logged in, tapping the keyboard with one finger. The screen was cracked in the corner, the picture a fuzzy mess in that section, but thankfully it still worked. Manoeuvring the mouse with my left hand wasn't easy, but I navigated to the camera system, selecting the files which were in six-hour increments. Six o'clock until midnight last night and what had already recorded, albeit intermittently, from midnight onwards. I right clicked and downloaded them to my computer hard drive, looking over my shoulder as the green bar ticked agonisingly slowly across the screen.

My jaw clenched, making my teeth ache in protest. It was taking too long, they would be back any minute and couldn't know what I'd done. Finally, the bar disappeared and I swiftly opened Outlook to access my email, attaching the two files to a new draft and typing in Stacey's email. I copied in Dom too; I regularly emailed him when I was working, especially if he was at home watching television. We'd have full-on conversations for hours until he went to bed, then I'd usually focus on my university work to pass the rest of my night shift.

NEED HELP
LAURA AND I HELD HOSTAGE
DEAD BODY IN UNIT 321, SASHA.
SEND POLICE

I clicked send, closed the programmes and logged out, just as I heard a tap on the glass door and turned to see Felix's grinning face pressed against it.

23

LUCA – NOW

I sat slumped on the kerb by the rusted road sign, the cold seeping into the backside of my jeans, clutching my side where Felix had shanked me. Blood dripped through my fingers. It was just a flesh wound, he'd said, it was self-defence to stop me beating the bastard to death and I would have kept going until my last breath. I didn't even know he was carrying, but he'd pulled the blade on me as we'd rolled around between the cars. I would have killed him, but he'd swore blind it wasn't Sasha in the suitcase as he'd made me walk away from the warehouse, staying a few steps behind with the flick knife outstretched. But Nina knew about the necklace, how else would she have known?

I couldn't do anything else but comply, I was dead

without medical help. That bitch stuck me with a lot of insulin and I already felt weird. It was a hard to describe, disconnected maybe, a little light-headed and my limbs strangely weightless. Just how quick was the stuff supposed to work, was I about to croak on the pavement? I was breathless too, but I wasn't sure if that was down to stress or pain; my stomach felt like it was on fire.

Maybe it was karma, collecting its payment, no hesitation, just boom. I couldn't deny I deserved whatever was coming to me, but Felix would get his too, I'd make sure of it.

I hung my head, massaging my temple. Sasha. The thought of her was like a poker in my heart. Such a beautiful girl, she never deserved this and it was all my fault. She was the most important person in my life and we'd got mixed up with Felix, over what? The lure of money and the promise of a better, more secure future. One that meant we'd never live in the poverty we came from again. We'd got caught up in something we couldn't control, the threat of violence ever present and I had to watch my back. I'd tried to watch hers too, but she was so vibrant, a free spirit, it was impossible to control how she behaved. But it was my job to protect her and I'd failed, something I'd never forgive myself for.

I hadn't meant to hurt that security guard, only wanted to put the old guy to sleep, but I didn't know my own strength. The sickening crack of his neck against the crook of my arm will haunt me forever. I'd gone too far, crossed a line and I needed to run. When tonight was over, if I made it, I had to leave, but where could I go? Not home to Poland, I'd never be welcomed back there, not without Sasha.

Fuck! I launched my baseball cap across the road like a frisbee, wincing as the wound stretched with my movement.

I was on my own, disposable, expendable. Hung out to dry because I had served my purpose, like Sasha. Unable to believe we'd bought a word Felix had said. Too caught up in our fresh start, embracing the people and the culture, in a place where everyone seemed to be our friend, or at least pretended to be.

When I'd met Felix at our local pub, I took him as some hippy, with his dreads and baggy clothes, but he seemed harmless enough. At first, I thought it was weird, him drinking alone, chatting to the bartender, but once he struck up a conversation, we couldn't shut him up. We thought he was sound, keen to get to know us despite being outsiders, buying rounds and happy to share advice on living in Crawley, suggesting the best spots to visit and those to avoid, decent restaurants, bars and places we might find work.

We saw him most weekdays. I'd pop in for a pint after helping out at a building site in East Grinstead where he'd said they took workers on a cash-in-hand basis. Sasha joined us and persisted on flirting with the landlord until she secured a few shifts behind the bar, both of us looking for full-time work but doing what we needed to get by, to pay for our shitty bedsit.

Felix mentioned his start-up almost as soon as he introduced himself. He imagined himself as an entrepreneur, in the process of developing a new gaming app that all the kids were going to love. Sasha thought it sounded like bullshit, but I thought it had scope. He'd said he needed finance to finish developing it, but didn't mention it much after that. A few weeks later, huddled around the table at our local, on our third round of drinks, he said he'd found a way to make easy money but was looking for people he could trust. It sounded so simple and our cut was more money than we'd dreamed of. A way to get out of the bedsit and into some proper accommodation. Looking back now, I doubt the app thing was even real.

Both of us got sucked in. By then, a month or so had passed and we hung out with Felix all the time. He helped us out with the deposit on our maisonette, sorted us some furniture, bought our trust. I thought he had a thing for Sasha, but it didn't faze me; she said she didn't see him like that. He wasn't a threat at the start, not all the time things were going well. Not when the money was coming in and Felix was taking his hefty cut. Sasha was spending it like she'd become a footballer's wife overnight, but then growing up poor she was seduced by it, we both were.

I repositioned myself on the kerb, my backside numb, pulling my T-shirt down over my hands, which were starting to tremble. I watched them in the glare of the lamp post. No part of my body felt like my own. Sweat trickled in between my shoulder blades, dampening the back of my T-shirt. Where was the damn ambulance? In my country, it would have been here by now. I remembered being in the pub with Felix while he ranted about the government and how the country had gone to pot – too many relying on handouts, he'd said. We were brought up to stand on our own two feet and that was how Felix sucked us in. It wasn't charity, he'd said, but kindness and he'd killed us with it.

If Nina was right, Sasha was gone, the only light in the sky, my north star, my sun and moon. I wiped the tears away, dragging my sleeve roughly across my face. It wouldn't bring her back, nothing would, and I'd been stupid not to realise how deep in it we were, how dangerous these people could be and how either of us would never be allowed to leave. In the distance, I heard a siren, coming closer. I tried to stand, but my legs gave out beneath me and I crumpled like a sack of bricks to the pavement. The world seemed to spin and sweat dripped from my forehead into my eyes, blinding me. Was it the insulin or was I bleeding out?

I lay on my side, burning up, T-shirt now saturated, but there was still hope. I could hear the sirens blaring, yet I couldn't move. It was like I'd been paralysed. My vision started to fade, just as the blue lights approached, and I managed to raise my hand as the ambulance flew past in a haze of yellow. Had they seen me? Were they going to turn around? I let out a long breath, like a death rattle, my hand dropping to the kerb, where I tried to absorb its temperature. I was so hot, my insides turning to liquid. That bitch had killed me. I closed my eyes comforted by the knowledge I'd see Sasha soon.

24

2 A.M. – 6 A.M.

While Felix entered the keycode he must have got from Luca, I thrust my wrist back into the cord and tried to steady my breathing.

'Looks like it's just you and me now... well, until I find your friend,' he said with a grin as he emerged through the door, his perfectly straight teeth shining at me. Everything about him was off, other than the hair and the clothes he didn't look grungy at all, he smelt good too, unlike me. His teeth gleamed, skin un-blemished, even his nails were pristine.

I tried to place Felix's age, maybe older than Luca but definitely older than me, mid-twenties probably. Was he some privileged ex-public-school boy who'd adopted the dreadlocks and baggy clothes look to piss off his parents or was he trying to stand out and appear edgy in a tsunami of Nike tracksuits and Air Jordans? I couldn't work him out.

He leant on the counter, his posture relaxed as though he didn't have a care in the world. No mention of Luca, or the ambulance. The only evidence of a scuffle was his T-shirt pulled out of shape at the neck.

'Why don't you do us both a favour and give me the password, then we can all get out of here.'

Mortifyingly, my eyes welled as I nodded in defeat. Stacey and Dom had the files, it didn't matter that Felix was going to delete them, they were already out there, in the ether. I knew Dom wouldn't receive the email immediately, once the police had confirmed everything was okay here, he would have likely gone to bed, but at least he'd know what had happened. As for Stacey, I'd hoped she would have come to the warehouse when I hadn't answered, assuming that was her calling me back. Some on-call manager she was.

'My password is lovelybones02.' I sniffed, letting the pent-up frustration out as he wrote it on a Post-it note. I'd come so far but ultimately couldn't last the distance and had to pray Felix would be true to his word about all of us getting out of here.

I couldn't imagine not seeing Mum or Dom again, the thought broke my heart. And I wasn't going to let him hurt Laura. As long as she was quiet, he'd never find her. *Please hold on,* I begged her silently, hoping she'd got through to the police, but as they hadn't arrived, I guessed she hadn't.

'See, that wasn't so hard, was it?'

Felix leant over me, so close I inhaled the spicy scent of Armani on his purple T-shirt. Bringing the screen to life, he typed in my password and my desktop appeared. I felt my pulse rocket from his proximity, the hairs standing to attention on my arms. Felix's demeanour elicited a different kind of fear to Luca, there was no bravado, no muscles or threatening stance, just a quiet assurance he was in charge.

'*Lovely Bones*? After the book?' His breath smelt of cigarettes and my stomach rolled.

'It's my favourite,' I replied flatly, wondering if, like Susie Salmon, I'd be destined to wander Storage Queen after my murder, or perhaps Sasha would instead. We could create a sisterhood of roaming souls searching for revenge.

'Seen the movie?' he asked as though we were colleagues chatting at the coffee machine during a break.

I nodded.

'That dude, Stanley... whatshisname, chilling, isn't he?'

'Tucci,' I said.

Felix laughed, 'Yeah, that's it.'

He turned his attention back to the screen, navigating with the mouse.

'Is it this programme?' Felix asked, pointing to Lexis Security, a padlock symbol on the left of the screen, one app of many.

I nodded again and he double-clicked, finding the files easily and moving them to the rubbish bin before confirming deletion.

'They'll wonder why I've deleted them,' I said.

'I'm sure they will.' Felix smirked but didn't offer an opinion.

Surreptitiously, I checked Sasha's watch on my wrist, it was two in the morning, there were still maybe five hours until sunrise and four hours until Paul arrived for his shift. What would he find when he got here? Me, deceased, tied to my chair and a couple of cracked panes of glass with the only lead to go on being Sasha's code used to enter the building. That was until Stacey or Dom woke up and watched what I'd sent them. Before that, at least the codes would direct the police to search Sasha's unit, where, if she hadn't been moved, they'd find her body. The smell would be instantly recognisable as soon as they gained access.

'Luca didn't know Sasha was in the suitcase, did he?' The question burst from my lips, the desire to know gnawing at me.

Felix straightened, staring at me, unable to hide his surprise. Was it because I knew about her, or that I'd used Luca's name? It didn't matter, I had nothing left to lose now.

'No he didn't.'

I let those words settle. So it had been true. When I'd mentioned him killing somebody earlier and he'd told me it was an accident, he was talking about the security guard.

'He's her brother, you know.'

It was my turn to be surprised, I'd assumed before that they were a couple, that her death was an act of domestic violence.

'Her brother?' I repeated, making sure I hadn't misunderstood.

'Yep, they both came over here from Poland just over a year ago, invested in my start-up.'

The weight of what I'd done to Luca sat heavily on my shoulders, it was self-defence but made easier knowing he was a killer, that he was getting his just desserts. I remained quiet, wanting to ask who had killed Sasha but afraid to, in case the answer was standing right next to me.

Felix was happy to fill the silence. 'She used to be our go-to girl, our mule, bloody good at it too. Stunning yet great at flying under the radar and able to talk herself out of any situation. Until she decided she wanted a change of pace, but once you're in, well, it becomes complicated to get out.' He sighed dramatically, twisting one of his dreadlocks around his finger, leaning against the desk without a care in the world. Not someone who had tied me to a chair and was holding me hostage.

'Mule? As in drugs?' Now the contents of the storage unit made sense.

Felix chuckled, but it was hollow and without any mirth. He tapped his temple. 'Switched on, aren't you.'

He got to his feet and stretched, letting out a yawn. I stifled mine, the events of the past few hours had taken a toll. Most of the country was sleeping and no matter how many night shifts I worked, it still felt abnormal being awake as the witching hour approached.

Felix cleared his throat. 'It's okay, I found a replacement. Perhaps if I'd told Luca to take the suitcase somewhere else, you wouldn't have got caught up in all this.'

'You can let me go,' I offered, deliberately keeping Laura out of the conversation.

'What, after you tried to kill Luca?' he sniggered. 'Although that was quite ingenious, I have to say. But I'm afraid I can't do that, you know our names, seen our faces.'

'I won't tell anyone,' I said, my voice barely a whisper.

Inside, I despised myself, being reduced to begging for my life, but wouldn't anyone in the same situation? When it came down to it, I was only human. Anger bubbled in my belly at being in this situation although what I'd done to Luca weighed heavily on my mind. Was he sitting on a wall, waiting for the ambulance's arrival, starting to feel light-headed and maybe a little nauseous? Did his limbs feel disconnected, his vision blurry? How long would it take him to die from a heart attack or organ failure? It would be inevitable without intervention. I was being trained to save lives, not take them, but I'd believed he was a killer and he was trying to strangle me at the time.

Despite every muscle in my body aching and sore, a sense of self-preservation kicked in and I looked around for a way out, a weapon to use when Felix decided it was time to end our conversation, but the only thing in reach was a stapler and I wasn't going to do much damage with that.

'So why don't you tell me where your friend is hiding. We can go and get her, make her promise to keep quiet and then I'll let you go, how about that?'

I pressed my lips tightly together, he was mocking me. There was no way he was letting either of us out of here alive.

Felix waited a minute or so for his offer to sink in, but I remained stoic.

'Luca said you were a pain,' he sighed at my refusal to speak, 'but don't worry, I'll find her. I have my ways.'

Felix stood behind me, massaging my shoulders, drawing my hair away from my neck. His touch made my skin crawl and I fought the urge to free my hand and poke his eye out.

'I have an idea,' Felix said after a minute, his hands digging in to my tendons, jolting me from my revulsion. I looked up at him looming over me, watching his smile form, eyes disappearing into slits. 'Let's check out the roof, I bet there's a good view of the town from up there.' He sounded jovial, excited even, but all the air left my lungs.

It wasn't going to be quick, a shot in the head or a knife to the chest, no, Felix planned to throw me off the top and make it look like I'd committed suicide. I'd just broken up with my boyfriend after all, not that he knew that, but my heart broke at the thought of Dom believing he might be the reason I'd ended my life. Or my mum wishing she'd known what turmoil I had to be going through to leap from a four-storey building.

No, they'd have the email, the footage, they'd see me being hunted around the warehouse, the reason why exhaustion won out. Two bad hypoglycaemic attacks, the amount of stress my mind and body had gone through to stay alive this long. Laura would live, she'd tell everyone what had happened. Felix would never find her as long as she stayed hidden.

I blinked back tears. Would Mum and Dom forgive me, knowing I'd tried so hard, I'd fought for my life until I could fight no more? Was that what I was doing now, as Felix untied me and directed me towards the lift, because it looked like I was being compliant, making it easy for him.

'Third floor I'm guessing?' Felix said, punching the number. The lift didn't respond, still stuck on the first floor. I guessed it had to be reactivated.

'It's not working,' I mumbled and he rolled his eyes, nodding towards the stairwell.

We climbed, Felix humming to himself behind me,

but when we reached the third floor, he got out onto the landing and frowned.

'How do you get to the roof again?'

I could pretend I didn't know, but Luca had already told him I'd been up there.

'The access to the roof is from the other stairwell, we have to follow the corridor around.'

'Oh yeah,' he said, gesturing for me to go first.

I led the way, wanting to see if the unit I'd been hiding in was obviously unlocked. Not only that, but I was also intrigued as to whether, now the lights were back on, Luca had locked Sasha's unit, knowing there was a hammer in there that would be a good weapon. I kept my head bowed, hiding behind my dark messy hair, only raising my eyes when the unit approached. I'd closed it well enough, it wasn't obvious the padlock wasn't secure unless you really looked.

'Smells funny up here.' Felix wrinkled his nose as we turned the corner and passed unit three hundred and twenty-one, which was locked.

'That's Sasha,' I said bitterly, feeling fire rise up in my bruised chest.

'Oh,' he chuckled at his faux pas and I had to resist the urge to turn around and smack him.

I simmered until we reached the east stairwell,

opening the door to the stairs, strange to see the places I'd been skulking around in the dark now lit up.

'You first,' he said, gesturing with a flick of the wrist, only now I could see he held a flick knife. I shuddered, there was no way I could let him corner me on that roof with nowhere to run, no place to hide. Despite running on empty, I wasn't about to give up without a fight.

25

We'd taken a couple of steps up towards the roof when my moment came.

'Shit!' Felix hissed as he missed a step, too busy watching me to concentrate on his footing, barely righting himself before I swung around and pushed him as hard as I could in his pigeon chest. His hands flailed, the knife slicing through air as he began to fall, catching the top of my outstretched arm, the tip splitting my skin. It all happened in slow motion, the look of surprise on his weaselly face, both of us crying out in shock. Blood dripped from my arm as Felix tumbled backwards down the steps, hitting the landing, momentum keeping him somersaulting down towards the second floor.

Springing into action, I jumped down onto the landing and darted through the door to the third-floor corridor, running whilst trying to stem the bleeding. If it had been the other arm he, might have caught my glucose monitor, not that it was worth anything without my phone. I squeezed the wound, not wanting to be traced by blood droplets on the floor, but he'd nicked me good and it stung like hell. I dashed past Sasha's unit and around the corner to the west stairwell, flying down the stairs as fast as I could, but when I got to the bottom and peered through the porthole into reception, Felix was already there.

He'd beat me too it, limping around by my desk, injured from the fall down the stairs and tapping angrily on the keyboard now I'd given him the password. Was he trying to access the cameras to find out where I was? It was a smart move and he was obviously intelligent enough to know I'd try to leave the building as soon as I was away from him.

'Shit!' I mouthed, leaning my head back against the wall as I panted. I wouldn't be able to get past him and escape. Despite his fall, he'd got downstairs fast, the squirrelly little shit, shame he hadn't fallen all the way to the bottom and broken his neck.

My arm stung and I gripped it tightly, I needed to find something to wrap around the wound. While

Felix was distracted, I climbed the stairs back up to the third floor as quickly as I could to the unlocked unit, slipping inside and closing the door behind me. With the light working, I was able to fully appreciate how rammed it was. Boxes were stacked nearly to the ceiling at the back, with only the space by the door free. I opened up one of the bin bags I'd sat between earlier, relived to find clothing inside. Rooting through, I found a floaty scarf and wrapped it around my arm, tying it tightly. I didn't think the wound was too deep, all the nerves seemed untouched, and I wiggled my fingers to check everything was working as it should.

Lowering onto the floor, I prayed Felix wasn't on his way up here. Despite sprinting down the corridor, if he'd been watching the right camera at that exact moment, then I'd led him straight to my hiding place. Scanning the room, I looked for a weapon, but nothing immediately jumped out at me so I got back up and started opening boxes. I found books and picture frames, extension leads, various paint tins and cans, paintbrushes and rollers and then boxes of climbing gear, ropes, pulleys and helmets. Finally, I found some rusted tools and garden paraphernalia that I guess had once been in someone's shed.

Selecting a crowbar from the haul, it felt satisfyingly heavy in my grip, the weight of it a comfort. I'd managed to fight off Luca, perhaps I could do the same with Felix; he was half the size. An idea struck me on how I could even the odds. Felix was an altogether different beast to Luca. It seemed he either didn't know how or hadn't thought about turning the power off, and as much as I wanted to stay here, I thought of Laura wedged inside the vent, likely feeling claustrophobic and in an enormous amount of pain. I shouldn't be sitting here in relative comfort, when she was stuck in there. I had to keep trying to get out.

Venturing out into the corridor, exposed under the fluorescent lights with no place to hide, I moved quickly. Perhaps I could turn the tables, or at least try to lure him out of reception so I could escape. I shook the can of white spray paint, hearing the ball bearings rattle inside. Perhaps the owners of the unit I'd been using as a refuge dabbled in upcycling furniture. Regardless, it was just what I needed. With a renewed sense of purpose, I jogged to the end of the corridor, reached up as far as I could, standing on tiptoes and pointed the paint can towards the small dome camera, pressing down hard and covering it completely.

Coming back on myself, I sprayed the other two cameras and then marked a cross on the door of unit three hundred and twenty-one. Downstairs, I repeated my artwork on the second floor, trying hard to ignore the sharp pains in my ribs and stomach from the collision with Felix's car. If anything, they spurred me on. When I reached the first floor, I was more cautious, moving slower and listening in the stairwell for any sound of movement from below. I heard nothing, so backtracked to spray the cameras before stopping at the air vent.

'Laura,' I whispered. Through the metal grate, I saw her feet twitch.

'Nina, thank God! Get me out of here. The lights keep going out, I panicked.' Her voice was shrill and wobbled as though she was on the verge of a breakdown.

'I will, it's not safe yet. Have you been able to call the police?' If she still had no reception, I'd take the phone to the roof and call from there.

'The battery died.'

'Fuck's sake!' I hissed, looking to the ceiling for some divine inspiration.

'Nina, please, I don't want to stay in here, it's so dark and I'm frightened.'

Laura sounded like the little girl I'd met in the playground all those years ago, not the strong woman I'd seen her grow into.

'I just need a bit more time,' I pleaded, already

seeing her wiggle backwards towards the grate. 'You have to stay there.'

She didn't answer me, but her body stilled and I heard her sniffling.

'I'll come back, okay, I promise. I won't leave you,' I said, backing away.

Even if Felix had seen me on the cameras as I came down the floors spraying them, he would be reluctant to leave reception because if I outran him, I'd be free. With him guarding the only exit, I couldn't get out. I contemplated what his plan would be, because if I never attempted to escape, he'd have to come searching eventually, especially if, like Luca, he was intent on having no one able to identify him. He had witnesses to find and the clock was ticking.

Perhaps he wasn't looking on the cameras at all, maybe he had another plan to lure me out. It wasn't until I reached the bottom of the west stairwell, near to the lift, I saw why he was taking his time, what had garnered his attention. I gasped as I peeked through the circular window, recognising Dom's stance and well-worn blue hoody immediately. He looked so handsome with his wayward sandy hair and lopsided grin. I felt my eyes were deceiving me and fought the urge to throw open the door and run into his arms, but something stopped me.

It was the way he was talking to Felix, the relaxed manner, his hands in his pockets, which seemed strange. Did they know each other? He stood just at the entrance, the door kept trying to slide shut, but he was blocking it, letting the chilly air seep in. Had he come back for me? Had he seen my email after all?

I pulled the door a fraction and put my ear to the crack, straining to listen to their muffled voices midway through their conversation, intrigued to find out how Felix could explain being at Storage Queen in the middle of the night.

'She's my girlfriend.'

'That's Doctor Nina?' The incredulity in Felix's tone made me bristle, but I noted Dom didn't say ex-girlfriend and my heart sang. He had to still care to be here at almost three in the morning.

'She's not changed her mind about coming with us then?'

I screwed my face up. What was Felix on about?

Dom shook his head, grimacing. 'Afraid not, Drex.' The nickname sent shockwaves through me.

'Well, I'm not sure how the two of you are going to work out if you're coming travelling, mate!'

I choked on my breath, nearly hyperventilating in the stairwell. Felix was Dom's buddy from college? Drexl?

'She's taking her time, isn't she,' Dom said.

'Yeah she's upstairs, like I said, some issue with the unit my mate is renting out; there was a leak, some of his stuff got destroyed. We've been here hours, mate, bit pissed off now, to be honest. I'm knackered.' Felix's lies dripped from his tongue like honey, but he was still limping slightly, not fully recovered from his fall down the stairs.

Dom stepped further inside, the door closing now he wasn't standing in the way.

'That's whose car is out there then, your mate's?'

Felix frowned through the glass at Dom's question.

'Yeah, sure,' he said.

Dom must have meant Laura's car, but he wouldn't have recognised it as hers.

'Can you go get Nina for me? I've been trying to ring, but her phone is switched off. We had a row and I really want to speak to her,' Dom asked.

I furrowed my brow, had he seen the email or not? I couldn't tell. Was he here to rescue me or to patch things up? Should I step out into reception and confront Felix? With Dom's help, we should be able to overpower him, but my arm twinged as if reminding me Felix had a knife and he wasn't afraid to use it. Plus I had Laura to consider too. She was already a casualty of this night shift and I couldn't let there be another.

'Problem is, it's a hazardous substance, that's why I've been sent down here. I'm waiting for the men in the hazmat suits to turn up, thought you were them.' Felix chuckled, rubbing the back of his neck. He sounded convincing and I saw Dom's resolve crumble.

'Maybe I'll wait then, keep you company.'

Felix scratched his chin and a smile spread across my face, glad that Dom was a fly in his ointment. 'You could, but wouldn't you get Nina in trouble? I think the boss lady might be on her way.'

My lip curled and I pressed my nails into my palm. God he was good, as slippery as a fish out of water.

'Yeah, you're probably right. Funny bumping into you here though, mate.' Dom turned, visibly deflated, and headed back to the keypad. He knew the staff code, something which would likely get me sacked if Stacey found out, and I pictured Felix's face when he just let himself in.

'Don't leave,' I whispered, hoping my message would send telepathically. Wanting nothing more than to run after him, beg him to end my nightmare shift.

'Yeah, what are the chances! I tell you what, as soon as she's dealt with the mess, I'll get her to ring you.' Felix slapped Dom on the shoulder in a brotherly gesture that made me want to rip his arm from the socket.

'Cheers, mate. You excited? Three weeks tomorrow.' The impish grin on Dom's face crushed me. He had no idea what he'd inadvertently got involved in being friends with Felix, the pair an unlikely combination. I would never have put them together but Dom had said they just got chatting on the first day of their college course and hit it off.

'Hell yeah! It's going to be a wild ride,' Felix replied, his eyes glinting.

All the muscles in my neck constricted, my jaw so tight I thought my teeth would shatter.

Over my dead body.

26

As soon as Dom left, I kicked myself for not making a run for it, for grasping the second chance of escape, but I was desperate to protect him. What would he have done if I'd burst through that door into reception telling him to run? How would Felix have reacted? Were him and Dom really friends? I wasn't sure a man like that was capable of having them. If he was happy to throw me off the roof to protect himself, what would another life matter. I couldn't be responsible for Dom getting caught up in my mess and I had to stay alive so I could warn him not to go to Thailand. What-ever Felix was up to, and it didn't sound like he was going on the tourist trail, I wasn't about to let Dom get duped.

Felix seemed unfazed by Dom's unexpected arrival and I watched him return to my computer and frown at the screen, perhaps looking at the cameras, trying to work out why all of a sudden he couldn't see anything on them, not on the corridors anyway. Only the one in reception facing the entrance and the car park would be visible now. At least I couldn't be tracked as I moved around the warehouse. What I needed to do was lure him away from reception so I could get out and go for help, but how?

Through the window, I watched him pace, likely in two minds whether he should attempt to find me and Laura, leaving reception unguarded? Luca must have told him there was only one way into the building with the fire exit door jammed, but now we were stuck, neither one of us wanting to leave our posts. He glanced towards the stairwell and I ducked down below the porthole out of sight, my body trembling. Had he seen me?

Knuckles white, I gripped the door handle, waiting for it to turn, for Felix to barge in, as every nerve ending in my body fired. With Dom's arrival, he'd been seen here and whatever came afterwards, there was a living witness, someone who could place him in the right place at the right time. Would Felix expect Dom to cover for him in the aftermath? Were they that close? Whatever happened, I had to make it out of here. Dom had to be warned, if he went to Thailand and Felix slipped something into his bag to bring back, I'd never forgive myself. I wasn't about to have years of incarceration in a foreign prison on my conscience. Dom had to know what Felix had made Sasha do.

I peeked through the window again. Felix was still pacing but now concentrating on his phone. I wished I had mine, but it was probably at the hospital by now, in Luca's pocket. I was still reeling from Felix's revelation that Luca and Sasha were siblings. How must he feel now, knowing the suitcase he'd dragged up to the unit had his dead sister's body inside? I had no doubt he was devastated and if I hadn't injected him, he would have likely killed Felix in the car park. I couldn't pity him, he'd killed the security guard, accident or not. All I felt was regret, as I suspected he did too.

Despite knowing I was safe for now in the stairwell, my hands still had a tremor. No doubt my blood sugar was dropping again. The gel I'd had would only last so long. I needed carbs, slow release that would keep me steady, and I kicked myself again for not eating all the macaroni cheese. Not only that, but giving myself too much insulin for what I'd eaten. Even so, it was the least of my worries at the moment.

I had to act, to do something. I wasn't going to stay here and wait to become a victim of Felix's wrath. I had to find a way to get him out of reception, so I ventured around the back of the stairwell, where Luca had gone to turn the power off. Behind the stairs, now in the brightly lit space, I found a housing unit for what looked like industrial-sized fuses. The sheet metal covering had been removed and propped up against the wall. I couldn't really make head nor tail of it. It was on a much grander scale than what we had under the stairs at home and none of the switches were labelled. On the right, a red lever sat in an upright position. If I pulled it down, would it cut the power? Is that all that Luca had done?

Indecision made me fidget and I tucked the crowbar under my arm, as I looked intently at the lever, running through my options. How would it help me get out? Without electricity I couldn't use the keypad, the entrance wouldn't open and I would be no better off. Plus I'd be wandering around in the dark again, whereas Felix had his phone and Luca's torch somewhere. He'd have the advantage. On the other hand, it might make him leave reception to investigate, enabling me to turn the power back on and make a dash for it.

I was about to come up with another plan to lure him away, but footsteps approaching the door forced me to act. Just as the hinges creaked and Felix stepped inside the stairwell, I yanked at the stiff lever, pulling it down and plunging us both into darkness.

Holding my breath, I was terrified to move a muscle. I didn't know if Felix could tell I was hiding in here, whether he knew where the fuse box was or had heard me pull the lever. He cursed loudly over by the door, but I detected panic in his tone, which gave me a hit of satisfaction. I was in control now. I'd navigated the warehouse in the dark already; this was my domain. With Luca gone and the cameras disabled, finally Felix and I were on more of a level playing field, but he still had the knife.

I waited for him to move, but it seemed, like me, he was frozen to the spot and my jubilation began to fade. A second later, I heard shuffling and Felix's light from his phone beamed right in my eyes, inches away. Startled, I let out a yelp, instinctively raising the can of paint and spraying it directly into the light.

'Fuck!' he screamed, dropping his phone and covering his eyes, smearing white paint over his face.

I raised the crowbar, whipping it across Felix's side,

and he crumpled to his knees, both of us scrabbling for the phone, coating the floor and our knees with slippery paint. I got to it first, but as I stood, Felix lashed out, punching me in the stomach, slamming the air out of me, and the phone flew from my hand. It skittered across the floor and crashed into the wall, where the light petered out.

Through the glass in the fire exit door, despite the sun not having risen yet, the sky had moved from a midnight blue to a slate grey, providing some respite from the darkness. It disappeared when Dom's silhouette pressed against the glass from outside, his hands cupped trying to peer in and I rattled the lever, unable to shout or even straighten as I gasped for breath. Yet my heart lifted at the sight of him in such close proximity. He hadn't left. I had no idea how much he'd seen, if anything at all. Dropping to my knees, I searched the floor for the crowbar while Felix went for the phone, both of us fumbling around until Felix's shadowy form pulled himself up and staggered towards me. The fire exit shook, Dom's futile attempts to get in the warehouse, as Felix snarled, baring his teeth.

'Fucking whore,' he spat, white paint illuminated his face, making him look crazy. He was nearly on me before he lost his footing and slipped, landing hard on one knee like he was going to propose. I grabbed the chance to haul myself up the stairs by the banister, unable to move at any great speed and terrified he'd be up and after me in seconds. As I climbed, desperately trying to think of somewhere nearby to hide, I recalled the lift was out of action on the first floor.

Feeling my way, I found the doors were still stuck open and I gingerly tapped my foot, edging it forwards to make sure there was floor beneath me to tread on. Once satisfied I wasn't about to drop down an empty shaft, I moved inside and pressed my back against the controls, a sharp pain stabbing my intestines. Felix's punch felt like it had mangled my bowel and I winced as I tried to straighten my back, hunching forwards lessened the pain. If Luca's kick to the kidneys hadn't done it before, I had no doubt now I'd be urinating blood the next time I went to the toilet, imagining my naked body purple in places like Sasha's.

I listened for Felix lurching up the stairs in the dark, spluttering expletives with every step, but I saw no sign of light. His phone must have broken when it hit the wall and perhaps he couldn't find the torch. Either way, it worked better for me. I flattened myself against the side of the lift as much as was possible, hoping he wouldn't fall in here by accident, but his footsteps moved slowly past, dragging along the opposite wall. I held my breath, not daring to make a sound.

'Nina!' Felix yelled as I squeezed my eyes shut, bladder straining with fear. He sounded incandescent with rage as he stalked down the corridor and I pictured Jack Nicholson, the unhinged look on his face dragging the axe behind him. Felix was no Jack Nicholson, but even a crazed skinny eco-warrior could be terrifying in the dark. He wouldn't hold back if he got his hands on me, but unlike Luca, I had a feeling Felix would enjoy humiliating me and inflicting pain.

Please stay quiet, Laura, I prayed, knowing he'd reach the vent soon, hoping she wouldn't give herself away. *Just hold on, a little longer.* I promised myself I'd get her out of here without any more harm and I intended to keep it.

For now I was free, away from Felix's clutches, but for how long? He wasn't what I bargained for when I saw him but, in truth, he scared me more than Luca. I hoped the spray paint was burning his retinas, forever impairing his vision, but there was no time to gloat at my small victory. I had to rescue Laura and myself from this nightmare.

27

Feeling as though I was on some kind of reconnaissance mission, as soon as I could no longer hear Felix, I crept back down the stairs, clinging to the banister. My intention was to turn the power back on and get the hell out of the warehouse, but he must have known as I'd barely reached the ground floor before I heard him descending the stairs behind me. He must have double-backed and not descended the west stairwell like I'd envisaged. The first thing he'd do when his rage subsided, if he couldn't find me, would be to turn the power on, if he knew how to, because he was just as trapped as I was with it off.

Abandoning my initial plan, I bypassed the fuse box and moved towards the door to reception, trying to be as quiet as I could. The floor at the bottom was slippery and I skidded, the face of Sasha's watch clattering against the metal banister sounding like an explosion in the silence.

'I hear you, Nina, and I'm coming.' The threat rang down the stairwell from the darkness above and I heard his pace quicken. I shuddered, treading on something hard in my bid to get away. Felix's footsteps grew louder and I reached down, brushing my fingers against the crowbar I'd lost in the scuffle, protruding out from the bottom step.

Should I wait here and catch Felix as came down the stairs? Then a better idea popped into my head of how to get rid of him, this time maybe permanently.

'You can't hide from me,' he shouted, almost on the final staircase, giving me just enough time to slip into reception, where it was so quiet you could hear a pin drop. Where had I last seen the torch? Luca had had it when he'd turned the power back on, when Felix arrived and they went to the desk. I crept over there, the pain in my stomach now a constant ache. It was like the worse period cramps I'd ever experienced. My head lightly throbbed and all my muscles groaned every time I moved from the bruises I'd incurred. There wouldn't be enough painkillers in the world for how banged up I felt right now, but I had no choice but to keep going.

When I reached the desk, I ran my hands across the surface, finding my stapler and Post-it notes, then the landline handset minus its cord. Near the monitor stand, my fingers grazed the torch and I clicked it on, whipping it towards the west stairwell, shoulders clenched as though Felix had snuck up on me when I hadn't been paying attention. He hadn't emerged yet, likely disorientated in the dark, or trying to find the fuse box, knowing we'd both been in the stairwell when it had gone off. I knew I didn't have long before he'd creak open that door and I switched the torch off so as not to draw attention to myself.

With the crowbar and torch, I took the door to my right through the east stairwell and began climbing as Felix shouted my name. I'd never been able to tolerate the step machine at the gym and given the amount of floors I'd climbed the past few hours, I was surprised my muscles hadn't seized up completely. Hamstrings screaming at me with each step, I'd grown sluggish, energy depleted. I needed some sustenance, some calories for all the energy I'd spent fighting for my life. More than anything, I needed to rest, but there was no option but to keep moving. Even if Dom had called the police again and managed to convince them he wasn't a crank after the first call-out had been closed, it could take ages for them to arrive. Was he still wandering around outside, trying to find a way in? Even if he was, I couldn't depend on Laura and I being rescued, I had to be the one to rescue us.

I fumbled in my pocket for the Polos, all fingers and thumbs in my haste, and they slipped through my fingers, tumbling down the stairs like tiny pennies.

'Shit!' I hissed. There was no point in wasting time trying to find them. Felix must not be far behind me, maybe he had seen the torchlight. That was fine, I wanted him to follow. Unless he'd given up and was going to wait in some dark corner for me to come to him. Did he still have the knife? He was dangerous and needed dealing with, but I was too broken for another physical fight where he would overpower me with ease. I had to use my smarts to beat him and that's just what I was going to do.

I was moving so slowly, it seemed to take forever, but I finally reached the second floor and made my way around the corridor to the west side. When I reached the doors to the lift shaft, I put the torch on the floor, the beam directed down the corridor, and got to work.

I'd not used a crowbar before, not for what it was properly made for anyway, but wedged the point between the lift doors and heaved. Initially, there was resistance and the doors stayed glued together, but little by little, I managed to force them further apart. By the time I'd got them fully open, I was a sweaty mess.

Shining the torch into the dark cavern, I could see the roof of the lift stuck motionless on the first floor, maybe seven or eight feet below where I was standing. I wasn't sure the fall would do much damage to Felix, but at least he would be contained long enough for me to escape.

With my plan hatched and ready, I had to lure him up here, but how? I moved the torch so its beam was pointing away from the lift, making sure it wasn't obvious the shaft was empty. There was only one way to get him here and that was to make noise, so I got down on the floor and began to scream, rolling around which aggravated my bruised stomach and likely cracked ribs. Writhing in pain I barely had to act. I carried on for a few minutes, stopping periodically to listen for any sign of Felix until my throat felt like sandpaper. If he believed I was injured and giving away my location, surely he'd come to investigate. Unless he was suspicious, but I thought the idea of catching me unarmed and immobilised would be too delicious for him to ignore.

I didn't have to wait long and I heard his footsteps coming from the east stairwell before I saw him appear around the corner. He limped down the corridor, his arms by his side, red-faced and wearing a sneer as I clutched my ankle, whimpering theatrically.

'Had an accident, Nina?'

I'd tucked the crowbar underneath me, the iron digging into my back. It was out of sight, but even knowing I had it, my mouth went dry. Had I made a terrible mistake enticing him up here?

'I've hurt my ankle,' I whined, trying to sound as pitiful as possible. Felix had to believe I wasn't a threat.

He moved slow, reaching into his back pocket and pulling out the knife, brandishing it towards me when he was feet away.

'Well, at least I don't have to chase you any more.' He smirked, stopping to tilt his head to one side. His shadow was magnified on the adjacent wall, like a vampire as he edged closer, coming in for the kill. My entire body quaked, but it wasn't an act. I'd deleted the footage, I was surplus to requirements. The only card I had to play was where I'd hidden Laura, but I'd never tell him that.

Just a few steps. That's all I needed and once he was in reach, I jolted upright and swung the crowbar at his calves with my right hand before he had a chance to jump out of the way. He crumpled in the opposite direction towards the lift, putting his hands out to catch himself, but with the lift doors open, he just met air. The point of the bar snagged on his baggy jeans and was wrenched out of my hand with the momentum. It, with Felix, went through the open doors and over the edge, falling into the shaft and hitting the roof of the lift on the floor below with a loud thud.

28

I crawled on my hands and knees towards the torch, scrabbling noises coming from behind me, then Felix laughing manically from the depths of the shaft.

'Oh Nina, you're going to fucking die tonight,' he said between bursts, 'I am going to enjoy killing you, sweetheart.'

Pulling myself to my feet, lips pressed so tightly together they almost disappeared, I edged towards the lift shaft, terrified of what was awaiting me below. Peering down, I pointed the juddering beam of the torch onto Felix, catching the glistening whites of his eyes bulging from his crimson face.

The crowbar came hurtling towards me and I jumped backwards, the point narrowly missing my toes as it hooked onto the edge. Felix swung from it, trying to climb out of his pit. *Shit!*

I let out a scream as panic shot through me and the corridor seemed to tilt. Knowing he wouldn't be contained for long, I ran for the stairs, breath ragged. Flying down them at speed, the beam of the torch bounced around the stairwell as I jumped two or three steps at a time, sending painful jolts through my stomach and compounding the ache from my ribs. The sudden explosion of frantic energy propelled me forwards until I reached the paint-smeared ground level, slipping onto my hands and knees. The jolt in my wrist as I connected with the concrete made me howl and I laid there stunned for a minute with pins and needles running the length of my arm. After the pain subsided, I crawled to the fuse box.

With the torch in my mouth shining at the lever, I tried to force it upwards but could find little strength in my damaged right wrist.

'Come on!' I yelled before eventually it gave and glorious light flooded the paint-ridden stairwell. Tears of relief spilt from my eyes as I put the torch in my back pocket and pulled open the door to reception, erupting uncontrollably when I saw Dom in the car park through the glass doors, illuminated by the glow of the floodlights. He stood, brow furrowed, concentrating as he entered my security code into the keypad outside. His eyes were ringed with purple hues and it was obvious he'd not slept all night, but I couldn't tell from his exhausted face if he'd seen the scuffle by the fire exit or my email. His blank expression gave nothing away.

It didn't matter, he was here and my shoulders wracked with sobs. The doors slid open and our eyes met, the corners of Dom's mouth rising as he crossed the threshold and paused to take me in. His smile melted away as he looked first at my tear-streaked face, then at the scarf around my arm, blood crusted beneath the knot where it had dripped. Heart swelling, I wanted to reassure him, tell him, despite my appearance, I was fine, but I didn't get the chance. In my peripheral vision, Felix emerged from the opposite stairwell, moving at speed across reception to intercept him. Mind spiralling with too much emotion, I couldn't comprehend what was happening. Was Felix going to pretend everything was fine, spin Dom another story about the substance leak I'd apparently been dealing with?

Everything seemed to move in slow motion as I tried to figure out how on earth Felix would explain the state of me, the egg-sized lump on my forehead or the gash on my arm. How would he account for the both of us being covered in white paint, looking bruised and battered.

Not taking my eyes off Dom, I tried to silently convey my message, my lips parting in an attempt to shout. *We aren't safe.* Petrified that if I bolted for the exit Felix would hurt him, he would get there first.

Dom followed my gaze, turning to face him head on, but Felix lowered his arm and I caught a glint of silver in his hand as, head down, he rushed at him. The pair collided before Dom even had a chance to react. It wasn't an interception but an attack. A hollow scream left my lips as Dom hit the floor, bowled over as Felix staggered but regained his balance. Straightening and rolling his shoulders back, he wiped his arm across his mouth. Paint stained his eyes and he looked like a Halloween ghoul despite having attempted to wash it off.

'Nina! Finally!' he exclaimed, turning towards me, arms outstretched in a greeting meant for old friends. He looked as banged up as I did, dragging his leg behind as he came towards me with bloodshot eyes, his purple T-shirt stretched out of shape and covered in grease from the lift shaft.

'Nina,' Dom whispered, choking my name out. It was barely audible but pulled my attention immediately. Over Felix's shoulder, I saw him writhing on the floor, face taut with shock. His hands covered his stomach and I gasped to see his fingers wrapped around the ivory handle of Felix's knife sticking out of him. He made short grunting noises, the colour already draining from his cheeks.

'I was just about to give Dom an update on that nightmare leak you've been dealing with, but I guess I won't need to now.' Felix shrugged, chuckling to himself like he'd completely lost all sense of reality.

'No,' I cried, my voice echoing around reception. I wanted to run to Dom, the blood already blooming outwards, staining his blue hoody a dark russet, but Felix stood between us, blocking my path. 'Don't touch it,' I shouted, ignoring Felix edging closer as I watched Dom tentatively gripping the handle of the knife now slick with sticky blood, my insides curdling at what he might do. 'Don't pull it out.'

'Listen to Doctor Nina,' Felix sneered and seeing the look on his smug face, I lost control.

I yanked the torch out of the back of my jeans and swung it at Felix, wishing I still had the crowbar. He dodged, stepping backwards, a tiny incredulous laugh escaping his lips as though I was entertainment.

'Easy tiger, you could hurt someone with that.'

'I intend to,' I snarled, his sarcasm compounding my fury, swinging again like I was on the battlefield, adrenaline cutting through the pain in my arm and wrist. All thoughts of leaving were evaporated now Dom had been hurt. I wanted vengeance. I wanted to make Felix pay for what he'd done to me, to Dom and to Sasha.

Despite his injured leg, Felix was quick, darting out of reach every time I tried to hit him. My shoulders protested and I tired easily, hampered by my throbbing wrist and weak arm, where Felix had sliced me with the knife. The knife that now pierced the stomach of my boyfriend.

'How could you. I thought you were friends!' I screamed, spittle flying from my mouth. Frustration at not being able to land a blow pulsed through me.

'Yeah, but he stuck his nose in, didn't he. Right little pair of busybodies you two.'

I wanted to wipe that condescending grin off his weasel face.

'You murdered Sasha too, didn't you?'

Felix shrugged, not even trying to deny it.

'How could you do this to us?' I screeched.

'Suck it up, sweetheart. My next mule is about to die, so I guess we've all had a shitty day,' he retorted, jumping back as I swiped at him again.

We danced around reception, Felix light and quick on his feet. Dom had rolled onto his side by the door, his entire body shaking. I didn't see the fist coming when Felix stepped towards me, too busy looking at Dom, whose bloodied hands were still on the knife. I'd raised my arm to swing again, but my nose exploded before I could. Blood filled my throat and I spluttered, dropping the torch with a clang before I tumbled to the floor after it.

Pain spread through my skull, hammering my cheekbones from the inside. Forehead on fire, my eyes blurred with tears and I could barely see. I regurgitated blood onto the floor and crawled towards Dom like he was my homing beacon, scooting up to him and wrapping myself around him from behind. It felt so good to touch him, to breathe him in, the smell of fabric softener and aftershave ruined by the metallic reek of blood.

'I'm sorry,' he gasped, blood already leaking onto his lips, but before I could ask him what he was sorry for, Felix began wrapping some thin blue rope he'd found discarded in one of the trolleys around us, wrenching us together like sardines.

My lungs were crushed against Dom's back and he winced as Felix pulled it tighter, securing it with a knot. Visibly shaking, Dom's skin was ashen and I feared he was losing too much blood. Once we were bound, Felix walked to the entrance and tapped at the keypad to open the door, then walked out into the car park without a backward glance. Where was he going? Was he leaving us here to die or did he plan to come back and finish us off? Either way we had to make the most of his absence.

'Come on,' I heaved, 'we have to try to get up.' Our escape teased us, the early-morning breeze wafted in, ruffling our hair, but perspiration covered every inch of my skin.

'I can't,' Dom grimaced and I couldn't shift him, every movement was excruciating.

'I think I'm having a low,' I wheezed as I tried to get purchase and hoist him up, but it was no good, he was too heavy and with him sat in between my legs, facing away from me, I was in the wrong position to gain any leverage, only managing to shuffle a few inches backwards. Palpitations grew in my chest and my lips tingled followed by an avalanche of irritation at not being able to move Dom. It was definitely a low.

Felix approached the door again and my heart sank at the sight of him. He carried a red can retrieved from his car, swinging it but giving us no time to prepare as he sloshed petrol upwards, spraying us. Dom screamed out in pain as the petrol filtered through his hoody to his wound and my arm smarted as soon as the cut was splashed. Eyes stinging, I tried to cover my head, but the liquid kept coming, the smell making vomit crawl up my throat, bile mixing with blood.

The assault abruptly ended and Felix tilted the can, pouring a line of petrol backwards towards the door.

'Let's see if we can't smoke your friend out, eh.' He winked at me and my throat constricted. 'Either way, none of you are getting out of here.' Awarding us a toothy grin, he re-entered the code to open the door, a blast of air ballooning his T-shirt outwards. 'Well, tonight's been fun and it's a shame you won't get to see Thailand, mate,' he said, shrugging at Dom, 'but you all enjoy roasting your marshmallows.'

Stepping backwards over the threshold without taking his eyes off us, he waited for the door to close before raising his hand in a mock salute, shutting us in and him out.

29

'Where's he going?' Dom croaked, his voice just above a whisper. He was weak, the life draining out of him before my eyes, it was heartbreaking and frustration mounted with each passing second that there was nothing I could do.

I buried my face in his soft hair. 'No idea.' I sounded like I was underwater now my nose was broken.

We watched, eyes like saucers, as Felix sloshed the last of the petrol along the bottom of the sliding door, running the entire width of the entrance before stepping back to admire his handiwork. His painted eyes gleamed and he tossed his dreadlocks back, awarding me a smug grin.

'Dom, where's your phone?' I said urgently, unable to pull my eyes away from Felix.

'In the car,' he wheezed. We watched through the glass as he pulled a cigarette packet out of his pocket.

'Shit!' What was wrong with people, usually everyone was glued to their mobiles as if their life depended on it. All I needed was one damn working phone!

Felix popped the cigarette in his mouth and cupped his hands to light it. Reality hit and panic ripped through me like a tornado, my chest threatening to burst from its cavity. I hadn't come this far to be burned alive.

'Move, now!' I shrieked, trying to shuffle backwards on my behind away from the petrol like a baby yet to walk, dragging Dom with me.

'Aarrgghh,' Dom cried out, starting to pant, one hand gingerly on his stomach, cupping the knife, the other supporting his weight as I pulled. We managed a couple of feet in a strange version of row, row, row your boat like we were at a kid's party as we attempted to move in sync, making little progress before the door ignited, lighting up the entrance and the gloom outside like a Catherine wheel before the sun could appear. Felix grinned as he watched the fire take hold.

I had to drag Dom away from the flames, but we

weren't moving nearly fast enough. The fire had already broached inside, licking the metal frames of the doors as they bubbled and blackened. Instead of creating a fire-free exit, the glass cracked but remained in place. Further popping sounds echoed around reception like it was about to implode.

'Dom, I need you,' I cried, tears welling up. I knew my blood sugar was dropping. I felt weak, my head swam and the signals from my brain struggled to connect to my limbs.

'I'm trying,' he wheezed, his trainers squeaking on the floor as we moved. We were losing valuable time as the flames grew, the accelerant going up so fast. A second later, the trail of petrol ignited and seemed to sprint towards us at lightning speed. Dom scrabbled, panic overtaking the pain he was in, bashing his head into my chin in the process, making my face ring. He lifted his forearm to shield his face as the heat seemed to explode in front of us. I concentrated on the thin rope binding us together, all the shuffling had loosened it a little, and I wriggled downwards, trying to force my arm inside to coax it over my head. If I could get out, I'd be able to drag Dom to safety, find the extinguisher and put out the fire.

Dom yelped, legs flailing as flames licked the hem of his jeans, quickly engulfing his lower leg. I moved faster, pulling at the rope and inching out from beneath it, my T-shirt tangled and rising up too. The tight rope caught the edge of my blood glucose monitor and I felt the canula rip from my skin as I pulled it up over my arm. Gritting my teeth, I pushed the T-shirt over my head, finally free of the rope, and threw it over Dom's thrashing leg, extinguishing the fire. Grabbing him beneath the armpits, I heaved him backwards until we reached the door to the west stairwell and away from the flames. Overhead, the shrill smoke alarm began wailing, so loud I had to pause and put my hands over my ears. The explosion of heat was overwhelming and I feared my skin was going to melt away.

Sprinklers I didn't even know were there erupted with water and I shrieked as we were drowned in heavy rainfall. Black smoke consumed the air, blocking the windows and shrouding our view to the car park. I could no longer see Felix, he'd left us to burn. My eyes stung and I grabbed for Dom, who was practically sitting on my lap but no longer responding. Wriggling out from beneath him, I found he'd lost consciousness and it was only a matter of time before both of us succumbed to smoke inhalation even if the sprinklers were putting out the fire.

'Dom,' I whimpered, trying to shake him awake.

He mumbled something incoherent and his eyelids fluttered but didn't open.

Concerned about the smoke filling reception, I
dragged Dom into the west stairwell, propping him up
as best I could at the bottom of the stairs and checking
he was still breathing. On the ground, the white-
painted imprints from our trainers, a map to my
struggle with Felix, were disintegrating in the forming
puddles. I was dripping with sweat and the water
cooled my skin, turning my nude bra translucent. If
Dom was conscious, he would have made a smutty
joke about me picking the worst time to try to seduce
him. I clung to that thought, that we'd have those
stupid interactions again; I had to because I needed
Dom to live.

We had a chance now, as the air was clearer inside
the stairwell due to the doors being fireproof, and I
glanced up the brightly lit stairs that looked insur-
mountable. There was no way I'd be able to get Dom
up them. He was too heavy and I too exhausted. I had
to go and get Laura too, but at least she wasn't in im-
minent danger, not from the smoke or her arm, not
like Dom with his wound. The sprinklers were doing
their job, the flames diminished and the whole
building wasn't about to go up with us being trapped
inside. But she must be panicking with the alarm and

the sprinklers going, not to mention in agony with her arm, and I felt torn about leaving her there to deal with Dom. At least the alarm would mean the emergency services had to be on their way.

My hands shook as the hypoglycaemic attack took hold, making me dizzy, and I struggled to hold onto any rational thought, but I'd get some sugar in a minute, Dom needed me now. His hands hung limply by his sides and I tried my best to assess his wound. The knife still protruded from his stomach, hoody pinned in place by the blade making it difficult to peel it away for a better look. A dark patch circled further out from the handle, steeped into the surrounding fabric. If I was sure of anything, it was that removing the knife would be the worst thing to do right now.

With the blade intact, the blood loss would be minimal; if removed without medical intervention, it could be catastrophic, although I had no idea if it had punctured any internal organs. The blade had been small, a flick knife, I remembered that much, my arm twinging at the memory, yet it was razor sharp and still able to cause damage. With no scissors to cut his hoody away, I couldn't get a proper look without tugging at his wound and I didn't want to cause Dom any more pain.

The burn on his leg wasn't that bad I discovered as

I eased the hem of his charred jeans up. The smell of petrol emanated from both of our clothes but our saviour had been the sprinklers, without them we would be charred corpses by now. Dom's ankle, although red and angry, hadn't blistered yet and could have been so much worse. I was grateful the denim hadn't melted and welded to his leg.

'Dom, can you hear me?' I said, projecting my nasally voice, but it didn't rouse him. My nose was completely blocked where the blood had clotted and shooting pains rocketed around my skull, but I couldn't think about that now, I had to get us out of here.

When I turned back towards reception, the circular porthole window was black, swirls of smoke moved ethereally against the glass, but I couldn't see anything still on fire.

Dom stirred, his eyes blinking open as I was about to pull open the door.

'I'll be right back,' I said, resting my hand on his shoulder. 'I'm going to try to find a way out.' Clamping the Storage Queen T-shirt over my face, I opened the door to reception. Plumes of smoke pushed into the stairwell and I shut the door behind me as fast as I could, hearing a faint cough from Dom. It was hard to see amongst the smoke, and the stench of burnt plastic forced its way into my blocked nose, making me choke. Bile crept up my throat and I fought the urge to be sick.

Compressing the T-shirt tighter over my mouth, avoiding my busted nose, towards the entrance I saw outside was still smouldering, flames continued to lick the frame, but at least the sprinklers had taken care of the fire inside. I sloshed my way over to the keypad, the black plastic casing and the numbers had melted, while smoke puffed from the top. It was useless, even with the power on the doors wouldn't open now unless forced.

Smoke devoured my lungs and as soon as I started to cough, I couldn't stop. It wasn't safe in here. The fire had been put out, but the air was thick with black toxic smoke and little oxygen remained. We weren't getting out this way.

Turning back towards the west stairwell, I kicked something hard, bruising my toes, and it shot across the floor. It was the crowbar; Felix must have brought it back down from the lift shaft with him, before favouring the knife as his weapon of choice.

I took it with me, knowing I might be able to use it to get out, but surely the fire brigade had to come soon. The alarm was going crazy and seemed louder in reception than anywhere else. I prayed someone in the surrounding area would see a building was on fire and black smoke spilling into the skyline. They had to, because Dom needed an ambulance. He couldn't wait.

30

Starting to feel light-headed, I stumbled towards the stairwell where Dom lay injured, reaching inside my pocket but coming up empty. I'd momentarily forgotten I'd lost the Polos earlier in my race to get away from Felix. It was the only source of sugar I had on me, and I was torn between retrieving Stacey's box of treats and getting back to Dom. I wasn't sure my lungs could cope with any more time inside reception.

I wanted to ask Dom about Felix and whether he knew Luca, but back in the stairwell he'd slipped into unconsciousness again. Thankfully, when I pressed two fingers against his neck, his pulse remained strong. His skin was ice cold, our clothes drenched from the continuous torrent from the sprinklers that wasn't slowing. Water sloshed around the floor and the noise from the siren on top of the downpour was making my brain rattle.

I patted Dom's cheeks trying to wake him, but he was unresponsive, his eyelids didn't even flutter. We were running out of time. Desperation tore through me and I swung the crowbar at the fire exit door, again and again, further shattering the glass, although, frustratingly, as with the windows, it remained intact. Kicking and hitting repeatedly, finally some of it began to dislodge. Clean crisp air wafted through the tiny holes I'd created and I brought my face close, inhaling them hungrily, wishing I could do the same for Dom, but my arms were like spaghetti and I didn't want to try to lift him until we had a way out.

Slumping down for a second to catch my breath, shoulders screaming, I wasn't sure I could get back up. I was out of energy and sweat poured down my grimy face. I didn't have the strength to keep swinging. I looked back at Dom, who, despite having no colour in his face, looked peaceful, as though he'd just dozed off on the sofa after a large Sunday roast and a pint at his local.

It was no good, I needed sugar and fast. Kicking the door in was our escape and I knew I was close to getting the pane out, but if I fell unconscious too, Dom would die, and none of us would get out of here. All the energy I'd expended trying to get the glass dislodged pitched me closer to being consumed by a hypoglycaemic attack. I cursed my stupid body, my useless pancreas and all the *'what doesn't kill you makes you stronger'* mantras I'd ever heard. It was bullshit. Laura was trapped upstairs, terrified and in pain and Dom could be minutes away from dying, yet I couldn't go on without sugar.

Dragging myself back into reception, water still streamed from the heavens, soaking through the last remaining dry patches of my jeans. My trainers squelched, absolutely sodden, and each step towards the reception counter with my T-shirt wrapped around my face was like wading through treacle. It was hard to see further than a few feet in front of me with so much smoke and even harder to breathe. I coughed and wheezed with every intake, my broken ribs excruciating, wanting to move as fast as possible, but my body would not comply.

My brain, slow to connect the dots, remembered I should be lower to the ground. Smoke rose as high as it could go, so it was safer nearer the floor, where the air was cleaner. I dropped to my knees, crawling through the puddles, my wrist and arm flinching with each movement, struggling to take my weight.

I was bleeding again, all the swinging with the crowbar had reopened the wound to my arm and drops of blood trickled down my frozen skin onto my wrist, diluting immediately. Icy water dripped from my stringy waves, cascading down my neck and chest, creating goosebumps which covered my entire body. I wished I had a top on, freezing in my bra. I'd always hated cold showers, to me they were a form of torture, but at least the water helped to keep me alert. However, what I wouldn't give to be somewhere warm and dry right now, a place where the people I loved weren't in danger. Their lives depending on me.

As I crawled closer to the reception desk, I saw the top of the yellow gloss counter had partly melted in the heat. The stink of scorched plastic was revolting, but the fire hadn't spread out further. Felix had wasted his petrol pouring it on us and the door, so not much else away from that had time to go up before the sprinklers unleashed their torrent. Thank goodness there were no soft furnishings to fuel the fire because Stacey had petitioned to get a purple sofa inside reception, which I secretly guessed she'd use for napping on her night shifts.

Everything electrical had been pretty much ruined and when I rounded the counter and got to the desk, the hard drive of my computer was smoking. Water had leaked into the air vents and it looked like it had short-circuited, the LEDs no longer flashed and the monitor was dead. It was lucky I'd sent Stacey and Dom that camera footage when I had, but at least it would be backed up on the cloud. Perhaps I should have emailed Mum instead. Would she have seen it and reacted sooner? Maybe, but there was no point in considering the what ifs, they didn't help us now.

The smoke was overwhelming and I started to cough, becoming distracted from the task, my mind as foggy as the room. Pushing aside the T-shirt, I heaved onto the floor, vomit rushing up and spewing out of my mouth, but still I couldn't catch my breath. There was nowhere for the smoke to go, no open windows, it just swirled menacingly above my head, sucking the life from my lungs with every second. Dizziness took hold and I slumped forwards, the last of my energy dissipating. Sugar, I needed sugar and fast, forcing myself onwards when it would be easier to lay and let the smoke get me, to finally give in.

Focus, Nina. My hands shook uncontrollably as I riffled through the drawer of my desk, pushing aside the crisps and Pot Noodles, trying not to listen to the voice in my head telling me I was going to die. It felt like my life was on a timer, the seconds ticking down to zero.

'Thank God,' I cried before coughing again, clutching the plastic Tupperware to my body as though it was a newborn. Now I needed air. With my belly flat to the floor, I ignored the pain in my ribs, held my breath and slithered like an army soldier to the east stairwell. Only because it was closer than the west where Dom was and I needed a minute to breathe and to eat.

As soon as I pushed through the door, I welcomed the lighter air and took shelter beneath the stairs, which provided some cover from the sprinklers, taking a second to inflate my lungs and clear out the grey mucus. Once I'd finished coughing and could finally inhale without wincing, I wrenched open the box and ripped into a packet of Haribo, barely tasting the gluey colourful mixture before swallowing. I was on to another in seconds, shovelling it in, wanting my blood sugar to rocket instantly.

It never did, it was always a slow and frustrating climb to normality, yet I needed to get back to Dom, to get him out of here. Pins and needles consumed my legs, the temperature of the bitter water had seeped right down to my bones, but my head remained woolly, demanding sleep, a natural rehabilitation while my blood glucose levelled out. Fighting the fatigue, I squeezed water from my hair, anything to keep moving so I wouldn't succumb. It had been hours without my phone, not that it mattered, the glucose monitor had ripped off my arm when I'd fought to get free of the rope. My blood sugar levels were just a guess now, but it felt like the worst hypo out of the three I'd had tonight. With my whole body quivering, I struggled to get my thoughts in order, like battling against a roaring tide in a dingy with one oar.

Get back to Dom, get out through the fire exit, I repeated like a chant so I wouldn't forget my purpose, teeth chattering with the cold. *Please could someone turn off the goddamn taps!* I was wet through and Dom was too, it would be sending his fragile body further into hypovolemic shock, with his blood pressure dangerously low. At least Felix had gone, believing he'd taken care of us. The only cars I saw through the glass were mine, Laura's Fiat, Dom's Beetle and Luca's Golf. There was no direct threat to run from any more, but Dom needed medical attention. Paul should be arriving in just under two hours, but it wasn't soon enough; Dom wouldn't live that long.

Surely Stacey would have been alerted to the fire alarm going off, she was the on-call manager and the emergency services had to have been notified, so where the hell was the calvary? I pulled myself up onto the banister. Legs refusing to comply, they wobbled precariously beneath me. I was dizzy, exhausted and in pain with every movement, but I was going back to Dom even if I had to crawl on my hands and knees to get there.

I did exactly that, fearing my legs would give out. Back in reception, the smoke lingered, swirling ominously, and I delicately shielded my nose, wading through water on all fours back towards the west stairwell, where Dom was waiting. Outside, the sky had turned a murky grey, the sun ever so slowly making its entrance, signalling the nightmare was almost over. At least it would be when all three of us got out of here and it was down to me to make sure we did, alive.

31

When I reached Dom, he was still unresponsive and the circle of blood staining his hoody had spread outwards. He'd slumped further over, now resembling a drunk at a bus stop, his head leaning against the banister. Water dripped from his mop of curls, making his sandy hair look almost black. I wiped his face with my damp T-shirt before putting it back on. It didn't make me feel any warmer; if anything, the cold fabric against my skin had the opposite effect.

Kneeling between his legs, I felt for Dom's neck. He had a pulse – weaker but still there – and I prayed he'd hold on a little longer. I kissed his glacial cheek, tasting smoke and ash, hearing his breath coming out in rasps, willing him to stay strong before reluctantly reaching for the crowbar again. It felt like it weighed a ton, but I continued to swing it at the fire door until my shoulders crumpled.

Blood melted through the fabric of my makeshift bandage and cascaded down my arm in a stream rather than the trickle it had been before.

'Come on,' I cried, having made little progress. I sat and used my feet to kick at the glass. The sharp end of the crowbar had made small holes in the pane, but nothing we could get through. Every movement was laboured, like I was travelling in slow motion, the effort exhausting, but I couldn't stop. I began targeting the corners and edges to see if I could shift it that way, making small indentations and splits with each swing when I went back to using the crowbar.

Eventually, after what felt like forever and when I had nothing left to give, the glass gave way, shooting out of the frame and crashing onto the pavement outside, letting gloriously fresh air waft in. I stuck my head through the hole, the breeze taking my hair, looking at the tiny weeds shooting up between the cracks in the slabs. That's when I saw why we hadn't been able to get out. The fire door had been wedged shut with a sliver of wood slipped beneath the door. That bastard! Luca had planned it, trapping me inside. In a fleeting second of spitefulness, I hoped the insulin overdose I'd administered had sent him to hell before any paramedics reached him.

I grappled with the wood, jostling it back and forth, scraping my knuckles on the pavement until finally it came free. I'd done it. I'd got us out. My entire body sagged with relief, muscles loosening like a deflating balloon but there was no time to rest. I had my car keys, I just needed to get Laura to help me move Dom.

Leaning back on my knees, I attempted to stand, but my legs had gone numb and I jolted backwards when Felix's manic face appeared before me in the space where the glass had been.

'Where do you think you're going?'

Felix's trainer hit me square in the chest, sending me flying back inside, and I crashed against the side of the stairs, splashing water everywhere.

'It was good I came back to check. You two have had a lucky escape.'

'The fire brigade are coming,' I wheezed, clutching at straws, but was met with a sneer.

'Yeah? Where are they then?' He crouched down, forcing himself through the gap in the door and I grabbed the crowbar, making for the stairs, being careful not to knock Dom as I climbed over him.

'Come back here you, little bitch,' Felix shouted at

my back as I scurried upwards. I turned to see him wrench the knife out of Dom's stomach, wiping it on his hoody.

'No!' I yelled, but Dom didn't even flinch.

'And I forgot this,' Felix said, pointing it at me, starting to climb.

I hated leaving Dom behind, as vulnerable as he was. The wound needed pressure to stop the bleeding, but I knew I wouldn't be able to fight Felix off. My blood sugar was only just starting to rise and I had no strength left after getting through the glass. For once, good fortune was on my side as Felix skidded on the waterlogged stairs, giving me a good ten-second head start. I clambered up, heading for my hiding place on the third floor, knowing it was the only safe space where he might not find me. I couldn't believe he'd come back, just when we were so close to getting out of here. I'd finally found a way out and it had been snatched away. Was this nightmare night shift ever going to end?

When I reached the top, hamstrings pinging and my heart pounding, I paused to feel the vibrations of footsteps on the metal below because I couldn't hear anything over the siren. Felix had to be close and might have already reached the second floor, closing the gap between us. Without hesitating a second longer, I launched myself into the corridor, skidding on the puddles that had gathered on the concrete as the continuous siren echoed around the building. At least the lights were on, as the floor was like an ice rink. As I passed unit three hundred and twenty-one, the smell of Sasha was masked by a tinny odour that I was sure came from the sprinklers.

It was disorientating, nothing but a constant shrill scream with water pummelling down, each drop like a pinprick to my skin. All of my senses were overloaded at once. I slipped twice, jarring my knees, my trainers having zero grip on the wet floor. When I reached the unit, I raced inside, easing the door closed, trying to pant quietly, but I couldn't catch my breath.

Teeth chattering, I squeezed water from my hair and pulled my now sodden T-shirt over my head, discarding it on the floor. My trainers squeaked, pooling water every time I moved, and my jeans were soaked. I huddled between the bags, pulling out random clothes and layering them on top of me until I could start to feel my fingers again. I was too weak to fight, but I could hide. Using the clothes as camouflage, making sure I was completely covered, I chewed the inside of my cheek, waiting for Felix to burst into the unit any second.

Minutes passed with no sign of him, but I couldn't

relax, even though it was a relief to be back inside the musty space surrounded by someone else's belongings. At least it was dry and slowly I began to feel my extremities again. Clutching the crowbar to my chest, I listened for footsteps approaching but could hear nothing past the wailing siren. He must have come up by now, or perhaps he was searching for me on the floor below.

When the shivering became too much, I emerged from beneath the makeshift blanket of stale clothes and riffled through the bag for something to wear. I found a striped woolly jumper that could have fit another person inside as well as me. I wrinkled my nose, it was less than fresh, as though it had been stashed in a loft for years, but it didn't matter, it was dry and I was hardly smelling like roses.

Thrusting it over my head, I stayed by the door, waiting to strike in case it was thrown open and Felix barged in. Huddled in the corner, I ran through every possible scenario of what was going on outside, the siren wailing like background music making my ears ring. Surely someone must have got sick of the noise by now and called the emergency services, if nothing else than to get them to turn it off.

My stomach squirmed with thoughts of Dom bleeding out. Laura must be terrified, she might think

I'd deserted her as I hadn't returned in so long. Her arm would slowly be setting and would likely have to be rebroken when she got to the hospital before a cast was fitted. Guilt cloaked itself around me, it was all my fault, I'd brought her into this mess.

I'd believed our nightmare with Felix was over, that he was long gone after he'd sent us up in smoke, that he'd used the fire as a means to escape, to flee the scene so he wouldn't be caught. He must be desperate to get rid of us to come back to check we'd burnt to death. It was cowardly to hide here, I should have stayed with Dom, protected him, but I was in no condition to fight. Felix would have killed us both. My brain had kept me alive this long, that and my gut instinct, and I wasn't about to give up on either now.

I shivered in the itchy jumper, still trying to warm up, my skin felt like it was layered with frost. Would the fire brigade be on their way? If so, they were taking their time. I had no idea who was alerted if the alarm went off, Stacey I would think. I imagined her waddling up to reception with the entrance on fire. Cupping her hands over the glass to peer in, screeching 'what in the hell happened here?' Having to puff on her inhaler to stave off a stress-induced asthma attack when she saw water pouring from the ceiling and all the carnage inside.

It seemed silly to worry about the amount of damage to the building considering the circumstances, but it was unlikely I'd be getting the annual bonus Stacey mentioned in my interview. If I survived the rest of my shift, I doubted I'd still have a job anyway. How long were the sprinklers going to stay on for? Surely not indefinitely. I dreaded to think how many storage units had been flooded. How our customers could potentially lose thousands of pounds of stock or furniture, but I guessed we'd be insured.

My mind wandered, the siren making me crazy, and my ears thrummed, although the sound was slightly more muted in the unit. At least the floor wasn't wet in here, not yet anyway. What about Sasha's unit, was the suitcase sat like a floating island. It was a fabric suitcase, what if any of the vital DNA needed to convict her killer was washed away? I couldn't think about it, there was nothing I could do for Sasha now, I had to concentrate on dealing with Felix. I couldn't save Sasha but I could save Dom and Laura.

32

Was Felix still looking for me or had he cut his losses? At what point would he have had enough? He had to be terrified about us identifying him to still be here, likely exhausted having been up all night, cold and wet now too. With any luck, he'd get hypothermia. That fall down the lift shaft had to have hurt too, although he'd masked it well when Dom arrived. I knew from his limp he'd injured his leg, but that was from me pushing him down the stairs earlier. It was still good to know he had a weak point I could take advantage of and I needed all the help I could get.

Edging open the door to peer out at the water-logged corridor, my heart jumped into my mouth and I swiftly closed it when I saw Felix marching towards the stairwell. Thankfully, he'd already passed me, but my stomach lurched nonetheless. A few seconds earlier I'd have been caught red-handed, but he hadn't noticed the unit I was hiding in was unlocked. In the moment I'd glimpsed him, water dripped from his dreadlocks down his back as he walked, his T-shirt glued to his skinny frame. He looked as much of a drowned rat as I did. My hair was a bedraggled stringy mess, hanging limply over my ears, and every part of my body ached with bruises and worse. Banged-up head, cut arm, broken ribs and busted nose, damaged wrist, the list of areas giving me pain was endless. I wanted nothing more than to crawl into my bed at home, take half a packet of ibuprofen and sleep for a week, but Dom needed me and so did Laura.

The tremble in my hands was now a slight quiver, meaning my blood sugar levels were almost back on track, although I had an almighty headache to add to my list of ailments, but I wasn't about to roll over and give up now. I had to see it through to the end and that meant getting everyone out of here in one piece.

As I contemplated what to do, the siren abruptly stopped and the noise of the sprinklers ceased. Had firefighters arrived? Were they downstairs? Taking another peek through the crack in the door, I saw it had stopped raining outside. Although my ears still imagined they could hear the repetitive wail of the fire alarm, it was so deeply ingrained in my brain.

Concerned I'd be walking into a trap, I waited behind the door, looking through the crack until the corridor had been clear for a couple of minutes and I could hear nothing but the ringing in my ears. Creeping out of the unit, I kept the crowbar close, stepping around the now still puddles towards the west stairwell, intending to creep down the stairs, get Laura and get out of the fire exit unseen and unheard. I was eager to check on Dom, hoping he wouldn't have deteriorated.

I made it down to the first floor, the steps slick with water, having seen no sign of Felix. It seemed a bit too quiet and my muscles tensed, ready for attack. Surely after all that had happened tonight, it couldn't be this easy.

I peeked through the window in the door to the first-floor corridor when I heard a scream that turned my body rigid. Laura! I burst through the door and broke into a run down the corridor as the screams continued. She sounded petrified and I had to get to her before Felix caused irrevocable damage. I had no doubt he wouldn't hesitate, not after all the trouble we'd caused.

Felix's deeper tone followed another high-pitched

scream and there was no mistaking the exultation in his voice at finding one of us.

'Where is she?'

'I don't know,' Laura wailed, following by the sound of a palm smashing against skin.

Bile rose up in my throat, terror mixed with a hatred so intense I thought I might combust.

'I'm going to fucking tear your arm off if you don't tell me!' Felix shouted, followed by a shriek that pierced my eardrums, making the siren sound like a lullaby.

My eyes filled, listening to Laura being tortured, but I forced myself to slow as I reached the first corner, trying to keep my steps measured along the next stretch. I had to have the element of surprise.

I didn't need to worry; the sounds of my footsteps were masked by Laura's howls of agony as I imagined him manipulating her broken arm for information.

'Urrggh, you fucking pissed yourself,' Felix coughed, then retched, and I heard scuffling as I approached the next corner and peered around, but there was to be no surprising him.

Facing my direction, he stood over Laura, who was curled up on the floor, still cradling her arm, tucking it beneath her as much as she could to protect it. The grate to the vent had been discarded on the floor behind them, where I guessed Laura had kicked it down, although it wasn't clear if she'd wriggled out, or if he'd found her. Perhaps she'd given herself away as I almost had.

'Nice of you to join us,' Felix gloated, his lip curling as I stepped out fully from behind the wall, feeling exposed and vulnerable.

'Let her go.' With my arm at my side, I rolled the crowbar around in my hand like it was a snooker cue and I was getting ready to take my shot.

Felix raised the flick knife and sneered, showing no concern I had a weapon.

'Quite frankly, Nina,' he said, wiping his forehead with his sleeve, 'I'm cold, I'm wet and I want to go home, so if you can just fucking die already.'

'Ditto,' I replied, raising my eyebrows.

That amused him and he stepped over Laura towards me while I edged backwards.

'I came to bargain with you.' I pointed the crowbar at him and he stopped.

'What are you offering?' He asked, his arms outstretched as though he was about to curtsy, like it was some big joke.

'You need a mule, don't you? Upcoming trip in three weeks. Doesn't look like Dom will be flying anywhere, does it,' I said, thinking on my feet. 'I have a passport, I'll take his place.' I'd say whatever I needed to, if it meant we'd get out of here.

'*If* I let you all go?' Felix's sparse eyebrows crept higher on his forehead and he shook out his dread-locks, water still dripping from the ratty lengths.

'Yes,' I swallowed, my throat bone dry, muscles twitching with adrenaline as I lied through my teeth, 'if you let us all walk out of here right now.'

Felix carried on towards me, dragging his leg slightly and laughing now. Laughing so much he had to pause and hunch over, clutching his stomach the-atrically as my anger bubbled to the surface. Despite wanting to flee, I remained rooted to the spot, glad he was putting some distance between him and Laura. She attempted to sit up, her face ghostlike with streaks of mascara smeared down her cheeks, still clutching her arm.

'You must think I'm an idiot, Nina,' he sneered.

'I think you're desperate,' I retorted, rolling my shoulders back and projecting my nasally voice, 'be-cause you must work for someone, Felix, someone must be in charge of transporting drugs back into the country.' *And I doubt it's you, you little weasel.*

Felix grimaced, just for a second, before his ex-pression recovered, but I realised I was on to some-thing and pressed on.

'I'm guessing someone will be angry when you can't deliver what you've promised and no doubt you're too chicken shit to carry them yourself.'

His eyes narrowed at the insult and I realised I'd hit a nerve. He went along for the ride, enjoying the vacation to a hot climate with zero risk, getting others to do his dirty work for him while he creamed the profits.

'What do you know about it?' he snapped, but he reached for his ear, tugging at the lobe, and I knew I was on the right track.

Over his shoulder, I saw Laura slowly rise to her feet, trying to be as stealth-like as possible. I flicked my eyes back to Felix, keeping him focused, and continued talking.

'I think I know all I need to.'

'You don't know shit.' The bravado had been erased; he was angry now. I'd seen him for what he was, not some criminal mastermind but a pawn in a greater game, and I was sure he was as dispensable as the rest of us.

Behind him, Laura moved slow, picking up the grate and tiptoeing towards Felix, lifting it as high over her head as she could with her one good arm. The weight of it wobbling in her hand.

I raised my voice slightly, trying to drown out her

movements. 'Whatever, Felix. Can we come to an agreement because, like you, I'm cold and tired and just about done with this night shift.'

I'd barely got the last word out before Laura brought the metal grate down on the back of Felix's head and he crumpled to the floor.

33

The grate clattered to the concrete and Laura's legs went with it, buckling beneath her.

'We need to go,' I said, rushing past a groaning Felix and helping Laura up. She'd disabled him momentarily, but he wasn't unconscious. Laura wasn't strong enough with only one working arm to bring the grate down with any force. He lay face down on the wet concrete, clutching the back of his head, hands entwined in his dreadlocks, but I didn't see any blood. The heavy grate could have caused all sorts of damage, a fractured skull or swelling on the brain, but it hadn't broken the skin, and either way, I wasn't about to check his vitals. Not after everything he'd done. All

I could think about was getting out of the warehouse while we had a chance.

Laura's cheek bore a red handprint from Felix's palm, her eyes shiny with tears. She looked haunted by the night's events and I couldn't blame her. A few hours ago, she would have been chatting with customers and rushed off her feet, country and western music driving her mad. Now she was living the nightmare I'd endured for the best part of the night and it wasn't over yet. Not until we got off the premises and sought help.

'Are you okay?' I asked as we huddled together, moving as quickly as we could down the corridor, Laura's legs stiff from being immobile in the vent for so long.

'I'm sorry. I couldn't stay in there any longer,' she sobbed, wincing with pain and embarrassment. 'I wet myself.'

'I think we all have,' I replied, giving her a weak smile, which she managed to return, trying my best to lighten the mood. It was so good to have her near me, to be able to touch her, knowing that together we would be okay, we'd get through this.

'Let's get the fuck out of here, shall we,' Laura said.

Leaving her fear behind in the corridor, we made

our way determinedly down the stairs, moving faster as we heard the mumble of voices from below.

The ground-floor stairwell was full of paramedics, already strapping Dom to a stretcher. A tidal wave of relief washed over me at him getting the treatment he so desperately needed. Finally, there was light at the end of the tunnel.

'Jesus Christ!' Laura's hand rose to her mouth as she took in the sight of him, how he was clinging to life.

I remained on the stairs, giving the paramedics space as they manoeuvred him towards the door. 'He's got a wound to his abdomen, blade is about four inches, removed about twenty minutes ago. He's been unconscious for longer,' I shouted over their urgent voices, trying to give any information that might help.

One of them nodded to confirm they'd heard as they wheeled the trolley out of the fire exit to a waiting ambulance.

Laura was next, stepping down to a waiting paramedic, already casting his eyes over the arm she clutched to her body. He wrapped a blanket around her and led her out, signalling for me to follow. Through the door to reception, I could see firefighters inside, assessing the scene.

I glanced up the stairs, expecting to see Felix

emerge, but there was no sign of him. I had to tell someone he was up there, but when I turned back to finally leave the warehouse that had been my prison for hours, a dishevelled Stacey blocked my way.

'Oh, thank God,' I said, hardly daring to believe our nightmare was over. She grabbed me and pulled me into a hug before she spoke and I inhaled the musty smell of stale alcohol and sweat.

'What on earth happened?' she asked, holding me at arm's length to take me in. Her hair resembled a bird's nest and face devoid of make-up. She looked like she'd just been dragged from her bed, her mouth stained at the corners with red wine.

'Where have you been? I called you!'

'I... I fell asleep,' she stuttered, her cheeks flushed. 'I called back, but nobody answered.'

I pictured her at home in her pyjamas, an empty bottle of wine at her feet, fast asleep in front of the television, and indignation made me shake. I had no idea whether the blood loss and trauma would be too much for Dom to survive it and it could all have been avoided if she'd picked up the damn phone.

'What happened to that boy the paramedics took?' she asked, referring to Dom.

'Felix stabbed him,' I answered truthfully.

Stacey's brows drew together and she shook her

head in confusion. I waited for her to ask me who Felix was, but her face hardened to stone.

Frustration at her reaction bloomed inside me, my jaw clenched and I gripped her sleeve, trying to drag her to the exit by her puffy coat. 'Come on, we need to get out of here!' Trying to convey that we were all still in danger, but she seemed paralysed.

'Felix?' The name dropped from her mouth so innocently that it took me off guard.

I stepped backwards, releasing her. Did she know him? I couldn't take it all in, overwhelmed with the urge to get outside and check on Laura and Dom.

'We need to go Stacey.'

'Where is he?' she asked through cracked lips ignoring my pleas.

'Upstairs,' I said, taking another step out of the door. 'We can send the paramedics up to him.'

Stacey pushed past me and climbed the stairs. What the hell was she doing?

'You can't go up there, he's dangerous,' I shouted, but she didn't turn around.

34

I looked towards the opened fire exit door, marvelling
at just how easy it would be to walk through it, to leave
this godawful place, but I couldn't make my legs move.
Torn between finally being free but knowing I couldn't
let Stacey go up there alone. Felix could hurt her, he
had a knife and with the emergency services here, he
had nothing to lose. I listened to the noise of the
hustle and bustle going on in reception, checking the
area was safe, the blue flashing lights illuminating
the sky.

'Make your way outside please?' A firefighter in a
mask came through from reception and began
climbing the stairs, searching for people to evacuate,
but I couldn't follow his order. I watched as he

climbed all the way to the top, disappearing by the time I reached the first-floor corridor.

Stacey was already there, bent over Felix, who still lay on the floor, his legs curled up in the foetal position.

'Stacey, get away from him, he's dangerous,' I shouted down the corridor, but she shot me a look of such pure hatred it was almost physical and I recoiled. What was going on?

She unzipped her coat and knelt, tucking her hair behind her ear. 'My boy,' she said, stroking his head, leaning over him and talking gently in his ear.

I swallowed, feeling bile rise in my throat. *My boy?* No, he couldn't be.

Felix moved slightly, roused by the sound of her voice, and she leant back on her knees, turning her head towards me.

'What did you do to my son?' Her teeth were gritted, her stare boring a hole in my chest. I could feel the vitriol in her glare, it radiated off her in waves.

In that one sentence, it all made sense. How Felix knew his way around the building, the code to get in, why Sasha had rented a unit here. Was Stacey in on it or an innocent bystander in his criminal activity?

'Did you know Sasha stored drugs in unit three hundred and twenty-one?'

She scowled at me, then back at Felix, shaking her head and replying dismissively, 'I don't know any Sasha.'

'Yet you signed her agreement, she was your customer and she was Felix's mule. She's dead now, upstairs in her unit, he killed her.'

Stacey screwed her face up in confusion. Clearly she had no idea what I was talking about.

'Felix made her bring back drugs from Thailand and then he killed her when she wanted to stop. A man was here, Luca, he locked me in her unit with her dead body,' I shrieked, my body practically convulsing with pent-up anger.

'What did you do to my son?' Stacey demanded again, bellowing down the corridor.

I splayed my hands out, irritation making the vein in my neck twitch. Why wasn't she listening to me?

'He's been chasing me around here all night, he wanted to throw me off the roof, Stacey. I'm going to get the police.'

'Not my boy,' she replied flatly, still stroking his head, which he lifted slightly, mumbling something to her I couldn't hear.

She was in denial, either that or she knew everything and had turned a blind eye, but I was on a roll now, connecting dots I hadn't known existed.

'Is that where your brand-new BMW came from? Felix's drug money?'

'How dare you,' she shouted. 'Felix works hard, he's got his own company, a tech start-up. What you're saying is nonsense. If I should get the police for anyone, it should be you, he's got concussion.'

I'd been right thinking Felix was a mummy's boy and Stacey was refusing to accept the obvious, refusing to see the evidence right in front of her face. What more proof did I need?

'So I started the fire? I stabbed Dom and broke Laura's arm, did I? I inflicted all these bruises on myself?' I seethed, lifting my jumper to show my naked torso, my dignity all but disintegrated. Pointing to the bloodied patch on my arm, I added, 'He sliced my arm, Stacey, with the same knife he used on my boyfriend!'

'You didn't do that did you, Felix, what she's saying?' Stacey's tone was unsure now, whatever he'd muttered to her wasn't adding up with what she'd seen with her own eyes. Her hand stopped stroking his head and she rubbed at her face, the anger whooshing out of her like a punctured balloon. Finally, I thought I was getting somewhere.

Unfortunately for Felix, Dom and I were still alive, Laura too. Witnesses to what had happened over the course of the night shift, ones who would tell the police everything. The web was closing in and he knew it.

'I've got camera footage, Stacey, I emailed it to you, you can see it once the police are here. It proves what happened.'

Felix jolted upright, making his mother jump. She scooted backwards, looking at me, then back at her son, who was already getting to his feet. Had he been faking it, counting on his mum to get him out of this sticky situation, to fix everything. How many times had she covered for him before?

'What did you say?' he shouted, lips taut and white, eyes blazing.

'Calm down, Felix.' Stacey reached for him, but he roughly shrugged her off. She flinched and I saw in that moment, she was scared of him.

'Stacey, please, go and get the police,' I pleaded, hearing the wobble in my voice as Felix stalked down the corridor towards me. My heart rate skyrocketed as fear took control of my limbs.

'I'm going to fucking kill you, you lying bitch.' He broke into a jog, Stacey screaming his name, and I bolted for the stairwell. I got through the door but wasn't fast enough to get downstairs to safety before Felix caught my jumper, yanking me backwards, the flick knife pressed to my throat. 'Easy now,' he said, 'we're going up, not down.' He pulled me up, moving the blade to press it against my side, his hand squeezing the back of my neck, directing me like a puppet. I knew where he was taking me, I didn't even have to ask. Chin trembling I could disguise the terror I felt after having evaded Felix for hours he finally had me at his mercy.

Surely Stacey wouldn't let Felix hurt me. Despite him being her flesh and blood she'd do the right thing and go and get the police, wouldn't she? They had to be downstairs with the paramedics and the firemen, surely with an incident of this scale, multiple casualties, they would have been called.

'It's no good, Felix, the police are already downstairs,' I lied, not knowing for sure if they were. 'Laura and Dom got out, they'll tell them everything.'

His jaw flexed, but he didn't answer. We'd reached the second floor and kept climbing, up towards the third, towards the roof. My temples throbbed and my legs felt weak. *Help will be coming*, I told myself. It had to. I was hoping beyond hope that Stacey had nothing to do with tonight, that she was merely a pawn in her son's plan. Stacey obviously didn't want to believe that her precious boy Felix was a drug dealer. Had he spun her a story about his tech start-up, rolling in cash, flying out on business trips, and she'd never enquired further as to where the money was coming from? I felt pity for her, she'd had the rug well and truly pulled out from under her feet if she thought her son was some kind of entrepreneur. He was nothing more than a manipulator, a liar and a murderer.

I checked Sasha's watch; it was quarter to six on Saturday morning. In an ideal world, I'd soon be in my car, yawning, the radio switched on, waiting to merge with the early-morning traffic onto the main road to get home. As it was I didn't know how on earth the next fifteen minutes would pan out. Surely the firefighters would be checking the building. Laura would tell them I was still inside, even if Dom couldn't. Felix was unhinged and right now I didn't know which way Stacey was going to go. Blood was thicker than water, but what, she was powerless to stop him? I hadn't imagined her flinching, she was scared of him, that much was obvious. Had she known what her son was capable of and been on the receiving end of it before? Would she put herself between him and me if push came to shove? There's no sign she was following us and I hoped that meant she had gone in search of help because with Felix's hand at the back of my neck and the knife threatening to plunge into my side I could barely get my legs to work. They were like jelly and I feared they would give out on me any second, I was so frightened.

I should have followed Dom out, stayed with him. I hoped the paramedics could save him because he'd tried to save me; he knew something was wrong and wasn't prepared to be fobbed off by the police or Felix. I couldn't have that be the end of him. If he lived, maybe I would defer for a year and go travelling, make our relationship work. As much as I wanted to be a doctor, and I would be, tonight had shown me what was really important and I couldn't lose Dom, not now.

35

STACEY – FIVE MINUTES BEFORE

'Felix, wait,' I hollered down the corridor, watching his once beautiful brown locks now in those nasty rats' tails whip through the air behind him as he chased Nina. 'What are you going to do?'

'I'm going to fucking throw the bitch off the roof, that's what I'm going to do,' he spat his words out like they were venom and for the thousandth time since my handsome baby boy was born, my heart splintered into pieces.

What had happened to that chubby-faced toddler, even the spotty sullen teenager was an angel compared to what Felix had become. A monster, or rather a wolf in sheep's clothing because he could turn on the charm when necessary, to get what he wanted.

Quickly reverting to the detached man who'd stood before me just now, eyes dark and empty. Forever soulless, no matter how much love I poured into him.

He expected me to clear up his mess. Like so many messes I'd fixed before, smoothing things over, making excuses for him. I'd done it at school, when he'd been caught selling pills to kids so young it made me sick, and again at college when he was kicked out for assaulting his lecturer because she'd told him he was lazy. It wasn't the first time he'd hit a woman, that had been his sister Freya when he was seventeen and then I'd bore the brunt of his rage less than a year later.

Our relationship had fractured beyond repair after that, but I clung to the hope I could change him. A mother's love could do anything, couldn't it? I claimed mental health problems to anyone that tried to intervene. Told them we were seeking treatment and that he was under the care of a psychiatrist, but he'd never let me take him to one, no matter how much I begged.

I'd told so many lies over the years, to the authorities, to anyone who would listen, trying to protect him, believing that trouble always found him, not the other way around. When, in fact, the truth was he was out of control and had been for years. I blamed myself, I wasn't a strong enough parent and he didn't have a father figure to discipline him. Convinced he was the way he was because his dad had died when he was in his early teenage years, the death having affected him so much more than either of us cared to admit. It had broken our family and we had never recovered.

Graham, Felix's dad, had had a heart attack at home one December. I'd been Christmas shopping with Freya, and Felix had been home alone, upstairs playing on his Xbox. He'd had no idea his dad had passed away on the sofa a floor below, unable to hear him call out in pain as he'd had his headphones on. I'd turned to alcohol to numb the pain, something to lean on, and although I didn't drink half of what I used to, I never really gave it up.

I'd tried my best as a single parent, but the burden of grief was too heavy to carry alone. I'd tried to smother them with love to fill the void Graham left, but it didn't work for Felix. His heart had seemed to darken that day, his easy youth evaporated. He'd had to roll up his sleeves and be the man of the house for a while because his mother was drunk – something he often liked to remind me.

'No,' I said, my voice only audible to myself as a single tear rolled down my cheek. Enough was enough and this mess was one I couldn't sweep away, no matter how much the guilt ate me up inside. He'd stabbed the man downstairs and set fire to a building, if Nina was to be believed. I knew Felix had his flick knife with him and I'd seen the blood smeared on the ivory handle. He always carried it, a spontaneous gift from his father a few months before he died and one that I hadn't approved of. He'd gone too far this time and no amount of apologies or expensive gifts could persuade me otherwise. It was finally time for my son to be accountable for his actions, to stand on his own two feet. I wouldn't protect him any more.

'Felix,' I called into the empty corridor, but he was long gone, chasing a bloodied and bruised Nina, who looked like a train wreck. When I first saw the state of her, tiny slip of a thing, my stomach had lurched – what depraved lengths had my son gone to? Had he touched her, forced himself on her against her will? The shame enveloped me. I should have stopped him years ago, listened to my conscience, but I loved him so much, it tore me in two.

What had gone on tonight and why was Felix even here? I had so many questions. I'd never heard of the person Nina spoke of – Sasha, was it? – and what did she say about running drugs? I knew Felix smoked marijuana, he had done since he was in his late teens, but I just accepted it, the stink wafting from the garage every night. I'd tried to shield his younger sister from it, but even she knew what he was up to. I thought if that was the extent of his criminal activities, then I'd swallow it. I took comfort in the fact it could have been so much worse.

But I'd been wrong, blinkered by a need to protect my boy from the world that he was convinced was out to get him. In reality, I needed to protect the world from him. I couldn't change the past, but I could stop Felix from hurting anyone else. My feet seemed to move down the corridor of their own accord, the canvas shoes I'd thrown on when the call came, waking me before dawn, now soaked through. I'd had so many missed calls and voicemails, but one glass had turned into another until Freya had sent me to bed. *The fire alarm is going off. Security have been in touch. Emergency services are on their way.* The call galvanised me into action through my hangover fog. Felix's bed was empty and Freya had been pulled from sleep by the noise I'd made in my haste to get dressed and insisted she drove as I'd had too much wine and would have been over the limit.

We had been gobsmacked by what we'd seen when we drove up to reception, blue lights flashing, firefighters dousing the entrance with water and black smoke swirling. The building was a state, waterlogged and glass smashed. It didn't take a blind man to see the damage was immense and I'd have to answer for it, but when I saw the boy on the stretcher and Nina said Felix's name, my stomach had plummeted. He'd gone too far, although it broke me to admit it; he'd have to face the consequences.

The stairwell was quiet and I was torn between finding my son and going downstairs to get help. I hadn't seen any police when I'd arrived, just firemen and paramedics. Fear of what Felix would do to Nina if I didn't stop him made me climb the stairs, reluctantly pulling my phone from my pocket, every hair standing on end. My fingers hovered over the screen, knowing what I had to do but unable to bring myself to dial those three numbers. He would see it as the ultimate betrayal and making that call I'd be saying goodbye to a future with my son, but what choice did I have? Who knew what he was capable of if he got his hands on Nina – murder, if she was to be believed.

The thought of him snapping her tiny neck forced my fingers to move and the call handler answered quickly before thoughts of hanging up could enter my mind.

'Hello, which emergency service do you require?'

'Police please.'

36

6 A.M. – 7 A.M.

On the stairs, the water had finally started to dissipate, it dripped through the holes in the metal criss-cross pattern down to the floor below, making the once heavy downpour now a drizzle. Felix's knife pressed into the wool of the jumper, the point working its way through and grazing my skin. He pressed himself close to me, manoeuvring me like I was a marionette, his steps matching mine until we reached the hatch that would take us to the roof.

My throat closed up at the thought of the long drop. Felix had been determined to make sure Dom, Laura and I didn't get out of here, using any means necessary, and he was furious two of us had. Whatever plan he had for his mum to rescue him from this situation, I'd put a spanner in the works. I still couldn't believe they were related, but I'd sown the seed of doubt with Stacey that her son wasn't all he claimed to be and had to pray she came to the right conclusion. If Stacey chose to side with her son, that didn't bear thinking about. What if she turned a blind eye and buried her head in the sand? I didn't know her well, but she had always been fair. She could be a stickler for the rules and I thought she had strong morals, but if it was a choice between me as her co-worker and her son, I didn't stand a chance, even if she wanted to do the right thing.

More than anything, I just wanted this hellish night to be over, but as soon as I opened the roof hatch, the sirens below gave me hope. Laura would have told them I was still in here, surely they'd be searching for me. There was an amber hue on the horizon, the sun slowly rising, signalling the official arrival of the weekend. The wind had dropped, yet I shivered in damp denim, the oversized jumper was thin and not doing much to keep me warm as Felix marched me closer to the edge. Mist drifted below the skyline, and the dawn chorus of nearby nesting birds rang out, but as he pushed me against the railing, my eyes bulged and I gripped on with everything I had.

'Told you there's a great view,' he said, his hands over mine as a light breeze ruffled my hair.

I struggled against him watching as a stream of yellow hats and uniforms scurried below. It was so far down. Not survivable and the sheer sight of the drop made my knees buckle but up here so high, the adrenaline ravaged my body like wildfire.

'If you're planning on jumping, it would save me the hassle of throwing you over.' I could hear the smirk on his face.

'It's over, Felix. Laura got out; even if you kill me, everyone will know what you did,' I said, unable to hide the tremor in my voice, but he just barked out a laugh over my shoulder.

He was so flippant, cold and callous, I couldn't get my head around it. Was he even human?

'I won't make it easy for you,' I shouted, every muscle clenched so tight I was like a tiny ball of rage.

'You fucking ruined everything,' he snarled, gripping my shoulder and forcing me to bend over the railing, the metal digging through my jumper and into my skin. The tip of the knife he pressed to my side pierced the skin in my struggle and I howled, more out of fear of him inching it deeper than because it hurt.

I pushed against him, trying to lean backwards, all

my weight on my heels, but still my trainers slid closer to the edge and I feared I'd slip beneath the railing. Felix, as skinny as he was, weighed more than me and was trying to force me the other way, over the top, and the vein in my neck bulged as I felt the railing wobble. A single drop of sweat fell from my forehead down into the abyss below as panic and desperation hit. After everything I'd gone through tonight, it couldn't end like this. I wasn't about to let Felix throw me over the edge and claim I'd jumped. I couldn't let him get away with hurting the ones I loved.

'You bastard,' I screamed, throwing my head backwards with as much force as I could, my skull connecting with Felix's nose, a surge of hate exploding from me. I heard the crack of the cartilage, the knife dropping from his hand onto the felt. It bounced and flew over the edge. Thrusting my elbow upwards into his gut, Felix released my shoulder, staggering backwards, but grabbed at my jumper, pulling me with him.

We fell together, scrabbling on the floor like two children fighting over their favourite toy. My injured ribs felt like Felix had dug the knife in he was threatening me with before, pain shot around my chest making me gasp as we struggled. I kicked out at his bad leg, hearing a sharp intake of breath. He responded just as viciously, digging his fingers into my upper arm, where his knife had gouged me. I shrieked as blood seeped into my sleeve.

'Felix, stop!' Stacey's cry came from feet away, wind blew her hair around her pink shiny cheeks.

Her son ignored her pleas as though she wasn't there. I kicked at his groin and rolled further away from the edge. He curled up in pain, clutching his crown jewels as a steady stream of blood flowed from his ruptured nose.

Stacey's screams rang in my ears as I got to my feet, using my advantage to boot him in the back, caught up in a frenzy of adrenaline and the need for vengeance. In that moment I wanted to hurt him, I wanted to kill him for what he'd done.

My hair yanked backwards, strands tearing from my scalp as Stacey threw me aside like a rag doll. I panted, trying to catch my breath as I lay on the felt, anger dissipating. I had no energy left and closed my eyes, feeling as though I might pass out until a cry from Stacey made my lids fly open. I looked up to see Felix was up and running towards me, his eyes bulging like a madman.

37

Stacey fell onto her hip after Felix shoved her aside, letting out a yelp of pain and rolling around in her puffy coat like a caterpillar as she tried to get to her feet. Felix paid her no attention, his vitriol directed at me.

'Bitch!' His face was puce and he was on me with two short strides.

My hands went up to shield my head, but I wasn't quick enough. The kick to my cheek left my ears ringing and vision blurred, seeing two of Felix as he dragged me towards the edge, dreadlocks dangling over our faces. My eyes slowly focused on the clouds over his shoulder, drifting away and taking the fading moon with it.

'Just fucking die, would you.' He choked out the words as I rolled onto my belly and dragged my nails across the floor, grit turning them black, jumper snagging on the felt and riding up. He was like a caged animal, cornered with nothing left to lose.

The hatch opened and I watched as a yellow helmet slowly emerged, someone was climbing up, coming to save me.

'Felix, don't do this,' Stacey wailed, upright now as muffled shouts sounded from across the roof.

Felix's face was covered in blood, still dripping from his nose, and he grunted like a wild thing as my legs went over the edge of the building. I grabbed the railing with my right hand, clinging on to the only anchor I had keeping me on the roof. Its thin metal pole giving me little comfort.

The drop to the tarmac took my breath away and fear strangled my thoughts, making the blood swim faster in my veins. He'd won, despite my fighting to stay on the roof, he was stronger. Tense shouts drifted up, the uniforms staring at the roof in horror at what was unfolding. I squeezed the metal pole until the blood left my knuckles, ignoring the burn in my palm as I tried to swing my leg back onto the roof, but my efforts were uncoordinated. When the sole of my trainer made contact, Felix kicked it away, preventing me from climbing up before going for my hand. I wouldn't be able to hold on much longer and Felix was already bent down, trying to peel my fingers away from the metal, to send me plummeting down.

'It doesn't matter if you kill me,' I yelled, 'everyone will know what you did.'

Reaching up and grabbing wildly with my left hand, I caught hold of Felix's T-shirt. Unsteady in his crouch and taken by surprise, he lurched sideways and rolled over the edge, his eyes like saucers and lips parted in a silent scream. Catching my arm as he fell, I screamed in pain as the jolt from his weight wrenched my left shoulder from its socket. Stacey shrieked from somewhere on the roof and a second later she was on her stomach, her upper body on the edge, trying to reach for her son.

'I can't hold on!' I screamed.

Shooting pains tore through my arm. Dislocated, it hung limply with Felix at the end of it, his paint-streaked face now ashen, gripping my wrist with both hands as he clung on for his life. White spittle gathered at the corners of his mouth and he panted for breath. The two of us dangled from the roof, four storeys up as the fire brigade hustled below. Police and more ambulances had arrived now, the car park a mass of vehicles with blue flashing lights, but I couldn't do more than glance down, terrified of how high up we were.

My shoulder seared with a pain I'd never experienced before and I could feel my fingers loosening around the railing. Barely having been able to take Felix's weight for more than ten seconds, a mass of hands suddenly gripped my arm and began trying to pull us up. I gasped for air, my chest compressed against the edge of the building, the jumper catching on felt as I was wrenched upwards.

My shoulder was in agony, the ligaments torn and muscles spasming each tiny jolt of Felix's weight as they heaved, sending waves of nausea through me, and I swallowed down the bile that threatened to explode out of my mouth. Felix's hand slid down my wrist until it connected with Sasha's watch, the leather digging into my skin as he clawed me with his fingernails. Strong hands reached for us, but terror morphed his features, his eyes bulged and spittle leaked from his lips as Sasha's watch was ripped clean from my wrist and the weight on my arm evaporated.

Luckily for him, two men already had hold of Felix when the clasp broke and he was pulled back onto the roof seconds after I was. The both of us sat feet apart as a whirlwind of yellow jackets seemed to whizz around, providing blankets and trying to help us to stand. I shook with relief at having something firm beneath my feet, my life having flashed before my eyes in the seconds I dangled from the roof. Thank god for the emergency services, they had saved my life. I prayed they'd be able to do the same for Dom. Anger bubbled in my stomach at him being caught in the crossfire, forcing its way up my throat like bitter vomit.

'You almost killed Dom,' I cried while Stacey knelt down and wrapped her arms around her son, burying her head in his shoulder.

'Really, you're worried about him?' He let out a tiny snort. 'He knows everything; why do you think he was so keen for you to join us on our trip to Thailand?'

The world seemed to shift as the gravity of Felix's words took shape, floating in the air before pummelling my brain like bullets.

'What?' I said as I was practically carried away towards the hatch, unable to pull my eyes away from his smug face.

'Don't waste your tears on him, Nina. You were always going to be the mule,' he shouted over the din.

I looked into the depths of Felix's eyes, searching his dilated pupils. Was he telling me the truth? Had I been living a complete lie all these months, believing Dom loved me?

38

FELIX – EARLIER

'Will you be home for dinner?' My mum's annoying voice filled the hallway as I put my trainers on, forcing my feet in because I'd left the laces tied. She'd just got in from work, coming home as I was going out, no doubt ready to sink into a bottle of red as soon as her coat was off. It wasn't an accident we were passing in the hallway, she drove me up the wall and when she was home, I tried to be out, or in my room so as to interact with her as little as possible.

'I don't know yet,' I replied, unable to hide my irritation.

'It's fajita Friday, it's your favourite,' she said in her saccharine tone and I ground my teeth together. I wasn't fucking twelve any more, yet she still treated me like I was a child.

'I'll eat out, don't wait up.' I slammed the door without waiting for a response and lingered on the step, hearing Freya call through from the lounge, asking Mum about her day as she took her shoes off and offering to make her a brew. Perfect fucking Freya, the golden child.

I needed to move out, get my own place; it wasn't as if I didn't have the cash. I spent more time at Luca's than I did here, but there were perks to living at home. Who else was going to do my washing, and I couldn't be arsed to cook my own meals. Plus, she liked having me around, she'd said so herself. The truth was, she wanted to keep her beady eye on me, but it served a purpose. Freya reckoned I treated the place like a hotel, but I paid my way, didn't I, why should I help out if I was paying for the privilege? Women, they always wanted something and it was never simple or straightforward, they were a pain in the arse, the lot of them.

My mood brightened as I got in the car and revved the engine, listening to it roar. Screw the neighbours. The supercharged Mitsubishi Evo made a hell of a racket, but it was my pride and joy. Like shit off a shovel, it had cost me a pretty penny, but the amount I was raking in, I could afford it.

We had another trip in three weeks' time and I needed to prep Sasha. This one was going to be different; I'd been given a new contact, which was why we were flying out with a couple of extra pairs of hands, but as long as the cargo got back in one piece, it was good enough for me.

I'd roped in my old college mate Dom. He thought we were going on a six-month hedonistic adventure to find ourselves, the sap, but I'd come up with a reason we needed to return home after a couple of weeks. We had both started the agriculture course, on a mission to save the planet but didn't last the distance, neither of us could stomach the tutor, he was a right tosser. Dom was a decent bloke though, a bit wet but nice enough, and we'd kept in touch, a beer here, a curry there. So when I'd offered him the chance to come, subsidising his flight, he'd jumped at the opportunity for the trip of a lifetime. He wouldn't have any idea he was carrying on the way back, or his girlfriend, if Dom managed to convince her to join us. The more the merrier, as far as I was concerned. The more gear we got through security, the more money for me when we got back to the UK.

No one could beat Sasha though, she'd been a godsend. That girl was like a little doll and she could charm the birds from the trees. It was my idea to pose as a couple on the last trip, bloody worked too, she loved a bit of role play, especially when she was so drunk she couldn't even stand. In fact, I'd had more successful runs since she came along than any of the others before her and as long as she didn't get itchy feet, things would be fine. Luca did as he was told, the meathead, but Sasha, she had dreams, aspirations, she'd told me on a hot, sweaty night in Thailand. Ones that need stamping on pretty quickly.

I threw the car into gear and floored the accelerator, zooming down our little cul-de-sac and around the green at the end. No reason why the whole street couldn't appreciate my enormous exhaust. In fact, I felt a bit peckish, not for poxy fajitas though. I rolled my eyes as I turned onto the main road heading for Luca's. Maybe Chinese, some prawn balls might hit the spot. Sasha loved them so I'd pick up a cheeky banquet on the way down there. Might even be able convince her to go for a drink or ten. She was fun when she'd had a few and couldn't really say no. I re-arranged my crotch, already feeling the stirring.

Life was good, business was great and Kanye blasted through my sound system, the bass reverberating through the car. I lit a cigarette, lowering the tinted windows, remembering I had to meet with Tommy later to shift the last lot of gear before our next trip. Couldn't keep him waiting; he didn't say much, but there was something about his softly spoken voice that freaked me out. I'd missed a delivery once, the last mule, some slut who was willing to do anything for a free holiday with some pills thrown in, got made as we went through security. I sniggered, she was still in Bangkok as far as I knew, weaving fucking baskets or something in a cell with around forty other women, never to see the light of day. Drug trafficking came with a hefty sentence. I'd scarpered quick and was never even questioned, but Tommy was not happy when I got home. I was minutes away from a pasting until I offered him fifty per cent off the next shipment. Then Sasha and her dumb brother had walked into my life and, hey presto, everything came up smelling of roses. That first trip she did was the most lucrative ever and I knew I was onto a winner.

39

6 A.M. – 7 A.M.

'I'm Jill, a paramedic. Are you hurt?' A woman in a green uniform had come through the hatch and joined the firefighter in assisting me across the roof. My body felt like it was made of liquid and I could barely stand. I had no words, my breath catching in my throat as the enormity of my night sank in. Finally it was over. Felix and Luca couldn't hurt us any more. I wept with relief at being on solid ground, even though it was the roof; it was something I'd convinced myself I'd never feel again.

'Are you hurt?' she repeated the question, stopping so she could look at my face.

'I'm Nina,' I eventually stuttered, pain shooting

through my shoulder and back, adding, 'my shoulder.' Directing her to where the feeling was slowly coming back, tingling with pins and needles. 'I need some sugar, I'm diabetic.' My legs felt wholly unconnected and I was glad when another firefighter appeared at the bottom of the ladder to help me down back into the building, lifting me as though I weighed nothing. 'How's Dom and Laura?' I sobbed to Jill, utterly overwhelmed with emotion now that I was finally safe.

'Your friends? They're with my colleagues, they're rushing the man to hospital now.' Bursting with gratitude at my rescue, I couldn't stop crying and thanking the firefighter with the kind eyes before he said goodbye, another paramedic taking over to help Jill. He'd saved my life, grabbing my wrist when I was a second away from letting go of the railing.

The next twenty minutes were a blur. Paul rushed over when I emerged through the blackened entrance where the glass had been smashed through. The air in reception had cleared, but the building stank of burnt plastic and looked a mess. Water pooled on the floor and dripped from every surface. It was like a tsunami had hit Storage Queen while I'd been upstairs. The police were talking to who I assumed was a tearful Stacey's daughter, Freya, as she hurried over to join

Felix and Stacey as they came down after me, cloaked in blankets.

Paul bombarded me with questions I barely heard as Jill escorted me to a waiting ambulance and took charge, helping me onto the gurney and clipping an oxygen monitor to the end of my finger.

'My shoulder,' I whimpered, clutching my arm close to my chest like Laura had, the pain excruciating.

'It's okay, honey, it looks to be dislocated. I'll put a sling on it and we'll get them to pop it back in at the hospital. Here's some gas and air, it'll help with the pain.' She put a mask over my face and the relief was immediate with one long inhale.

'Stacey's sweets saved me,' I said woozily, smiling at Paul, who sat opposite me in the ambulance as the paramedic placed a sling on my arm and began prodding the lump on my forehead.

'I'm so glad you're okay, I couldn't believe it when I turned up for work and they were putting a fire out! What happened?'

'Stacey's son happened,' I replied, the words leaving a bad taste in my mouth, 'and the building's a wreck.' I blinked slowly as the gas and air began to take full effect.

The paramedic used a finger pricker to check my glucose levels and immediately removed my mask so I could ingest a disgusting-tasting gel.

'It's fast-acting, should bring you up quickly,' she said, placing the mask back on.

'Don't worry about the building,' Paul said, smiling, his ears going pink before adding, 'you need to rest now, you've had quite the shock.'

'At least you're going to have the day off,' I mumbled, chuckling to myself, delirious with the gas and air.

I didn't think I'd ever had such a lengthy conversation with Paul, usually we'd just exchange a few words in the handover before I rushed out of the door, eager to get home. He'd recommend me a Netflix show to watch on my next shift and I'd let him know if there was any leftover food from my night's stash for him to binge on. I'd never taken much notice of his floppy brown fringe and strong jawline. Laura would think he was gorgeous or maybe it was just the gas and air softening my focus.

'I need to cut this jumper off to get to the wound on your arm and check for other injuries,' the paramedic said, eyeing Paul, who blushed crimson and jumped up, knocking his head on the roof of the ambulance.

'I'll be off,' he said, nibbling on his lower lip, and I sensed he was reluctant to leave me alone despite the paramedic wanting to get to work with her scissors.

'It's okay,' I mumbled through my haze, 'I'll be fine.' I waved my hand with the oxygen monitor attached.

'If you're sure. Do you want me to call someone for you?'

I nodded. 'My mum. Give me your phone, I'll type in the number.'

Paul dutifully dug his mobile out of his pocket and I slowly keyed in the digits, hoping I'd remembered them correctly.

'I'll ring her now.'

'Thank you,' I said, as he opened the door to the ambulance.

'Before you go, Paul, can you give Stacey a message for me.'

He turned, waiting for me to speak. I had so much I wanted to say to her but no idea where to start, or even how to feel. There was one thing I was sure of, though.

'Sure, what is it?' he prompted as my eyelids fluttered. I wanted nothing more than to close them and drift off.

'Tell her, no more night shifts.'

His mouth slowly curled upwards into a grin, blue eyes shimmering.

'No more night shifts,' he repeated, chuckling to himself as he climbed down from the ambulance and the door swung shut.

40

As I sampled the finest gas and air the NHS had to offer, I questioned Jill on the way to the hospital, trying in vain to stay awake, and found out Felix had been assessed by one of her colleagues for a sprained ankle and concussion before being driven to the hospital. They'd known he'd need further treatment and would potentially have to be admitted, even just for observation.

Despite Felix's protestations at needing medical assistance and attempt to flee once he reached stable ground, Laura had already named him as both the cause of the building fire and Dom's injuries. The police had arrested him on site and escorted the ambulance he was in to the hospital, having deemed him a flight risk because he'd already tried to leave the scene.

According to the paramedic driving the ambulance, she'd heard he was already blaming everything on *some bloke called Luke or Lucas* to anyone who'd listen, claiming it was a case of mistaken identity and he was in the wrong place at the wrong time. No doubt he was hoping his mum would back up his story, but I'd been a witness to the night's events and intended to tell the police everything as soon as I could, even if Stacey didn't.

Due to his extensive injuries, Dom had been flown by air ambulance to the Royal Sussex County Hospital in Brighton. I was given limited updates on his condition due to not being his next of kin and it was frustrating, to say the least, but I couldn't fault the NHS staff, their treatment and kindness had been amazing.

A fantastic team of doctors and nurses tended to me when I arrived at East Surrey hospital. My shoulder was put back into its socket and thankfully an X-ray confirmed I wouldn't need any surgery, just plenty of rest to heal. The X-ray also showed I had three broken ribs that would mend with time. I had oxygen administered for smoke inhalation, four stitches put in the gash in my arm, various cuts and bruises assessed, as well as my nose, which thankfully wasn't broken, and finally a CT scan to check for swelling to the brain. I spent an agonising four hours being patched up, in between periods of waiting, filled with anxiety at whether Dom had survived the knife wound Felix had inflicted. I didn't know whether what Felix had said on the roof was true, I didn't want to believe a word of it and I couldn't switch off how worried I was about him.

Laura came to find me once she was finally discharged. Her arm had been broken again and reset with lots of pain relief. Like me, she wore a sling, but also a pretty pink cast. She burst into tears as soon as she saw me, relieved I was all right and had managed to get out of the warehouse safely. She told me she'd been shouting at everyone that I was still inside and they had to find me.

We had cups of hot chocolate from the vending machine and talked through the events of the night, Laura waving me away as I apologised for dragging her into it all. Once we'd had a good cry and numerous one-armed hugs, she got me to sign her cast, insisting I be the first. I wrote *Love you Sling Sister,* which made her giggle. A little while later, her mum came to collect her and she made me promise I'd message her when I was sent home.

Eventually, once I'd had something to eat and

been given some insulin, I was discharged with a new pen and a plethora of painkillers. A uniformed police officer was waiting to take my statement in a side room the hospital found for us after I'd been reunited with a very tearful mum. She'd hugged me for five whole minutes until I begged to be released, horrified at the state of my battered and bruised body.

The interview took another hour, where, despite flagging from lack of sleep, I told them about my night shift hour by hour. From Luca's arrival with his suitcase, him hunting me around the warehouse, then about Felix and the footage I'd sent to Stacey and Dom which proved my record of events up until the power was turned off. Mum listened to every word, disturbed by my account, and I was glad she was there to hold my hand while I relived it through a haze of tears. Finally, I told them where they could find the body of Luca's sister, Polish citizen Sasha Cizmarova.

Luca, as it turned out, had been admitted earlier that evening after an ambulance had been called to the industrial estate. He'd been brought in, treated with lots of fast-acting glucose, put on a drip and moved to a ward in another wing for observation, where, after my statement was taken in conjunction with Laura's, he was swiftly arrested. Despite everything he'd done, I was relieved to learn I didn't have his death on my conscience.

I'd been honest about everything, including injecting him with insulin during our struggle. Showing the bruising around my neck as evidence of his near strangulation and the desperation I'd felt, fighting for my life, especially after finding the body of the poor security guard. They could have charged me with grievous bodily harm as a minimum but told me because it was self-defence it was unlikely they'd proceed.

Eventually, I was allowed home and, utterly exhausted, Mum bundled me into the car. I messaged Laura from Mum's phone during the short drive, to tell her I was finally going home. She was messaging from her bed, having taken painkillers, and was waiting for them to kick in, still reeling from the trauma she'd been through. When I crawled into my bed with a hot-water bottle, an ice pack for my nose, tea and a hot cross bun that Mum delivered, my entire body hurt, but the relief at being home and safe was indescribable. It was impossible to get comfortable, no matter what position I lay in, even with strong painkillers, and I feared I wouldn't sleep, but I could barely keep my eyes open.

When I woke on Saturday evening, having slept

the entire day away, the night before seemed like a dream, or, rather, a nightmare. It wasn't until I stood in front of the mirror in my underwear after a hot bath that reality came crashing back in. We were all lucky to have survived, although I was still waiting to hear if Dom had pulled through.

I spent the rest of the weekend resting, my bruises turning from an angry red to a violent purple. Mum looked as though she was going to burst into tears every time she glimpsed any of them, so I purposely kept myself covered up. I couldn't do anything about the bump on my forehead though, which thankfully had shrunk in size but now had an attractive yellow hue. I stayed in my pyjamas, glued to the internet and the local news channel, absorbing any information I could on the incident and Dom's progress, but hardly anything was reported.

However, gossip was rife on local Facebook posts about Felix and Stacey, with some far-fetched theories being thrown around that I chose to ignore. Mum took the weekend off and Laura came round to visit on Sunday afternoon. We ordered a takeaway and watched a movie, something funny and light-hearted, trying to get back to some sort of normality, although it was much more subdued than our usual evenings in.

Dom, we'd heard through friends of his family, was awake but still in intensive care. He hadn't yet been in contact with me and all I wanted to know was the truth, but it wasn't until Monday when I had a visit from the police to give me an update and return my phone, which Luca had stolen, that I learnt anything new. As a result of the camera footage and mine and Dom's matching statements, Felix's initial charges were murder and two counts of attempted murder, as well as arson. The drug trafficking was still being investigated.

Sasha's body was covered in his DNA, but it was Luca who broke during interrogation, telling the officers everything. He was heartbroken at learning his sister was dead. They were very close, the pair of them coming to the UK for a better life, where they'd been persuaded by Felix into joining his 'get rich quick' scheme transporting heroin from Thailand back into the country. His contact out there had bribed a worker at the airport and got them specific flights, ensuring security would look the other way. They'd quickly got caught up, swayed by Felix's charm, his promise to keep them safe and the cash thrown at them. After the first successful trip, they believed it was easy money until Sasha built up her nest egg and wanted to stop. That was when Felix had turned up at Sasha's flat to find her leaving for Manchester and killed her in a fit of rage at his perfect operation going down the toilet. Felix had hit Sasha with a hammer and put her in a suitcase, removing her from the flat and passing her to Luca at a neutral location, claiming he'd been jumped on the street by some junkie and it had been self-defence.

He'd instructed Luca to put the suitcase in the storage unit until he figured out where to take it for disposal. Under Felix's direction, Sasha's unit had been rented as an anonymous location to store the heroin they brought back from Thailand before being cut and sold on to dealers. He intended, Luca said, to enlarge his operation and recruit more smugglers as it had been going well, so the unit would come in handy for future trips and a larger supply. Stacey would be none the wiser.

The police disclosed that messages between Dom and Felix found on Felix's phone proved that Dom wasn't aware of the smuggling operation. Relief washed over me when I learned our relationship hadn't been a lie. He'd come back to Storage Queen that night to patch things up between us, calling the police when he'd arrived to find the power out and unable to contact me on the phone. When he returned, he genuinely believed Felix, who he'd known for a few years, about the leak, only realising something was wrong later.

When the police left, I sent Dom a message to let him know I'd come to the hospital as soon as he was up to receiving visitors. I didn't know if we'd get back together, but we had lots to unpack about that night and I wanted to thank him for risking his life to save mine.

EPILOGUE

It took a while for Dom to recover, but I helped as much as I could, visiting him in hospital and then at home once he was discharged. He admitted he'd made a mistake, he'd known it as soon as he'd driven away from my house that night, apologising that he'd given me an ultimatum about Thailand. I forgave him, happy to have him back in my life, and we talked about the lucky escape he'd had, not going to Thailand, where he could have inadvertently carried heroin back for Felix, or, as he called him, Drexl. I asked him why he called him that and he told me Drexl was a character in the classic nineties film *True Romance* that Felix was obsessed with. Gary Oldman's character was a white man with long dreadlocks and had inspired Felix's look. He thought it made him look like a gangster. I'd never made the connection, even though I'd seen the film.

Dom felt betrayed by his old friend. He'd known Felix was a little wild but not violent like he'd proven that night at Storage Queen. The incident never hit the national news due to coverage being focused on riots in the Midlands after a pregnant woman was killed in a police chase. Other than a few articles in the *Brighton Argus*, the world quickly moved on to much bigger things. If only it had been so easy for me, the nightmares continued for a while and I found it hard to trust any strangers that came into my life, fearing they had a hidden agenda. Slowly with everyone's help I began to put it behind me.

Laura had her cast on for six weeks, but her broken arm healed and our combined trauma bound us closer than ever before. She made sure I didn't retreat back into my shell and with Dom we agreed to book a holiday during our respective summer breaks from university, spending a week on a beach in Croatia. I'd written to Sasha's parents, sending my condolences. Despite never knowing Sasha before she died, I felt as though, in part, I owed my life to her. From the Polo mints to the watch, she'd been with me that night, keeping me alive.

Luca, short for Lucjan, had been charged with the manslaughter of the security guard who'd visited Storage Queen once I'd pressed the panic button, as well as actual bodily harm and false imprisonment. He was remanded in custody in the UK pending trial along with Felix.

Stacey had reported to the local press that she knew nothing of her son's criminal activities. She apologised publicly on his behalf and resigned from Storage Queen with immediate effect. Surprisingly, I still had my job, and despite what I'd said to Paul in a waft of gas and air fumes, I resumed working the night shifts. Sheer determination at not letting Felix or Luca dictate my future made me go back. I wasn't prepared to let my fear of working alone control me. As a precaution, they implemented a new procedure to follow. All evening and overnight visits were by appointment and ID was to be presented on arrival for access to be allowed. On top of that, more cameras were installed in reception and all stairwells.

It made me feel much safer and I'd had a small payout in compensation from Storage Queen, which I'd used as a deposit on a flat with Dom. He kept apologising for his selfishness, getting caught up in the idea of our first holiday together unable to understand why I didn't feel the same way. Since then he'd been nothing but supportive of my commitment to my university degree. Mum had taken the news of the flat well, better than expected, and I'd signed her up to a couple of dating apps for when she felt ready to get out there. She'd helped us move in and redecorate, buying us a house plant that I was bound to kill, but the thought was there.

We'd been practically inseparable until then and the four of us – Dom, Laura, Mum and I – were more protective over each other than ever. My studies were still going well, I'd aced my most recent assignments and one of my lecturers had whispered that I was close to being at the top of the class. I was on my way to becoming the doctor I'd always dreamed of being and nothing was going to stop me.

* * *

MORE FROM GEMMA ROGERS

Another book from Gemma Rogers, *The Honeymoon*, is available to order now here: https://mybook.to/HoneymoonBackAd

AUTHOR'S NOTE

Excerpt taken from www.diabetes.org.uk

Type I diabetes

If you have type I diabetes, your blood sugar is too high because your body can't make a hormone called insulin. Fewer than one in ten people in the UK who have diabetes have type I diabetes. There is nothing you can do to prevent yourself or others developing type I diabetes. The exact causes are not known.

Although it's often diagnosed in childhood, people can develop type I diabetes at any age. You are at a slightly higher risk of type I diabetes if your mother, father, brother or sister has it.

Insulin is the main treatment for type 1 diabetes. You can't live without insulin injections or using an insulin pump. Checking and managing your blood sugar levels is important to help you reduce your risk of serious short- or long-term health problems. These are called diabetes complications.

There is currently no cure for type 1 diabetes, but we're funding lots of research to help find new treatments and a cure.

Type 1 diabetes is a bit of a juggling act. My husband, who has been diabetic for over twenty years, describes it as walking a tightrope. If your blood sugar level is too high, you need insulin to bring it down to a normal level. Too much insulin and your blood sugar level may go too low, like Nina in the book, and you will need sugar to raise it again. Counting carbs is something both my husband and now my youngest daughter must do at every meal, for every snack, to determine how many units of insulin are needed to keep balancing on that tightrope.

It's a constant battle and one fought daily and during the night too because it doesn't stop when you're asleep. My youngest daughter's recent diagnosis was part of the inspiration for this book, how scary it is if you're diabetic and caught or trapped somewhere without insulin or sugar, where there's an actual possibility you might die if you can't get to either of them. Of course, The Night Shift is just fiction, a worst case scenario, but I hope it helps to raise awareness of the dangers. There are millions of diabetics living healthy and fulfilling lives, my daughter is just one of them and she certainly doesn't let it define her.

ACKNOWLEDGEMENTS

Thank you to all my readers, from the ones who have been with me from the beginning and the new ones I've picked up along the way. I can't believe this is book eleven already! I have so many more in me to write and I'm thrilled I get to share this with all of you.

It's been a bit of a year for the Rogers' family, so thank you to my amazing husband who is my rock and takes on so much while I'm shut away writing. To my beautiful and resilient teenage daughters who are growing up too fast, I'm so lucky to be your mum.

A special mention goes to Mark Fearn, the first reader of *The Night Shift* and the only one I trusted to tell me the truth when I was having a wobble! I love our banter and I'm so glad we met. Looking forward to seeing you again at Capital Crime, if not before!

Another shout-out to Sharon Groves who helped with my storage unit research. Thank you for allowing me a tour and answering my insane questions.

As always, a huge thank you to the fantastic team

at Boldwood Books, especially my editor Caroline Ridding. I can't imagine having anyone else, please can I keep you. And the fabulous Jade Craddock, my eagle-eyed copyeditor, forever! Massive thanks as well to my proofreader Arbaiah Aird, for being so on the ball and spotting all the things I'd missed.

ABOUT THE AUTHOR

Gemma Rogers was inspired to write gritty thrillers by a traumatic event in her past. Her debut novel *Stalker*, released in 2019, marked the beginning of her writing career. Gemma lives in West Sussex with her husband and two daughters.

Sign up to Gemma Rogers's newsletter to read the first chapter of her upcoming thriller!

Follow Gemma on social media:

ALSO BY GEMMA ROGERS

Stalker

The Secret

The Teacher

The Mistake

The Babysitter

The Feud

The Neighbour

The Flatmate

The Good Wife

The Honeymoon

The Night Shift

THE

Murder

LIST

THE MURDER LIST IS A NEWSLETTER DEDICATED TO SPINE-CHILLING FICTION AND GRIPPING PAGE-TURNERS!

SIGN UP TO MAKE SURE YOU'RE ON OUR HIT LIST FOR EXCLUSIVE DEALS, AUTHOR CONTENT, AND COMPETITIONS.

SIGN UP TO OUR NEWSLETTER

BIT.LY/THEMURDERLISTNEWS

Boldwood

Boldwood Books is an award-winning fiction publishing company seeking out the best stories from around the world.

Find out more at www.boldwoodbooks.com

Join our reader community for brilliant books, competitions and offers!

Follow us

@BoldwoodBooks

@TheBoldBookClub

Sign up to our weekly deals newsletter

https://bit.ly/BoldwoodBNewsletter